Blood on the Priaire

Blood on the Prairie

A Novel of the Sioux Uprising

Steven Merrill Ulmen

Eagle Entertainment USA
Mankato, Minnesota

Public domain and fair use information used in this novel was obtained from the following sources:

    1. *The Ancestry, Life, and Times of Hon. Henry Hastings Sibley*, LL.D. by Nathaniel West, D.D. Pioneer Press Publishing Company, St. Paul, Minnesota, 1889

    2. *Minnesota in the Civil and Indian Wars 1861-1865 & Minnesota in the Civil and Indian Wars,* Volume II, Official Reports and Correspondence. Prepared, Compiled, Edited, and Published under the Supervision of the Board of Commissioners. Appointed by the Act of the Legislature of Minnesota of April 16, 1889 and April 22, 1892, St. Paul, Minn. Electrotyped and printed for the State by the Pioneer Press Company 1890 & 1893.

    3. *Bury My Heart at Wounded Knee* - Chapter 3 - "Little Crow's War" - Holt, Rinehart, and Winston, June 1971.

    4. Public domain song lyrcs and cover images obtained from a number of sources.

Cover Art Design by David Hoffman

ISBN: 978-0-615-24796-0

Pre-press by North Star Press, St. Cloud, Minnesota

Published by Eagle Entertainment USA
130 Teton Lane #2
Mankato, Minnesota 56001

Library of Congress Catalog Number: 2008908448

Dedication

To my Ida Mae, two Matthews, Angela, Amanda, Laura, Pauly, and now, Sophia Pearl.

1

"TASTE THIS," THE COOK SAID, plopping a scoop of a rather gray, oozing concoction onto the mess kit of the big fellow standing before him.

For a moment, the man stared at the spreading lump as if deciding if it was edible. Then he shrugged and said, "Okay." He spooned the mass into his mouth and chewed slowly, his tentative effort becoming joyful. He swallowed and smacked his lips. "Don't know what you did to make hardtack and salt pork taste this good, Sarge."

Mess Sergeant Aloysius Bodine grinned. "Thanks, Ryker," he said to Toby Ryker, the chief scout for the Sixth Minnesota Regiment. "It ain't hardtack, though. It's bread that pork's sitting on, and I kneaded the dough myself just this morning, but I tried simmering the salt pork with a bit of broth and a dollop of cream."

"You kneaded the dough this morning? I need dough every morning," Ryker replied dryly. "Noon and night too, most days."

Sergeant Bodine rolled his eyes. "You're so clever, Ryker."

Totally unabashed, Ryker said, "Yeah, I know."

"You missed morning mess again."

"Yeah. Been out on the trail."

The Sixth Regiment, stationed at Fort Snelling, really had very little to keep them occupied these days. With the Civil War starting to boil up in the east and south, the soldiers were antsy, itching to get into the action, but they had to wait to be called up, and sitting at Fort Snelling provided little for them to do until they got that call. That gave Sergeant Bodine the time and motivation to experiment with rations.

But the Sixth kept their scouts busy just the same because the war to the south was not the only concern of the Minnesota army. They had another front to watch.

"Hey, Ryker, want some plum jelly on a heel of bread?"

"Plum jelly? How'd we get so dog-gone lucky?"

"That's a darned good question. It was a mix-up at the quartermaster's I'm sure."

"Well thank you, Mr. Quartermaster, sir," Ryker said, grinning. He held out his mess kit. "I believe I would like some of that jelly, and maybe some more of that doctored salt pork, too. Serve it up, will ya, Sarge?"

"You betcha, coming right up." The cook put two slices of bread on Ryker's mess-kit tray then smashed a boxelder bug crawling across the table with his army-issue ladle. He wiped the implement across his apron, knocking the just-departed vermin onto the floor, and then dipped the same ladle into a large pot, lifting out a generous portion of the steaming gray concoction onto the two rough-cut slices of bread. He then sawed off another chunk of bread and smeared it with dark-red jelly. This he plopped right on top of the pork mixture, which, of course, began soaking into the bottom side of the crust. "I'm sure glad I signed on with the First and will be heading south soon." He waved the flies away from the jelly and the bread. "I want to do battle with something besides these blasted bugs."

"Yeah, if it weren't for my folks, I'd be happier joining you rather than hanging around here with precious little to do." Ryker slapped at a mosquito, then dug his spoon into the pork.

Sergeant Bodine cocked an eye at him. "What's your folks got to do with it, you big ignoramus? You ain't no young, snot-nosed recruit."

Looking crazier than a rabid coyote, Ryker leaned over the table at the cook. Ryker was a big man, and the cook wasn't, so Ryker loomed over him. He slammed his fist on the table, looking like he was ready to rip the smaller man apart. "What did you just call me?"

Bodine looked up into Ryker's face, spat a dark stream of chewing tobacco out the side of his mouth onto the floor and said, "A big ignoramus. Yup, them was my exact words."

Ryker sat down again and adjusted his hat. "Yeah, okay, that's what I thought you said, but I just wanted to make sure, you low-down, stupid, mangy, buck-toothed, slack-jawed little runt."

Bodine grinned, showing a gap on his upper left side, and Ryker grinned back at the cook, who was his best friend. Truth was, Ryker loved to eat, so it was hardly surprising he chose a cook to chum around with, although the way the two of them carried on most of the time like a couple of naughty, name-calling schoolboys, nobody would suspect they were buddies. It was also a plus that Ryker wasn't all that fussy about what exactly he ate, which, at the fort, was pretty much whatever Bodine plunked down in front of him.

"Actually, this is pretty good slop," Ryker said, spooning a generous portion into his mouth. "What you call it, Sarge?"

"Spiced pork and milk."

Ryker narrowed his eyes a moment, his dripping spoon half-way to his mouth. "You can't call it that. Pork with milk? Yuck! Sounds like breakfast food! You got to call it something that folks'll at least want to eat."

"But it really is spiced pork and milk."

"Yeah, and hardtack is really very stale biscuits, but no one calls them that 'cause no one'd eat 'em. Call this something like . . . Pork Bodine."

"I can't attach my name to it. How'd that convince anyone to eat it? No, but how about . . ." he stirred the concoction with the ladle, "let's see, used my secret ingredients that only I know what they are, lest some big chief scout I know blabs the recipe all over the place."

3

"Come on now, admit it," Ryker said. "You don't have the foggiest idea what those spices are. I know you, a dash of this, a pinch of that."

Ignoring Ryker, Bodine doodled with the mixture some more. "If'n a feller was to smash up this pork a little bit and made it red, it would look kind of like smoked ham." His head cocked to one side as he peered into the pot. "Spices and ham . . ." His eyes lit up. "I know! I'll call it SPAM!

Ryker arched an eyebrow. "SPAM? You really have no imagination at all, do you, Bodine?"

"I reckon you're right, you big ox." Bodine sighed. "But if this stuff takes off and becomes part of the army menu, I hope they remember that it was my idea first. I can make some big money off this recipe if the whole army uses it."

"You're always inventing some kind of stew or another. This is just the first that's actually edible." Ryker smirked at Bodine. "'Course, can't go by what I'd eat, though, ya know. Why, I've been known to eat ripe raccoon kilt by a fox a week before, which I went and wrestled the haunch away from an aged bobcat with no teeth, and who'd touch that, for cripes sake?"

Bodine made like he was going to backhand Ryker with his ladle. "But you sure do like my spiced pork, right?"

Ryker grinned.

"Say, when do you think we'll be mustered to fight in Mister Lincoln's war?" Bodine asked, changing to the more serious subject all the soldiers had on their minds.

Ryker thought about that a moment as he chewed. "We won't escape it for long, that's certain. You'll be riding some train south before you know it. If it weren't for my folks, I'd be itchin' to take on them Johnny Rebs myself. But, hey, when they finally do get us Minnesota boys into the action, we'll whup their butts in a few months, free their darkies, and have this Civil War nonsense over and done with right quick. Bit of action, bit of glory, yessireebob."

"Guess you're right about that. But Ryker, I didn't know you had folks, least not anybody who'd own up to birthing you. Where your folks at then?"

"Quite a bit north, shore of a big lake, Mille Lacs, they call it. My pap 'n' mam, though, they's both up in years."

"That's no surprise, cuz you are, too. But what in tarnation they do way up there? That's just Indian country, ain't it?"

"Mostly, but there's a few white folks over to Hinckley. They fish and hunt . . . well, that's what my pap used to do. Now . . ." Ryker took another bite of the pork concoction and waved his spoon at Bodine until he swallowed. "See, my grandpappy trapped and traded with Hudson's Bay for many a year, and so did his pappy, way back when heck was a pup. Grandpappy died on the trail, some accident when he was canoeing white water with a load of hides. Pappy mighta been a trapper, too, but the fur trade wasn't what it used to be, nothing like the stories Grandpappy used to tell of his pap, that's for danged sure." He smiled and shook his head fondly at the remembrance. "So, anyway, my pappy took to fishing and hunting so's at least he could feed us, and cuz there was still some hide buyers about who paid cash money for pelts. But he's an old codger now. Got the rheumatiz, he does. He just turned sixty."

"Sixty? Your pappy's sixty years old?" The cook looked surprised. "Geez, I just hope I have a long life like that."

"Yeah, but he's pretty much just skin and bone these days. Born back in ought-two, he was. He's so danged old that . . ." Ryker gestured to Bodine to ask what that meant.

Bodine rolled his eyes and sighed again. "Oh, all right! How danged old is he?"

"He's so danged old that he's got moss growing on his north side." Ryker chuckled as Bodine shook his head sadly. "My mama, Fawn, is a bit younger. Pure blooded Chippewa, too."

Certain he'd caught the scout in a bold-faced lie, Bodine squinted at Ryker shrewdly. "Go on! You got that thatch of fiery red hair sticking out over your ears, and your mama's full Indian? No Indian I ever knew, pure or half-blood, had anything but black hair."

5

"Yeah, well, my mam's pure Chippewa. She turned fifty-six this year. She was just thirteen when I was hatched, too.'

"They's both old, then," the cook said.

"Yeah, I know," Ryker replied, sobering. "They're the only thing holding me back from going south to war. I don't think I could stand it if I went off and they died needing my help."

"You're a sentimental old fool. You know, you ain't exactly a spring chicken anymore yourself."

"Yeah, I'm forty-two." Ryker pulled a flask from his boot and took a swig. "Shucks, though, Al, considering how long my pa's lasted, I'm just hitting my prime."

Sergeant Bodine watched him tip back his flask. "Ain't it a little early in the day to be suckin' on that John Barleycorn?"

"What do you mean? It's nigh onto ten o'clock, for cripes sake, and I've been up since before dawn! For me, it's got to be . . ." he counted off on his fingers, "It's nigh two in the afternoon."

The cook laughed. "Ryker, if you weren't such a darn good scout, Colonel Crooks would have drummed you out of the military a long time ago. They don't keep men in their forties, 'less they's a general or something."

"Well, scouting's different. The army's always going to need good scouts, and young squirts like we're signing up these days don't have the know-how to be a scout. That's where growin' up amongst the Indians helped me. I learned a lot about trackin' and trailin' from my Pappy Oliver, and from traipsin' around in the woods with my mam's people. And speaking of Indians, I don't like what I'm hearing out there."

"Ah, them dumbbells ain't anything to fret about."

"Don't fool yourself, Al. My ma's folks are Chippewa. They're mostly trappers and fisherman. They don't pick fights 'less they have to. Around here, they're Dakotas though. They're warriors from old times. There's lots of them camped 'round about Yellow Medicine and Redwood, and they aren't pleased. They're saying the treaties they made with the government aren't being honored. Rations are doggone slow in getting delivered, what with the war going on in the south. They's hungry and getting sick, and they blame us for it. They think we stole their land and their hunting way of life, and by cracky, they're right about that." Ryker shook his finger at Bodine. "So just don't go foolin' yourself into believing they can't stir up a passel of trouble."

"Aw, they don't have the spunk to raise hell no more," the cook said, licking the pork off the back of his ladle.

"Some don't, but some do, mark my words. Black Wolf and Cut Nose, for instance. They never did cotton to us much in the first place, and they's been stirring things up amongst the tribes, organizing the young warriors. They're trouble. Some of the more experienced leaders, like Little Crow, have a hard time controlling them."

"You know what I think? I think you worry way too much."

"Hope you're right," Ryker replied, noticing even Bodine didn't sound all that convinced when he said it, "but I doubt you are. I think one of these here fine days we're going to find ourselves right in the middle of an Indian war the likes of which has never been seen. And if that happens, a lot of folks'll end up dead, both white and red."

"Folks are dead, both white and red," Bodine snapped his fingers to the rhythm of the rhyme and grinned at Ryker. "Such poetry outta your ignorant mouth."

"You won't think this is so doggoned funny when you got a Dakota arrow stuck outta your ear and you're walking around with your scalp tucked away in your back pocket, Al."

Commissary Sergeant William McCauly interrupted the two men when he stepped out of the headquarters building across from the open doors of the mess hall with packages and letters in hand, and hollered, "Mail call!"

Both men turned to look as soldiers gathered in front of McCauly. "Gonna go see if you got a letter there, Ryker?" Bodine asked.

"Naw, I never get nothin' but, you know, it's fun to see the young recruits get excited when they get letters from their sweethearts, so maybe I'll mosey over."

"You got a sweetheart, Ryker?"

"Not so much. Just Big Faye, my girly-friend over yonder in St. Paul," Ryker said.

"Seems I remember you saying she's a healthy-sized heifer." Amused at his own comment, Bodine let out with a high-pitched, contagious giggle, and Ryker caught the fever from him.

"It's true," Ryker said, chuckling. "She'd dress out about three hundred, but she's comfortable, and she's always available when I'm in the mood. She don't write, though. Never going to get a real letter from her, although that one time she posted me a perfumed hanky of hers. Swiped it across her ass, most likely."

"You're such a romantic devil that I can't understand why the women aren't swarming all over you like flies in an outhouse," Bodine said as the scout left the mess hall.

"Can't figure that out neither," Ryker hollered over his shoulder.

"Tobias Ryker!" Sergeant McCauley waved a letter in his general direction. "This came in for you, Toby."

"Yeah, you heard me with Sergeant Bodine, didn't ya? Teasin' me just ain't right. Gets a man's hopes—"

McCauly looked at him deadpan. "I ain't teasing, man. Here."

"Well as I live and breathe," Ryker exclaimed, taking the letter gingerly as if it were fine china. He recognized his mother's handwriting on the envelope. Having learned to read and write from missionaries, her writing was nicer than his. For a long moment, the big man stood there, a boulder in the stream of soldiers trying to get their mail.

Mister Tobias Ryker
Fort Snelling, Minnesota

Finally, Ryker put the letter protectively in his pocket and headed to the barracks where he went straightaway to the corner bunk he occupied when not out on maneuvers. No one else was in the barracks just now, so he sat on his bunk and carefully opened the envelope, almost fearing what was inside, and expecting bad news.

Dear son Toby,
Your father is not well. He suffered apoplexy and is not long
for this world. I don't know if this will reach you or if you can
come before it is too late, but please try. Please come quickly.
I pray you get here in time.

Your mother, Fawn

Ryker drew a deep breath. He always knew that one day, such a letter would come, but it was still a shock because now that he held the message in his hand, it was real. At first his mind was a jumble of emotions,
thinking of his family, of his childhood, of nothing in particular. Then his
head began to clear. He had to get authorization from the commander of
the Sixth Minnesota Regiment to take a leave from his duties. Not knowing what his father's condition really was, the duration of the leave he'd
need wasn't certain. He had a good horse, one used to long days and hard
riding, but it would still take him easily four to six days to get there. And
what would he find at the end of the trail? Would Oliver still be alive? If so,
would he linger? What would become of Fawn? Being an only child, all
these thoughts weighed heavily upon him. He would have to make deci-
sions on how to provide for his mother if his father passed.

Sighing again, he pulled the flask from his boot, took a snort,
adjusted his hat, and headed towards the Fort Snelling post headquarters
building. After hearing his story, Ryker's commander, Colonel William
Crooks, readily gave him his leave, saying as all was quiet to report back at
his leisure, since he had seen continuous service for several months. Within
the hour, Ryker was packed and heading north toward Mille Lacs.

"I'M SORRY, BUT THE STORAGE BINS are empty," Indian Agent
T.J. Galbraith said to the contingent of Dakota Sioux who had come
into his office at the Yellow Medicine Agency on the Minnesota River.

"The White Father promised us food," Little Crow, a Dakota
chief said. He motioned to those standing with him. "We are hungry.

Our children are sick and starving. Some have died. We need the food we were promised."

"But until the food and the money gets here, there's nothing I can do." As he spoke, he watched Trader Andrew Myrick enter the office and move to his side. Emboldened by Myrick's presence, he said loudly, "You have to understand, Little Crow. I requisitioned supplies for my own staff here at the agency what . . ." he looked at Myrick, "two, two and a half months ago, I think it was, and I was assured that it would be here by now. But even that hasn't arrived."

Myrick, looking hateful, glared at the Indians and nodded.

"You have to understand, Little Crow, there's a war going on," Galbraith added. "It's a big, important war. The White Fa . . . President Lincoln has a lot on his mind. More than your needs. So, what do you expect me to do about the food? Your treaty of Traverse des Sioux is not a government priority right now."

An angry man, taller than Little Crow and younger than many of the elders that crowded the office, pushed to the front. "We know there is food in the storehouse. My men saw when it was delivered and locked up days ago. Is this what you call honoring the treaty?"

Galbraith seemed taken aback by that information, but he hesitated only a moment. "But the money disbursement isn't here, Black Wolf. Until *both* are here so you can settle up with the traders, nothing leaves my warehouse."

"That's right," Myrick said, taking a step toward Black Wolf. "If you're so damn hungry, go outside and eat grass. The prairie is full of it."

The angry young warrior lunged toward Myrick, but Little Crow grabbed him and spoke to him in Dakota, and he stepped back. "We'll see who eats grass," he muttered.

Then Little Crow leaned over Galbraith's desk and looked him hard in the eyes. "You need to understand," he said in a harsh whisper, "that when men are hungry, they help themselves."

Galbraith turned red and puffed up in anger. "That would break the treaty. If you do that, you'll get nothing but trouble from the settlers and from the government in Washington. They'll send soldiers."

Black Wolf, sneering, said , "Lincoln's soldiers are too busy fighting your own people to protect a few settlers who lose some cows."

For a long moment the Dakota delegation and Galbraith and Myrick, with nothing but the desk between them, stared each other down. Then Galbraith broke eye contact. Softly, he said, "Look, I think I can get some emergency supplies delivered up here from Mankato. It'll take three days, though, at least. I'll also check at the Redwood Agency and see if they can spare some rations to tide us over until then. I'll ride down there myself yet today."

Black Wolf said, "Do you have any food in your house?"

Galbraith frowned. "My house? Well, I—"

"Give us that. Give us what you have, so we can feed our children today."

"I can't do that," Galbraith said. "That food is for me. I'll starve without it."

"Is it okay to starve Indians, but not okay for the Indian agent to starve along with us?"

Galbraith stammered, his face turning fiery red in anger and his hands balling into fists.

Little Crow motioned to the others. "Come. We'll get not so much as a crumb of bread to eat here today."

Once out of sight of Galbraith's residence and the chiefs, Black Wolf gathered his warriors around him. "Get what weapons you have. Tonight we're going to butcher a couple of the white man's cattle. That's the only way we'll see government food anytime soon."

UNDER THE COVER OF DARKNESS, Black Wolf and a dozen warriors dressed and painted for the hunt. They stole downstream along the shoreline of the Minnesota River toward a couple of homesteads. En route they chanced upon several deer and shot two yearlings. Had this been simply a hunting expedition, they might have taken their kill back to camp right then and there. But Black Wolf had a different mission in mind, and it had more to do with retribution than finding food. Besides, two young deer would not come close to feeding everyone back at camp.

They came to a fenced field and killed two young steers so quickly and quietly, that the rest of the herd never bawled an alarm. The Indians quartered the steers and dragged the meat off with them. On the way back, loaded down with beef, they heard the dull clank of an iron bell and chanced upon a milk cow come loose from somewhere, a rope dangling from her halter. Laughing, the men led her off as well.

Back at their camp near the Yellow Medicine Agency, they danced the rest of the night away as the women cooked the meat on huge fires. All in camp feasted on the bounty of the hunt, and the young men boasted of their boldness and cunning.

In the next days, when the promised emergency supplies failed to arrive to sustain them, Little Crow continued to press Agent Galbraith, coming to his office each morning. At the same time, the night raids continued, even increased. The Indians ranged ever further from the agency, taking what they needed from the settlers. Word passed among the various tribes about what they were doing. Black Wolf developed a following among some of the bands, mostly young warriors disgruntled with their treatment by the government. Factions developed within the Indian nations themselves, with some wanting to go to war and some wishing to remain loyal to the federal government.

Little Crow, who had been to Washington, had traveled across the country to get there, knew in his heart that the Indians could not win against the whites. But a young warrior like Black Wolf held nothing but disdain for Little Crow and those who held out against war.

"HEY, GALBRAITH, THOSE STINKING INDIANS of yours have been looting our stock," said Morgan Wandersee, one of several irate homesteaders congregated at the headquarters of the Indian agent after the night raids left them with losses.

12

"What do you expect me to do? I don't have the firepower to contain them," Galbraith replied.

"Haven't you been feeding them?" said Walter Quiram. "You're supposed to feed them so they don't do this kind of thing. Have you been selling their rations like folks are saying?"

Galbraith huffed indignantly. "I resent that. How can I sell what I don't have? A partial shipment arrived last week, but it was only about a third of what was ordered. With the war on, that's the way things are. It's not my fault."

"Who's going to pay for our livestock?" Wandersee asked. "My prize milk cow is gone, and I'll bet my last gold dollar she ended up on a spit at a Sioux bonfire."

Galbraith scratched his chin. "Submit a claim to me, and I'll pass it on up the line and see what I can do."

"Washington's going to fart around until these damn Indians go on the warpath and folks start getting killed. What then?" Clement Rasmussen said.

"If that happens, I'll be the first one to make tracks for Fort Ridgely, Clem, and I suggest you gather up your wife and kids and do the same," Gilbraith replied, looking around the room at the others. "That goes for the rest of you, too. There will be blood on the prairie, settler's blood, if that happens, none of your families will be safe from it. But I sure hope it doesn't come down to that."

"You'd better do more than hope," Wandersee said. "It's your duty to take care of these redskins, keep them away from our livestock. If you can't handle the job, maybe we need a new Indian agent."

Ryker sat with his mother in the small kitchen of his parents' cabin on the west shore of Lake Mille Lacs. It had taken more than a week to make the necessary arrangements, another to make the trip north. Still, his mother was astounded that he had come so quickly.

"He bleeds some through his nose," Fawn told him with concern. "At first there was blood in his eyes too, but that stopped. He still bleeds through his nose though."

"Probably relieving pressure in his head," Ryker said, trying to sound confident. "That's good, Ma."

Mother and son looked at each other, both knowing it wasn't good at all. Then they both turned to look across the cabin to where the sick man lay on the rope bed piled with balsam boughs. "Let me wake him," Fawn said. "He'll be so thrilled to see you."

"Easy, Pappy," the scout said, sitting down next to Oliver Ryker's deathbed. He offered his invalid father a sip of water from the gray metal dipper that rested in a pail on the rough table next to him. The elder Ryker had lost much weight and was not taking food.

"Toby, promise me . . . take good care of your mam," Oliver managed to say with words that were slow and a bit slurred because he was so weak. "She's been my world . . . forty-some years. I don't want to worry . . . how she'll get by. Promise me, son."

"Of course, Pappy."

His father took another sip of water, then waved the dipper away.

"You got . . . any whiskey?" Oliver said.

Toby grinned. "A man can surely die an agonizing death drinking nothing but pure water. Sure, Pappy," Ryker said, removing his flask from his haversack.

After Oliver took a healthy swig, he licked his lips. "Good. Must be . . . Kentucky whiskey."

Ryker grinned. "Sure is, Pappy. This here's Old Heaven Hill sippin' whiskey. You told me to buy nothing but the best, except if I was broke, and then, to steal nothing but the best. Remember?"

Oliver looked puzzled. "I don't recollect . . . not okay to steal, Toby."

Ryker patted his father's bony hand, remembering how powerful those hands had once been. "Not to worry, Pappy. I work for the army. I never had to steal no bottle of whiskey in my whole danged life. Just pulling your leg, I was."

Oliver looked seriously at his son. "Toby, they's not doing right . . . by the Indians. Don't get mixed up in that."

"Well, Pappy, I do what I can. There are problems on both sides, but I try to be fair in my dealings with everybody."

"Good, that's good. Always remember . . . half Indian."

"I will, Pappy. It's mighty tough sometimes, but I will."

"Good. You . . . always a good boy." Oliver looked his son over. "Good man. You've grown . . . right stout there, lad."

"I'm a fatty-fatty-two-by-four, you mean," Ryker said, chuckling. "Yeah, I've put on a pound or two since I was a strapping young lad. I eat too danged good in the cavalry."

Oliver smiled slightly.

"Big Faye thinks I got a big hinder. I tried to explain to her that a fellow can't drive a spike with a tack hammer."

"Big Faye?" Fawn looked at him quizzically.

"Yeah, my girly-friend. Faye Knutson is her name. She and I met at a church social at the cathedral in St. Paul. We take walks along the river sometimes, and go out to eat at fancy restaurants."

"I think that's wonderful you have a woman friend," Fawn said.

Oliver Ryker squinted at his son. "I'm sixty . . . old as dirt, but I can still spot a fib. Big Faye a . . . she a night woman?"

"Oliver, shame on you!" said Fawn sharply. "We raised Toby better than that. You wouldn't engage in any hanky-panky with a loose woman, would you, Toby?"

"Um, why, of course not, Mama," Ryker said, looking down at the floor. He could feel himself blushing.

"There, see what you did, Oliver? You embarrassed our son. I certainly hope you're happy." Although just five-foot-two, Fawn demonstrated yet again who wore the pants in the Ryker household.

Oliver sighed. He winked at Ryker. "Don't go . . . too many picnics."

"I won't, Pappy. Anyway, Big Faye, she calls me her 'lard-ass soldier boy.' It's a term of affection."

"I wouldn't exactly say you're fat," Fawn said, patting Ryker's stout shoulders and trying to ignore his double chin and protruding belly.

"What exactly *would* you say about me, Mama?"

"I'd say you've just always been a big-boned man with a healthy appetite."

"Thanks, Mama, you're very kind."

Oliver grew serious. "You should . . . butcher the shoat. After I'm gone . . . folks will show up . . . they'll be hungry."

"Oh, there won't be that many who come. Surely a few chickens—" Fawn said.

"Butcher the shoat."

"Yes, sir," Ryker said.

Oliver nodded. Even in the short time Ryker had been there, his father had seemed to grow paler, weaker. "Think I'll . . . sleep now, son. If'n I don't wake . . . obliged you came."

Oliver Ryker was a man who had planned everything out all throughout his long life. He now closed his eyes and fell into a deep slumber, as there was nothing left for him to do. An hour later, his breathing ceased and his heart stopped, and he joined his British ancestors across the Great Divide.

"He waited for you," Fawn said. "He loved you very much, you know. All he's talked about this last month has been holding on until you got here."

Ryker hugged and kissed his mother tenderly then pressed his cheek against her head. The two of them, with tears in their eyes, silently looked at the still form on the bed. Abruptly, Fawn stiffened and pulled herself away. That was Fawn; unlike Ryker, who freely displayed his feelings, she viewed any display of emotion, even with her own family, as a sign of weakness. She'd learned early, when the Sioux raided their camp when she was a child, that the weak were easy prey, and she vowed never to put herself in danger.

IF FAWN BELIEVED THAT NO ONE would come to pay their respects to her husband, this was one of the few times she found herself mistaken, for word of Oliver's death spread quickly up and down the shores of Lake Mille Lacs. From miles away they came—hunters, fishermen, traders, woodsmen, settlers, and even merchants from as far away as Hinckley who knew Oliver Ryker as the reliable, trustworthy fisherman he had always been. The Chippewa too came in great abundance, setting up their wigwams near the small cabin that Oliver and Fawn called home.

When the feasting began, Oliver was proven correct about the shoat. It was right to butcher it and roast it on the spit, and besides the pork, Ryker hunted down three deer and bought a half side of beef from a farmer nearby as well. All parties reminisced about Oliver's good nature, his helpfulness, his fine deeds, and his fair dealings. No one actually mourned his death, however, because after all, he was sixty. They laid him out for a few days and toasted him night and day, then, before he got ripe, they buried him back of the house. Father Louis Bouvier, a French missionary serving the area, officiated at the services. All the ceremonies took eight days from the time Oliver closed his eyes for the last time. The day after that, cabin fever set in, and the restless scout paced the floor of the small, rustic, Ryker home.

"Toby, you don't have to stay here on my account," Fawn said.

"But Pappy said I was to look out for you after he was gone."

"I know what he said, but don't you fret about it," she replied. "I can take care of myself just fine, thank you very much. I can hunt and fish and I'm in fine health, and don't forget that my people are nearby. I am still Ojibwe. I'll always have a place with them."

"Mama, you would return to the tribe?"

"Yes, when the time comes. Maybe next year I'll move with them onto the reservation."

"I'd feel better about that," Ryker said. "Thinking about you alone . . ."

"You go on now," Fawn said firmly. "Go back to the military. That's your life. That's where you belong."

17

Toby turned, then paused. He faced his mother again. "There's trouble brewin', Ma, not only with Mister Lincoln's war, but with the Dakota on our western border."

Fawn spat on the ground. "They're Sioux, and they're savages," Fawn said. "I never did like them. A bunch of hot-heads and renegades. They aren't so tough, though. We Ojibwe pushed them out of northern Minnesota without much trouble."

"Black Wolf and Cut Nose are stirring them up."

"Black Wolf's a heathen. His father was honorable, but Black Wolf is not. He's a lazy, drunken excuse for a man! Cut Nose—I don't know much about him. Look to Little Crow for better leadership."

"Now, Mama," Ryker replied. "This ain't all their doings."

"Maybe not, but I don't trust them, especially Black Wolf," Fawn said. "You be careful around him. If you can, put a bullet in his head."

"Now Mama . . ."

"You're just like your father, very tolerant. That's admirable, but it can also be dangerous in this day and age. This isn't like the old days when you could trust your neighbors. Nowadays whenever I leave the cabin, I don't know if everything will be here when I get back." She retied the drawstring on Ryker's shirt and smoothed out the buckskin over his broad chest. "You got to look out for yourself these days."

"I will, Mama," Ryker said, kissing her. "And I promise I'll be better about writing to you."

"Letters are iffy. I was lucky to find a trader heading to Fort Snelling. Just keep me in your thoughts, as I will you. That's enough, and if our paths happen to cross, it will be a cause to rejoice."

"You're wise, Mama."

"Shush now." Fawn turned away, took out a handkerchief, and dabbed at her eyes. "I don't want you to remember your mother as a weeping old woman." She handed over a fringed buckskin coat, pants, and leggings, hand-stitched and beaded in Ojibwe designs, which she had made especially for him.

18

"Mama . . ." Ryker said in a whisper, overcome at the beauty, the craftsmanship of the outfit, and knowing it represented a labor of love that took many hours to create.

"Never forget your Indian heritage, Toby. Just as your father was proud of your British blood, I am proud of your Ojibwe blood. Your father's time is over, and my time . . . only the Great Spirit knows how long that will be. But your time is now. These are your days, so go back to the army, live an honorable life, and keep making me proud that you are my son."

The two embraced. Within the hour, Ryker was packed. After a final goodbye to Fawn, he headed south toward St. Paul on the Mississippi, and beyond, to his post at Fort Snelling. It was the last time he would see Fawn. Although neither said so, they both knew that.

2

SNOUT WRINKLED AND MOUTH hanging open, Ryker gawked about the grounds as he entered Fort Snelling. The place seemed so different. Many of the familiar faces were gone and were replaced by civilians roaming the commons, people who looked like they had come through a war themselves. Ryker shook his head in bewilderment as he entered the post headquarters, stood at attention, and saluted Colonel Crooks. "Scout Toby Ryker reporting back to duty, sir."

"Ryker, where the devil have you been?" Crooks didn't bother to return the salute.

"Up north, to home. My pappy died. You gave me my leave. Don't you remember?"

"Vaguely, but it seems like you've been gone forever."

"Only a month or so."

"Well, anyway, we're up to our necks here. I'm glad you're back. Black Wolf and a bunch of his renegades are on the warpath, looting and killing all over the western border. A courier from Fort Ridgely came in just this morning with the news."

"Black Wolf . . . I might have known," Ryker said. "I've been saying all along that he's trouble, but nobody listened."

20

"We're listening now. And on top of everything else, I'm short-handed here, since we got new orders and most of the regulars have been deployed to the south to fight in the Civil War. The Sioux knew how to time their massacre perfectly." Crooks motioned out the window. "Those civilians are some of the survivors. They keep straggling in off the prairie, and the stories they tell are horrible."

"What you want me to do, sir?"

"Stand by for further orders. Governor Ramsey approached Henry Sibley today requesting he take command of the state forces in the field and that he lead a campaign against the Sioux. Sibley agreed, and has been appointed to the militia at the rank of colonel and as commander of the Indian Expedition, so they are calling it. He'll need your services, as will we all."

"You got it, sir. Taking your leave," Ryker said, stepping back and saluting.

"Fine," Crooks said. "I knew I could count on you, Ryker."

ON THE MORNING OF MONDAY, August 18th, 1862, the Dakota Uprising began in earnest after first few isolated instances of thefts and deaths. It spread, over the next few weeks, from Otter Tail Lake and Fort Abercrombie on the Red River, south to the Iowa border, a distance of two hundred miles, and, eastward, from Big Stone Lake, on the western shore, to Forest City in Meeker County, an area of 20,000 square miles, embracing no less than eighteen counties with a population of 40,000 souls. Over this vast territory, the sky, at night, was illuminated with a the reflected glare from the conflagration of burning homes and towns. In a week, and mostly within the first forty-eight hours, 1,000 persons perished, and thousands more were sent running for their lives. A stream of 30,000 refugees rushed up the Minnesota Valley, seeking protection in the larger towns or heading to neighboring states. Not less than $2,000,000 worth of property was destroyed in a belt of two hundred and fifty miles, and in ten counties at the heart of the action, nothing was left.

21

"SIR, I WANT TO POWWOW with Little Crow," Ryker said, standing across the desk from his new commanding officer at Fort Snelling.

"That's very risky," Colonel Henry Hastings Sibley replied.

"For most, yes," Ryker agreed. "But Little Crow and I know one another from way back. He'll let me into his camp and will release me again unharmed."

Sibley eyed the scout cautiously. "Ryker, I've heard tell you're a good scout, but are you really that good?"

"My mama thinks I am," Ryker said, grinning. Then he lost his smile. "Little Crow knows I'll be honest with him and that I won't try and trick him." He squinted at Sibley. "And that's the truth, sir. I won't try to trick him. That's not how I do things."

"Okay, do what you can, and also try to find out where he is headed," Sibley said. "And if you can get him to release any prisoners, so much the better. Do you need a horse?"

Ryker shook his head. "I've got my big bay, Wino. I'll head out this evening. One of Little Crow's sentries is sure to spot me in no time and take me into camp."

"As soon as I'm able, I'm conducting a forced march to St. Peter, so report there upon your return."

"Yes, sir."

RYKER UNDERESTIMATED HOW DISTANT Little Crow's camp was, for he ended up following the Minnesota River west for several miles past Yellow Medicine River before coming upon a sentry, and then it was he who spotted the sentry, dozing astride an Appaloosa pony, rather than the other way around. Ryker recognized the man. Not being able to resist the temptation to have a little rough-and-tumble fun, he sneaked up on the Indian from behind, dragged him from the horse, and put his Bowie knife to the man's throat. "Boo!" he said.

The warrior flinched and would have cut himself on Ryker's knife had the scout not moved it out of the way in time. His name was Dancing Bear, and he and Ryker knew each other.

"For a great big fat man, you're sure quiet," Dancing Bear said.

"Yeah, and for a sentry, you sure don't pay very good attention to what's going on around you," Ryker replied, putting his knife away. "It's important I talk to Little Crow. Can you take me into camp?"

"I can, but I can't guarantee Black Wolf won't have you killed."

"I guess I'll have to take that risk. You know I'm with the cavalry. I'm scouting for them right now. But I'm still Toby Ryker, and my word is still good as ever."

"That might not be enough for Black Wolf," Dancing Bear said. "These are very different times than when you and I played card games together."

"They are," said Ryker. "And what's happening is bad for all."

Dancing Bear sighed. "That's the truth. My replacement will come soon. When he does, I'll take you into camp with me."

Ryker knew waiting with Dancing Bear posed a risk as well, if the replacement identified him as U.S. Army. To forstall that, he dismounted and stripped his big bay of its saddle. He also took off his hat. In the waning dusk, he didn't look all that different from his friend.

They heard a rider coming up from the river, the heavy pounding of hooves indicated that he was riding hard. When he reached the top of the rise, he paused. "Dancing Bear?" the man said in Dakota.

"I'm here," Dancing Bear replied.

"Who's with you?"

"Toby Ryker. He's a half-blood scout from the big fort in St. Paul."

"He's a scout!" The man said this as a curse.

"I need to speak with Little Crow," Ryker said, though his Dakota wasn't good.

"It might be better for you if I slit your throat here."

23

"Running Fox," said Dancing Bear, "Ryker is my friend. He's an honorable man. Little Crow knows him."

It was then agreed that Dancing Bear would lead Ryker into the camp. When they arrived at Little Crow's camp well after dark, the place was full of activity. Women were busy at the cooking fires, and the center of the camp was full of warriors telling tales around great fires. As Dancing Bear took him to Little Crow's tepee, they passed a guarded tent from which came the crying and whimpering of women and children. Hostages, Ryker assumed. He also knew he could do nothing about that at the moment. Dancing Bear took him directly to Little Crow's tipi where the two exchanged greetings. Little Crow ushered him quickly inside.

"It has been a long time since you and I have spoken," Little Crow said the next morning as he and Ryker sat by his fire. The chieftain wore a long-sleeved blouse even though the weather was very warm. He had been wounded in the arms as a young brave, and he usually hid his disfigured limbs.

"Several months," Ryker said. "In fact, better than a year."

"These are very desperate times for us."

"But you can't win in a war with the white army."

The chief looked at Ryker with sad and concerned eyes. "I have traveled across the country to the east to see the Lincoln. The train carried me faster than any horse can run, and it never tired. I saw many towns and cities so great that even the hills and trees have given way to the white man's tall buildings. So many people, like thistle down on the wind. The Indian cannot win against so many."

Ryker's attention was drawn to a shrill cry from a tepee, the same one he had heard the weeping emanate from. "You have hostages?"

The man nodded heavily. "Some women and children as is the custom of war. And some warriors have visited there. I do what I can to protect them, but, you must know, my views on avoiding war are not popular just now. The young warriors have blood in their teeth, successful attacks behind them. They're excited and full of boasting.

People have been killed, scalps taken, women used. War is not a nice thing."

"This will come to nothing, you know," Ryker said.

"I know," Little Crow replied. "I suppose you will tell the troops where I am."

"That's my job, but heck, they don't need me to show them the way. You've left such a wide trail that even a blind man could find you."

Little Crow looked around at his warriors. "It would never have come to this had the food come."

"Washington hasn't honored it's treaties. I know."

"They should have understood that Dakotas are warriors, and making war on our enemies is our way. You know that, and you also know that Washington hasn't been fair with us. The treaty of Traverse des Sioux we signed back in fifty-one isn't worth the paper it is written on. We starve, we get disease, we have nothing, and it isn't supposed to be this way. If Washington wished to kill us off entirely, they could hardly have done worse. This is what our lives have become."

"I won't try to defend Washington. What you say is true. The government has not treated you with honor. But," Ryker gestured toward the loud celebrating in the middle of camp, "what is the purpose of all this?"

"Men like Cut Nose and Black Wolf want to get everyone's attention, and with your Civil War on, they believe the government is too busy to stop us. There aren't enough soldiers." Little Crow leaned toward Ryker and whispered, "And the Confederates and even the British are providing us with supplies now. The more the warriors distract the army, the better the South fares in the war."

"But in the end, you know as well as I do that your way of life will never return," Ryker said. "The old days are over. They are gone, Little Crow. You have to adapt to the world as it has become, for you cannot change it back as it was in your father's time. And now the soldiers won't even let you go back to how it was just a year ago."

"Maybe the old days are over, maybe not. Maybe Washington will give our lands back to us, so we can hunt and fish once again."

"Sure, and maybe you will learn how to fly, but I doubt it."

"Well, what has been done cannot be undone, just as the lies in the treaties, and the failed promises, and the starvation and the plagues inflicted upon my people cannot be undone." Little Crow nodded at his warriors then looked at Ryker with a noble bearing. "At least, the mighty Dakota Nation has taken a stand. We are a proud people and not to be trifled with."

"True, you have done that. I can't support how you did it, but you made Washington sit up and take notice." Ryker arose. "I had best be getting back. Hank Sibley's been appointed as the commander of the Indian Expedition, so they call it, by Governor Ramsey. They made him a colonel. You remember Hank Sibley, don't you?"

"The Long Trader was our first governor," Little Crow said. "He was a friend of us Indians when he was a member of Congress. How ironic. Now he is out to kill us."

"Can you blame him after what's happened?"

"Not giving us our food had consequences. Responding to that lack has its consequences, as well. It's difficult to envision that all this isn't part of the government's plan to destroy us."

"Oh, I don't think—"

"Don't you? Black Wolf and Cut Nose are convinced that it is true, that the whites would like it very much not to have us here at all. They want our land for all the people who want to come here. I saw those people—so many people. Indian land must look like paradise to them. The government steals the land from us and all but gives it to their own people. It's hard not to believe that Black Wolf and Cut Nose aren't right. More people are following them than me now. Where is Long Trader now?"

"He's encamped at St. Peter with what soldiers haven't gone off south to fight in that war. Volunteers are mustering to help stop you. He has a few cannons, and some mounted cavalry, but most of his soldiers are on foot," Ryker said. "More are coming all the time to join the fight, though. I wouldn't advise you follow the river to the north."

Little Crow nodded. "Cut off up that way, huh?"

"Along the river, yeah, you are."

Little Crow crossed his arms, looking tired. *Here's a man who knows he's going to have to travel a difficult road*, thought Ryker. It surprised him when Little Crow took a philosophical view. "It will be interesting to see how this war plays out, the Dakota warriors, the mighty Dakota Nation and all our allies who have been cheated by Washington, against the United States war machine."

"If I was a betting man, I'd bet on the Minnesota settlers and the rag-tag army, Little Crow," Ryker said, his piercing blue eyes riveted to those of the Indian. "They may look helpless and too few, some may not have much to fight with, but no matter how you cut it, they are the future of this state rather than the past. The past is the way of life you and your fathers knew."

Little Crow gazed off across the prairie. The beating of war drums behind them and the wild whoops of the warriors, many of whom had enjoyed some of the spoils of war—liquor—as well as the continued weeping of women and children from the hostage tent seemed to dim in his ears. He dreamed of a past that was no more, and the sadness in his face deepened.

"Whatever happened to Galbraith, the Indian agent?" Ryker asked, changing the subject.

"Ran away. He knew Black Wolf would have killed him had he stayed. He's now Major Galbraith of the Renville Rangers over at Fort Ridgley. He's fighting us too." Little Crow motioned to an Indian woman and spoke in Dakota. The woman seemed surprised at what he said. When she hesitated, Little Crow spoke roughly. She disappeared into a tipi and returned moments later with a boy about ten years old. The lad appeared in shock. He wasn't crying; he just looked lost. "Black Wolf took this boy after killing his family. He had been hiding in the cellar and watched it. Black Wolf's men would've missed him, but they smoked him out when they set fire to the cabin. So, they brought him back here to camp, but he's touched in the head. Not even Black Wolf takes pleasure in killing a crazy boy who won't even scream. You can have him to take back to Sibley as a gift."

Ryker approached the lad and put an arm around him. The boy flinched at the touch and looked up at the six-foot-four-inch scout, but said nothing.

"I'll take the boy, Little Crow, and I'll tell Colonel Sibley of your kindness."

The chief shrugged. "It won't stop him from trying to kill us, or the warriors from trying to kill him."

Ryker did not comment to that. "Any other hostages you wish to release?"

A louder scream came from the hostage tent, and Little Crow pressed his eyes shut a moment. "I fear if I tried to stop what Black Wolf calls the spoils of war, I might be killed. I do what I can to keep the women and children alive, but I can't stop the warriors from taking out their anger on them. War is never a pretty thing, Ryker."

"Perhaps I could see them, get a list of names—?"

Little Crow just shook his head.

Ryker looked down at the silent boy under his arm. "Do you know this one's name?" Ryker asked.

"If he has one, I've not heard it. They just call him dummy."

Bending down to eye level with the lad, the scout put his hand on the boy's thin shoulders and said gently, "What is your name, son?"

The boy looked into Ryker's friendly eyes and studied him for several seconds. His mouth opened a bit as if he were trying to speak, to form a word, a name, but no sound came. Ryker couldn't be sure he wasn't just mimicking his own mouth movements. Then the boy broke off his gaze and looked blankly at the ground.

Ryker kept the boy at his side the next half hour as he prepared to depart Little Crow's camp. During that entire time, the boy still acted mute, almost as if in a trance, and Ryker wondered if he really was feeble-minded or if witnessing the massacre of his family had traumatized him. When at last he departed, with the lad sitting in the saddle ahead of him, he felt he was still on good terms with Little Crow, and the two vowed to keep in communication as much as they were able.

Little Crow had to know that Ryker would report his location to Sibley, but as the scout had put it, the path of destruction to the camp was hardly difficult to follow. Ryker had not questioned him about the tribe's war plans or where they were moving next. Nor did he pressure Little Crow as to how many captives he had or anything like that. It was all information that could be gathered in other ways. The two men parted with honor.

It took Ryker four hours to return to the shoreline of the Minnesota River with his young charge riding on the saddle in front of him. Little Crow's camp sat on the open prairie in Nicollet County near Swan Lake, a large slough where there was plenty of water and game. The chief ruled the prairie for the time being with no one to hamper his movement, so he could camp where he pleased. The scout saw a few Indian sentries about, but Little Crow had passed word that no harm was to come to him or the boy, so they did not try to interfere with their travel in any way.

By the time Ryker reached St. Peter the next day, the afternoon sun was low in the western sky. The boy, sitting behind him now, had said nothing the entire ride, but he clung to the scout protectively while the cavalry steed worked its way around the ravines of the Minnesota River ever eastward.

"I was wondering if I'd have to send a detail out after you," Sibley said after Ryker had ridden into the makeshift post at St. Peter and found the colonel.

"That wouldn't have been a good idea," Ryker said, dismounting. "Accomplished what I set out to do, and," he lifted the young boy to the ground, "brought this hostage back from Little Crow's camp. It was good of him to release this tadpole unharmed."

"Yes, I must give him credit for that." Bending down to eye level with the boy, Sibley could tell instantly that the lad was damaged. "Take him over to the infirmary. He needs proper care, much more than we can provide here."

"Yes, sir," Ryker said. "If it is all right with you sir, I'd like to look in on him now and again."

"Until we can move him, that's fine, but in a few days, I hope to have enough provisions to move upriver to Mankato, New Ulm, and west to Fort Ridgely." Sibley motioned to the boy. "That won't be where this boy needs to be. He probably should be in an insane asylum, I'm afraid."

Ryker did more than look in on the boy. When he took him to the infirmary, the boy followed willingly enough, but when the scout tried to leave him there, the youth became fearful and clung to him as though his survival depended upon it. Still the lad did not speak. Ryker talked to him softly and repeated several times that he would return shortly. The boy seemed to comprehend this and released his hold, but stared after him as he left the makeshift hospital, which was set up in a vacant building.

Quickly cleaning up and stowing his trail gear, Ryker went to chow, ate hurriedly, then kept his promise and returned to the infirmary. The boy was looking toward the door from which he exited and smiled as Ryker entered. A tray of food had been brought for him, and he had been cleaned up and given clean clothing. But he seemed incapable of doing anything—even feeding himself—on his own.

"You ain't touched your vittles here, sonny," Ryker said, sitting on the cot next to the boy and motioning to the boiled potatoes swimming in gravy with bits of beef floating in it. Alongside was a slice of bread and half a cob of fieldcorn. The potatoes were more numerous than pieces of beef, the gravy was salty, and the corn was tough with the lateness of the season, but it was vastly better than the hardtack and salt pork he'd had on the trail. "I et that same dinner over to the mess tent a bit ago," he told the boy. "It's real good." He picked up a forkful of the repast and offered it to the boy, who opened his mouth and tried some. As though something clicked inside him, the youth looked at the food then at Ryker and took the fork and began to eat ravenously.

"Atta boy. That's more like it," Ryker said. "My friend Bodine— you don't know him because he's down south feedin' our boys in the civil war now—he'd be proud to see you eating like this. I am too."

30

Continuing to speak softly, the scout sensed that the lad relaxed a bit as the meal warmed his insides. When finished, the boy belched then grinned. "It's the gravy what does that. I do that too." Never knowing a youngster this age who wasn't amused by bodily function humor, he decided to try an old trick. He leaned over as though to share a deep dark secret and whispered, "I fart, too. Here, I'll show you. Pull my finger." When the boy complied, Ryker let go with a blast capable of peeling the fancy paper off a Victorian parlor wall.

It worked, for by this time the lad was laughing, and Ryker thought he'd struck a chord with the boy. "It's good to see you laugh after what you been through. Can you tell me your name now?"

The boy hesitated and thought a moment then stammered and haltingly whispered, "Da-David Stew-wart." He swallowed, then said, "From near Henderson, dow-downriver." As though shocked at the sound of his voice, he broke down and wept.

Ryker hugged young David Stewart and allowed the grief to spill forth from the traumatized youth. The floodgates then opened, and the words began to tumble from the boy's mouth. The two ended up talking far into the night, with David telling in detail how he had happened to go to the cellar of their farm home moments before the raid to fetch some potatoes for his mother for supper. He heard the Indians ride up with their cries and war whoops and the firing of guns, and when he heard screams coming from upstairs, he climbed the steps and opened the cellar door just a crack. There he witnessed with horror the savage, bloody slaughter of his pregnant mother, his father, and his three older brothers as it took place in the kitchen. When his mother's lifeblood oozed toward him on the floor and, still warm, began to drip down upon him, he closed the door to blot out the screams.

David didn't remember going back down into the cellar. The next thing he recalled was being in the Sioux camp with Indians taunting him, poking at his private parts, and scraping scalping knives across his forehead. He remembered looking around and having no idea where he was. He'd been too scared to speak, could not scream, and seemed to

31

be paralyzed into total inaction. He was in a near-catatonic state because the horrors he witnessed temporarily affected his mind.

Little Crow, typical of many Indians, believed the boy possessed a mystical power and was favored by their Great Spirit. He feared his warriors would be punished by the Great Spirit if they harmed this special boy. Although David never realized it, this psychological defense mechanism had saved his life.

As good fortune would have it, David Stewart was not doomed to life in the state asylum. Like hundreds of other refugees from the Indian massacre, he went to live with relatives. In his case, he ended up in St. Paul with Martha and James Stewart, an aunt and uncle on his father's side. Although they adopted him and raised him as their own flesh and blood, he never forgot Ryker and considered the scout to be his savior, his hero. The young orphan boy resolved to join the horse soldiers when he was old enough to do so, and he and the scout were destined to cross trails for many years thereafter.

3

SITTING IN THE MESS TENT with Colonel Sibley, Colonel Crooks, and the other officers, Ryker reported on his rendezvous with Little Crow and told of the captives he knew were being held in the camp.

"What made Little Crow do it, Colonel Sibley, sir?" asked one of the junior officers. "I mean, I know they've had tough times on the rez and all, but shucks, the Sioux lived through tough times before. What finally brought them to this?"

Ryker knew many of the answers, but he also knew that Sibley was an elegant speaker, and he liked to hear the commander talk.

"In the first place," Sibley began, "Little Crow and the Indian bands implicated had, under pressure, been induced to transfer, by treaty, in 1837 and again in 1851 to the U.S. Government, the rights to all their immense lands both east and west of the Mississippi River."

"Funny, ain't it?" Ryker said. "That treaty back in fifty-one, the Treaty of Traverse des Sioux, was signed within spitting distance of where we now sit."

"That's right," Sibley replied. "Our own Governor Ramsey was in on that one. So the natives, by treaty, gave up the possession to the

33

lands, which contained the graves of their fathers from time immemori-al, and consented to move onto a reservation where they would be pro-tected from intrusion by the whites and generously provided for by the government, with all the instrumentalities required to render them happy, self-sustaining and contented. In express terms, the treaties guar-anteed that every promise made to the Indians would be faithfully per-formed, and the solemnity of the obligation on the part of the govern-ment was emphasized."

"And the government did take care of them, didn't it?" asked one of the young officers. "I mean, my family were pioneers. They worked damn hard. No one gave them a free ride."

"Is that how you see the situation with the Indians?" asked Sibley. "I've been a trader to the Indians, and I know for fact that almost nothing the government promised was delivered. The Indians were intensely dis-appointed when they found themselves deceived and transferred from their magnificent country, a paradise on earth that abounded with forests and lakes teeming with animal life and beautiful scenery unrivaled anywhere, to an open prairie from which the buffalo, elk, deer, and other game had been driven. On the reservation these proud people were forced to depend almost solely on the traders, many of which took advantage of the Indians, and the government for their daily bread. To aggravate this discontent of the provisions of the treaties being basely disregarded, appropriations by Congress for specific purposes were criminally merged into a general fund, annuities frequently suspended in whole or in part upon the slightest pre-text by the Indian Bureau, and payments deferred for months after their maturity, thereby causing great suffering to these wards of a great nation false to its own promises and to its trust."

"I had an inkling of that, but I never heard it explained all the way through," Ryker said.

"That's just the background. There's more," Sibley said.

"But that's what touched them off just now, ain't it?" Making sure Sibley couldn't see him do it, Ryker winked at the now smiling Colonel Crooks and the other officers.

"That's correct," Sibley replied. "These past summer months, Indian Agent Galbraith, the same man who now commands the troops at Fort Ridgely against these Indians, three times called for an assemblage of nearly seven thousand men, women, and children from the Yellow Medicine and the Redwood Agency reservations with the expectation that money, food, and clothing due them would be forthcoming, as he had been so advised by the Commissioner of Indian Affairs in Washington. Each time the tribes gathered, they were doomed to bitter disappointment, for the promised goods were not delivered. Meanwhile, the supply of eatables remained in the agency storehouses while officials ignored the piteous appeals for food, appeals so humiliating to the Indian's spirit. The begging and the buffalo dances brought nothing. Apart from other grievances, this state of affairs was enough to drive the warriors to desperation. Still, it was four youths arguing over a hen's eggs that precipitatied the Acton murders on Sunday the seventeenth of August. When those boys returned to the main camp at the Redwood and Yellow Medicine Agencies, they frankly admitted their crime, imploring their kindred to protect them from arrest and punishment at the hands of the whites. That was the beginning. The next night warriors—not boys this time—constituting the supreme authority of the bands, assembled to the number of one hundred and fifty, formed the plan and took the oath of destruction which they so faithfully executed on the eighteenth and nineteenth.

"As you know, it was an epoch of the most inhuman and remorseless butchery ever enacted upon the American continent. But remember, Ryker, that there was nothing left for the Indians to do. Their wives and children were dead or dying for want of food. They were either to die themselves, or exact, even at the cost of their own lives, a fire-lit, vengeful, bloody, and brutal atonement for all the wrongs inflicted upon them. And with the nation embroiled in the Civil War, the time was opportune. 'Time, at last, makes all things even.' As for Little Crow, he knows what all this will cost his people. But he can't stop this, and he knows that, too."

Sibley neglected to mention that of the $475,000 promised the Sioux in the treaty, he claimed $145,000 for his American Fur Company as overpayments to the Indians for hides purchased from them. The colonel amassed a personal fortune at the expense of the Indians, and along with claims of the other traders, left them with practically nothing as payment for their lands. In his fur trading days, and now again in his military appointment, Sibley benefitted from the same collusion with Governor Alexander Ramsey that he condemned in others. Ramsey was the principal negotiator of the treaty, and Sibley received nearly a third of the Sioux financial settlement. Ramsey appointed Sibley as the commander of the Indian Expedition. These actions were more political than they were coincidental.

"You feel strongly about this, don't you, sir?" Ryker said.

"Yes, I do."

"I do too, because I'm half Chippewa, you know."

"With your red hair, I never would have guessed it. I had you pegged to be a Swede."

"Yah-shure, by golly, you betcha," Ryker said, laughing. "Lots of folks mistake me for a Swede, but I'm half Indian and half British."

"Which half is which?"

"Huh?"

"You said you're half Indian, half British." This time it was Sibley who had a twinkle in his eye. "Which half is which?"

"Aw shucks, sir, now you're teasing me," Ryker said, blushing. "But I guess the honest answer is that I'm British on the outside and Indian on the inside."

This apparently wasn't the response Sibley had been expecting because he sobered quickly and studied the scout for a moment. "That is a very interesting observation." He cleared his throat. "Well, when it comes to this, even though I understand where Little Crow, Black Wolf, Cut Nose, and the others get their rage, I cannot condone it. They are killing Minnesotans who had no part in creating the injustices against them, except perhaps by living on land the Indians consider their own."

"This being true," said Ryker, "if it comes down to a battle, I'll shoot to kill Little Crow himself even though we are friends. He knows that too."

"For now, maybe you'd best stay out of his camp," said Sibley. "At least until I can establish formal, official communication with him."

"Yup, I reckon that probably is best. The way this war is heating up, I don't know that Little Crow could guarantee my safe passage if I was to venture in there again, unless I was under a flag of truce."

THE VERY NEXT DAY, THE COMMANDER sent for Ryker. "I need you to lead reinforcements to Colonel Flandrau at New Ulm. They're having a tough go of it there on account of Cut Nose."

"Yes, sir. I'll be ready to head out directly," Ryker said. "New Ulm's upriver about twenty miles or so on the other side of Mankato. We'll follow the shoreline up."

"Good idea," Sibley said. "Stay off the prairie. You have nowhere to hide on the open ground."

"I know it. With our small detail, we'd be ambushed for sure, and never make it to New Ulm if we went up on the prairie."

Within the hour, Ryker was at the head of a column of soldiers of the Sixth Minnesota, led by Colonel Crooks, heading southwest toward New Ulm. They followed the Minnesota River as Ryker said, but the going was slow because of the rough terrain. Several times Ryker advanced alone to scout out the various ravines and draws leading down to the river, for there was ample cover there to hide marauding Sioux. About midway between Mankato and New Ulm, the troops came upon yet another draw.

"I'll check it out, sir," Ryker said. "This won't take long." So saying, he dismounted and with a quick pace moved forward on foot to the east side of the hilly draw.

"Ryker can really move for such a large man," Colonel Crooks said to his aide, Captain Hiram Bailey.

"That he can," Bailey replied, watching as the buckskin-clad scout scurried deftly toward the draw. "You'd never guess him to be that agile from the size of him."

"Ryker's amazed me before," Crooks said. "We're darn lucky he is on our side rather than fighting with the Dakota."

"I know he's got feelings for the Indians, but I sure hope he doesn't let it get in the way of his duty."

Crooks reined in Prince, his high-spirited Arabian that had started to prance, and looked at Bailey. "You needn't fret on that account, Captain Bailey. Ryker's as loyal as the day is long."

When Ryker reached the top of the draw, he disappeared down the other side for several moments. The officers next saw him appear at the foot of the draw, scarcely two hundred feet ahead of the column. He motioned to them to come forward as all was clear.

"Good," Crooks said, raising his arm and signaling his troops to advance. "We ought to reach New Ulm by mid-day tomorrow."

AT NOON THE NEXT DAY, Colonel Crooks led the troops of the Sixth Minnesota into New Ulm, a settlement whose population consisted primarily of German immigrants. It had been ransacked by Cut Nose and 600 braves, and left with only twenty-five homes still standing.

They bivouacked in the center of what remained of the town until the next day, allowing the troops to rest from the forced march from St. Peter and to help care for the injured and to bury the dead. All about them was carnage, smoldering ruins of what once had been homes and businesses, and corpses, many mutilated, strewn everywhere. The screams of the injured were in the air, drowning out the grieving moans and cries of the widowed and orphaned.

After assisting with the gruesome tasks for several hours, Ryker approached Crooks with a request. "I'd like to scout around the area a bit, sir. Some friends of mine have a brewery on the Cottonwood River. I haven't seen them in town, so I'd like to check it out and make sure they are okay."

"The Schells Brewery," Crooks said. "I'm familiar with it. August Schell and his men make a fine German beer."

"That they do, and, if he's okay, I'll bring some back with me, sir," Ryker said, grinning. "That is, if Cut Nose hasn't burned the place to the ground."

A half hour later, Ryker approached the brewery and was amazed to see it was still standing. It looked like nothing had been touched. He made his way up to the main house and greeted the rotund German woman who answered his knock. "Good day, Theresa," he said, nodding to the amiable wife of August Schell, the brewmaster.

"Why, if it isn't Toby Ryker," Theresa Schell exclaimed. "You haven't been down this way since heck was a pup."

"That's true enough. The last time I was here was for Wilfahrt's wedding."

"I remember. Say, Toby, when are we going to host a wedding for you?"

"I doubt that'll ever happen. I still have Big Faye in St. Paul, but I don't think I'd make much of a father. Too footloose . . . want to stay on the move."

"A man should have a family. You need someone to carry on the Ryker family name."

Thought of his father's recent death came to Ryker. "You have a point there, Theresa. I'm all what's left of my line. Had a brother and two sisters, but they all died of the smallpox way back in twenty-three. I caught it too, but I was too danged ornery to die, though I still carry the pox marks." Ryker sighed. "Maybe some day."

"Well, when that some day comes, we'll host you."

"Much obliged." He glanced around. "Has Cut Nose done any damage out here?"

"Not a bit. They stayed in town and let us be."

"Well I'll be hornschwaggled," Ryker said as the lady of the house offered him a beer. "How'd you get so danged lucky?"

"The Sioux have no quarrel with us. It's the government starving them to death that they are rebelling against. Whenever they come here hungry, we always feed them, and they respect us for it. This war isn't Little Crow's fault, Toby."

"Yeah, I know that. The government hasn't honored the terms of their treaties with the Sioux." Ryker downed the last of the beer and belched. "Sorry, Theresa. Say, by the way, I know some troopers back in town who'd love some of this brew to wash the dirt out of their gullets."

"Head down to the plant, and tell August I said to give you a couple kegs."

"Much obliged."

Upon Ryker's arrival at the brewery, August Schell and his men were busy emptying their latest batch of beer into wooden kegs. "Hi Toby," Schell said. "I thought that was you I saw up to the house."

"Yup, came to town with the troops on the trail of Cut Nose."

"The Dakotas caused us no harm."

"That's what Theresa said. Say, would you mind taking some brew up to the troops? I can pay for it, and they would sure appreciate the chance to wet their whistles. They're camped in town."

August Schell was a politician first and a businessman second. "Will do, but you don't have to pay for it. Let's just say this is a donation to our brave soldiers courtesy of the Schells Brewery of New Ulm Minnesota. I'll load some up and deliver it in a couple hours."

"Thanks, August. I appreciate it."

"Have you been to town yet?"

"Parts of it I have, what's left of it."

"I hear tell there isn't much left," August said.

"I plan to survey the rest of it before I return to bivouac," Ryker replied. "I need to report to Colonel Crooks on what happened here."

"Well, don't make yourself a stranger, you big *weiner schnitzel*."

"I'll try not to, but with this war with the Dakotas, I don't know when I'll be back down this way. Take care of yourself and keep the wind at your back, you old *eselhengst*."

"Jackass!" said August, laughing. "Well, Toby Ryker, aren't you the one! Where'd you learn that German word?"

"That's what your neighbors in town are calling Cut Nose, or was that *you* they were talking about, August? I forget." The two men feigned boxing with each other a moment or two, then Ryker shook hands with Brewmaster Schell and headed back to the townsite of New Ulm.

After seeing that the Dakota had spared the Schells, Ryker entertained pleasant thoughts about the honor of the Dakota warriors, but upon entering New Ulm again, what he saw greatly disturbed him. Several more homesteads had been destroyed by fire. There was more death and destruction everywhere, with fresh corpses lying in the sun. When he passed the smoldering ruins of the outlying farms around New Ulm, he felt bad for the Germans because they certainly didn't deserve to die this way. He stopped and offered what condolences he could to the survivors of the attack and assured them that troops and reinforcements were at hand and encouraged everyone to seek shelter in the town. He said that Cut Nose and his renegades would be hunted down, and that they would pay dearly for this. It wasn't a great deal of comfort to the survivors, however. They responded little, and moved listlessly about the task of burying their dead.

When Ryker noticed that a crucifix had been hung in effigy outside a church, it made him angry. His face hardened as he looked upon the desecration. Although he counted Little Crow as an honorable chief, he had less of an opinion of Cut Nose. That Indian had gone too far this time. Ryker resolved then and there to do all in his power to halt this renegade leader, to bring him to justice, and to end this senseless slaughter.

Back at the bivouac, Ryker reported his findings to Colonel Crooks and to Colonel Frandrau, the latter a judge who came to the defense of the town. Hoping the troops at Fort Ridgely could fend off any further attacks for a few days, the two officers determined that the Sixth Minnesota regulars would escort the survivors away from the town and return to St. Peter as they were too late to save New Ulm anyway. From there, as soon as Sibley could garner adequate supplies and reinforcements, they planned to conduct a forced march to the relief of Fort Ridgely.

Of great concern to Crooks was the fact that the entire southern Minnesota River Valley was at risk from Cut Nose. Could he be stopped, or would he again move down the river to the north? Mankato, St. Peter, Henderson, which had already been attacked, Belle Plaine, and all the homesteads in between were at risk. The western frontier was totally unprotected clear up to Fort Abercrombie and beyond.

Ryker heard a wail come from the infirmary tent and turned to see a young man wearing a lawman's badge sitting on the edge of a cot. "What's wrong with him? He doesn't look injured."

"It's his mind that is injured," Crooks said. "The men found him on the edge of town by a cabin. John McQuiston is his name. He's a deputy marshal. His wife and children were killed, and their cabin burned. His family was tortured and mutilated. When he came upon the sight, he lost his mind with grief."

Ryker winced. "What will happen to him?"

"Likely he'll be committed to a state hospital for the insane, unless he gets lucky and comes around."

Ryker looked at the man again and saw a medic lead him away. "The poor devil, this will haunt him for life."

"That it will," Crooks said, heading toward his command tent while the scout shook his head.

The troops, after enjoying some fine Schell's beer, prepared to break camp and start the trek back to St. Peter with the survivors in tow. The same route was taken north down the river as had been taken south to town, and it was again slow going. This time, besides being slowed down by plodding oxen and heavy wagons filled with frightened, injured survivors and refugees, there were a couple of skirmishes with Sioux along the way, but few casualties were suffered on either side. Still their nearness kept Ryker on his toes.

The Sioux still held the plains, with some 1,200 warriors who attacked the settlers and soldiers at will. It appeared that no one could stop their advance, and that the Sioux were determined to wreak their own special style of vengeance upon anyone found on their land.

UPON THEIR ARRIVAL TWO DAYS LATER at St. Peter, Colonel Sibley had been busy. He had amassed troops and volunteers 1,400 strong, and armament for the force, and set up a soup kitchen as well to feed the victims of the massacre who continued to straggle in. It angered him to the point of rage at what had occurred at New Ulm. He felt frustrated and helpless that he couldn't provide assistance in time to save the town. At a meeting with his aides and top battlefield officers that evening, the decision was made to march on to Fort Ridgely the very next day and continue from there west along the river, where the heaviest concentration of Dakota warriors were camped.

Ryker, after attending the briefing with the officers, set up his pup tent that evening, suddenly weary with the weight of all the death he had witnessed. Part of him was still loyal to the Dakota because he knew what they had endured, but part of him was also angry at what they had done to the helpless pioneers. As he lay on his bedroll, he tried to put everything in perspective, to maintain a balance when all about him was out of balance. The words of his mother that the warrior Dakota were not to be trusted came back to him.

As he drifted off into a fitful sleep, visions of death came to him. More clashes between the Dakota war parties and the army would surely occur. Maybe he would die on the battlefield! He had not considered such a thing until now, but as vengeful as some of the warriors were, it loomed as a distinct possibility. Ryker knew that when it came right down to it, he was Ojibwe not Sioux, and Little Crow's warriors would kill him if he ventured into their path of wrath. He realized that there was no recourse but to fight the Dakota with all the zeal that he had, for they had nothing to lose and would fight to the death rather than surrender. Privation had turned to hate and festered into an infected wound. The only end to this was the destruction of those Sioux who had declared war on the settlers and the government. Their time was past, their way of life over, and any advantage they achieved would be fleeting, for Minnesota was now a state. The Dakotas couldn't destroy the entire state. In the end, their victories would be shallow and meaningless, for their culture could never conquer the larger culture leaning heavily on their borders. How sad it was.

4

THE NEXT DAY, AUGUST THE 26TH, Ryker led Colonel Sibley and the troops from St. Peter and across the plains until they reached the trail to Fort Ridgely, a federal fort located on the frontier west and upriver from New Ulm. Sibley decided to move across the plains now that he had a sizable fighting force, knowing that any attack by the Dakota could be overcome.

The ground was covered with the flowers of early fall, including the tiny white clover, the mustard-yellow goldenrod, the deep pink of thistle flower, and the small but hearty red blooms of the wild rose. Also dotting the prairie was ox-eye false sunflower, black-eyed susan, milk-weed, and the wiener-like stems of cattail in the sloughs. Near the tree lines along ravines and streams, sumac was beginning to change color toward a brilliant red. What prairie grass existed was drying out and turning brown.

Ryker saw great flocks of blackbirds preparing for migration, and solitary red-tailed hawks doing likewise. Although the ducks and geese had not yet begun to fly south, they too would take to the flyways within the next two months. The cheerful "mister-and-missus-c-b-b-b-s" trill of the wren had already fallen silent, as had the divebomb flights of swallows. Warblers had already vanished. He knew that all these signs meant autumn was just around the corner.

As Ryker moved along at the head of the column, most of which were foot soldiers, he kept a watchful eye not only for Dakota scouts, but also on the weather, for it appeared the day was turning into a weather breeder. He felt a storm coming up. He knew that out on the prairie, a violent storm could be even more dangerous than Indian warriors, and that the unprotected troops were at the mercy of the elements. If a tornado were to touch down, the soldiers had nowhere to go to escape it.

The air was muggy, the puffy white clouds yielding to a dark fast-moving cloud bank, carrying within it the threat of heavy rain. The wind kicked up, and Ryker scanned the horizon for signs of a funnel cloud forming. Then he saw what he hoped he wouldn't see. "Tornado!" he yelled, pointing to the base of a dark cloud, which began to move rapidly in a circular fashion and formed a funnel.

"Tornado!" a soldier repeated, and the warning echoed and re-echoed throughout the ranks.

"And we ain't got no cover," one of the troopers shouted.

"Quickly. Go due west," Sibley said to his officers. "According to my map, there's a ravine with a creek bed that drains into Clear Lake not a quarter of a mile from where we're standing." He pointed in that direction. "See? There's the tree line. We can take shelter there."

Ryker continued to watch the tornado form. "She's starting to drop!" he exclaimed, as the base of the tornado cloud began to dip towards the horizon. Within seconds, it was on the ground and heading toward them at a rapid rate. "We'll never make it to the ravine!" he shouted to Sibley through the roar of the wind now picking up around them.

Before Sibley could reply, rough-hewn shingles and boards from a barn to the west seemed to explode as the tornado ripped through it. Debris began flying through the air. "Flat on the ground, men!" hollered Sibley. So saying, he dismounted and dropped, lying flat and covering his head with his arms for protection. His troops did likewise, dropping in place and covering their heads.

"What about the horses, sir?" shouted Thomas Barton, the farrier with Captain Anderson's company of mounted men, better known as the Cullen Guard.

Sibley shouted back through the increasing wind. "Let them run. We'll deal with them after this is over!"

The tornado headed directly toward them. The loud wind turned into a roar, and the day turned dark as night while thunder and lightning rumbled and flashed across the sky.

"God, why have you forsaken us!" screamed Private Jacob Freeman. Against Sibley's orders, he stood up rather than taking advantage of what protection there was on the prairie by lying upon the ground. Shaking his fist towards the heavens, he let loose with a string of profanity against the Almighty. Just when it seemed the entire regiment would be destroyed, the tornado veered toward the northeast as though attracted to the waters of the Minnesota River.

"Well I'll be a monkey's uncle," Ryker exclaimed as debris dropped all over the troops. "We just got plumb lucky!" The fast moving tornado began moving away. Two minutes later, amidst still strong winds, the troops began to stir and glance about. Another three minutes, and they were able to stand and watch the tornado, which continued to depart well to the north.

Sibley's first concern was for his men. Roll call was taken by the various companies, and to everyone's amazement, there was but one casualty—Private Jacob Freeman, who had been screaming out oaths against the Almighty just minutes before. His skull had been fractured when it had been hit by the limb of a cottonwood tree. He died quickly. There were two cavalry steeds from the Cullen Guard that had to be put down because their legs had been broken, probably from stepping in prairie dog holes while running. Other than that, the other horses were none the worse for wear, although they were thoroughly spooked. Their supply wagon had been turned over, but the cannons had weathered the storm just fine, being pretty well immune to the flying debris and having escaped the full force of the tornadic winds.

STEVEN M. ULMEN

"Pack Private Freeman's remains along on a litter," Sibley said. "We're on due course toward Fort Ridgely, and I'm sure we'll encounter more bodies along the way, people killed not only by the Sioux, but also by this dad-blasted tornado. We'll bury all the victims we find in a mass grave."

As his staff moved out to fulfill Sibley's orders, Ryker approached and said, "Colonel, we'll need a burial detail before long."

"I'm afraid so," Sibley replied. "The risk of disease is high with all these dead bodies strewn about."

"There's a rise yonder." Ryker pointed off to the west.

"Let's make for it. We can bury the dead without the Dakota sneaking up on us."

By LATE AFTERNOON, THE SIXTH MINNESOTA encountered the corpses of more than twenty settlers on the prairie. They also rescued thirteen survivors from the Dakota's wrath, people they found wandering aimlessly on the open ground, some with severe wounds. The burial detail was kept busy digging a huge mass grave on the rise they'd spotted earlier, which, ironically, turned out to be the site of a Lutheran cemetery.

One wandering survivor was Reverend Oscar Thordsen, the Lutheran minister who was also the caretaker of this cemetery. He was unharmed, though most of the people he ministered to had not been as fortunate. He didn't realize it, but he was respected as a holy man by the Sioux, and that was what saved him. When he offered to conduct a funeral service for the dead, Sibley thanked him for his kind offer then stood next to the minister while the troopers lay the slain to rest.

"That man there is Jake Freeman," Thordsen said as the dead soldier was removed from a wagon. "He was a member of my flock. Look at his head! Did the Indians do that?"

"No, the tornado did," Sibley replied. "Private Freeman stuck his noggin in the path of a flying cottonwood branch."

47

"Heavens, the poor man," the minister said as he blessed the corpse. He flinched, however, upon recognizing the corpse of a pudgy, middle-aged man being lowered into the pit. "That is Milo Roemhildt. He's from south of here." Thordsen pointed at two other corpses. "And there are Malachi Hoffman and his wife, Ruth. And that one over there," he pointed to another body, "is Magnus Fasnacht, but he's Catholic. I don't want him buried with the Lutherans."

"Now just a doggone minute," Sibley said as the weary soldiers stared at the preacher and began muttering amongst themselves. "We're talking about dead citizens of Minnesota slaughtered by the same Indians who slaughtered the others buried here. What kind of a Christian are you anyway, Thordsen?"

"Yeah, dead is dead," said one of the soldiers wielding a shovel, "and they are all going to atone to the same God as you and I are."

Thordsen's lack of compassion and how his bigotry upset Colonel Sibley and the other troopers infuriated Ryker. The next thing he knew, he'd grasped the smaller man and put him in a headlock. Bending his fingers into a fist, he rubbed his knuckles rapidly over the minister's balding pate until it turned bright red.

"Ow! Ouch! Let go of me, you . . ." Thordsen let go with a string of profanity that was totally improper coming from a man of the cloth.

"I can see why the Indians let you be," Ryker said. "No self-respecting warrior would want to hang your hairless scalp on his lodge pole."

The soldiers began to laugh. "Atta boy, Ryker," a soldier hollered. "Keep it up."

"Yeah, give him what for," said another.

Sibley grinned, flexed his fingers, and pounded his fist into his free hand as he watched his scout torment the prejudicial minister. Then, glancing at the cheering soldiers and reflecting on the impropriety of this entire situation, he shook his head. "Ryker, unhand that minister this instant."

"Yes sir." Ryker stretched his arms wide, which released Thordsen's head and caused him to fall forward. The scout lifted his knee just in time to catch the minister in the face and knock him backwards onto the ground. "Oops, sorry, preacher, it's my game leg acting up. When it spasms, I can't control it."

"Ryker, enough!" said Sibley as the detail hooted and guffawed. "Reverend Thordsen may not be setting a very good Christian example, but that doesn't excuse us from stooping to his level. I'll take charge of this matter."

"Aye, sir," Ryker said, saluting. He bent over and helped the minister to his feet. "Are you okay, Reverend Thordsen? And more important, did this teach you anything?"

"Lutherans are buried here. This is hallowed ground!" Thordsen declared, still rubbing his head. "Lutheran ground! To bury a Catholic here is blasphemy! The church council will have my job! I'll have to search for another call!"

Sibley looked around. "What church council? They're all dead!"

"Well . . . they are here in spirit. I know their intent."

"See here, Reverend Thordsen," Sibley said, "and in your case, I use the term 'reverend' very loosely. I'm in command here, and this territory is under martial law. I don't care about your dead church council. The remains of these victims, Catholic, protestant, and even the three Sioux bodies we picked up will be buried here, right and proper. I order it! If you fail to comply with my order, you are subject to immediate arrest. I could even have you shot."

Reverend Thordsen gulped. He hemmed and hawed a bit then mumbled, "Oh, all right, those blasted Catholics and heathen redskins can be buried here with the Lutherans, but not a word of this outside of this gathering. Do you understand?"

"Other than listing the number of the dead in my official reports, understood," Sibley said. "Body count of the casualties must be recorded. Identification of those we've found is also recorded when we have that information. That's for the families."

Ryker glared at Reverend Thordsen. "Yeah, well, I'm not quite as military as the colonal. Maybe I'll just write a piece about your unchristian attitude for the St. Peter newspaper, you ornery Swedish jackass."

"Ryker, do I have to put you in irons? Stay out of this!" Sibley glared at the scout and waved down the laughter of the soldiers as Ryker took a bow toward them.

Glancing at Sibley, Ryker knew he'd pushed his luck as far as he dared to and looked away. "Aye, sir," he said.

Grumbling to himself, Reverend Thordsen looked from Ryker to Sibley and nodded his agreement.

Upon completion of the funeral service, the troops of the Sixth Minnesota Regiment moved out across the prairie. They arrived at Fort Ridgely three hours later where Sibley immediately set up a command post.

"Ryker, about that burial detail we discussed," Sibley said. "You know this territory like the back of your glove. Tomorrow, I want you to lead Major Joseph Brown, Captain Hiram Grant, and a detachment of a hundred and fifty men of Company A of the Third Minnesota Volunteers on a burial detail, relieve any other survivors and refugees you come across, and try and get a bearing on the Dakota. Bury all the bodies you find and proceed to Birch Coulee. As soon as the reinforcements and supplies I requisitioned arrive from Fort Snelling, we'll join you and help scout out that area. I want to inspect the territory as far north as Olivia before we mount an offensive against Little Crow."

"It ain't a pleasant task, but it is the right thing to do for these poor victims." Ryker saluted the commander. "Aye, sir, we'll head out come first light in the morning."

UNDER RYKER'S SCOUTING, Company A was kept busy. They found numerous corpses in various states of mutilation and decomposition strewn across the prairie, and after making records of them and identifying those they could, they buried them in shallow graves where they fell. At one juncture where a small pond sat surrounded by cotton-wood trees, the scout glanced up and saw several turkey vultures soaring in the sky. "Something's dead over there, sir."

"Just a deer carcass probably," Major Brown replied, "or maybe a dead horse or cow from the tornado."

Ryker, however, had a hunch. "Hold up here a minute, will you, sir? Want to check out Beaver Creek Marsh over yonder."

Major Brown, after conferring with Captain Grant, agreed this was a good idea and ordered the troops to take a fifteen-minute breather. He drew out his chaw of tobacco, bit off a chunk, and as an afterthought said: "Smoke, if you got the makings."

Riding ahead, Ryker's hunch was soon proven true. He saw the flies first—swarms of them—and then caught the odor of death. Upon closer examination, he found the remains of Captain John Marsh and twenty of his men, all killed in the original massacre of August the 18th, lying in the tall weeds next to the pond. They had been scalped and mutilated, and three mangy coyotes and several vultures now feasted on the remains.

With them, also dead, was a family consisting of a man and woman and three children. He later learned that this was the entire Prescott Johnson family, immigrants who had crossed the ocean just five years before to make a new life as homesteaders in the Minnesota Territory. Now, all they could homestead was a six-foot hole in the ground.

The detail came forward and buried the dead and were about to head out when Ryker, seeing the glint of metal against the sun, narrowed his steely eyes and squinted towards the west. There he saw a war party of Sioux following Beaver Creek, which drained into Beaver Creek Marsh, heading in their direction. He saw the leader, whom he immediately recognized as Little Crow, draw up his pony and stand tall in his saddle, looking toward him. The Indian raised his lance, and Ryker heard a shout, and the Indians dismounted and disappeared in the weeds. Even the horses were quickly out of view, but Ryker knew they were hiding behind a tall knoll above the ravine known as Birch Coulee in this part of the state. "We got company, sir," he said. "And I don't think they came to pay a social call."

51

No sooner had he gotten the words out of his mouth than the volunteers heard the report of a rifle and saw a miniball throw up a puff of dirt off to their right. "Behind the wagons, men," Major Brown shouted. "These savages want a piece of us. Let's give them what for!"

A skirmish ensued with Ryker and the troopers belly-down under the wagons firing back toward the Indians. Ryker took careful aim, pulled the trigger on his Hawken rifle, and saw an Indian seemingly jump into the air before collapsing to the ground on his back. Two other Indians did likewise, slain by bullets from volunteers under Brown's command.

Then the *whump* of a bullet penetrating flesh followed by a scream told Ryker that one less member of Company A would be enjoying supper tonight. He turned and saw Private George Colter, three feet to his right, lying flat on the ground, unmoving. "Georgie!" he cried to the young private with whom he had played a game of checkers just the night before. "Oh, Georgie, no!" He looked back toward the attackers. "Damn you, Little Crow." He crawled up beside the soldier and rolled him onto his back, and saw at once the scarlet trail that started above his heart and oozed down his chest toward his belly.

"T-Toby?" said Private Colter, the sound of bewilderment in his voice. He touched his hand to his bloodied blouse and stared at it, unbelieving. "Look what they done to me, Toby! They done killed me!"

"Easy now," Ryker said, fighting back his emotions. "Major Brown is here, and Colonel Sibley and the troops back at Fort Ridgely have heard the shooting echoing up the valley by now. They'll be along directly." But Ryker knew that even if the surgeon for the Sixth Minnesota had been right next to him though, it wouldn't save Private Colter. His number had been called.

"I feel warm, Toby." Colter's voice was softer as the strength drained from him along with his lifeblood. He coughed, and the blood from his ruptured lung gurgled out of his mouth.

Ryker was aware only of Private Colter even as the bullets whizzed around them. He pulled the soldier, who was not much more than a boy, to him and hugged him, rocking him in a soothing motion. "There now, Georgie, just don't you worry none."

"I-is it sundown?"

Ryker glanced down at the bloody chest. "Just about."

"Tell my Mama I died proud, Toby. Like a true Colter."

"That you are, Georgie." Ryker wept as Colter's eyes rolled back and his spirit left him.

Ryker continued to hold the lifeless body for how long he knew not, until the sound of gunfire brought him out of his reverie. He laid the body tenderly against the prairie grass and heard a yell emit from his throat. Cursing, he jumped up and ran towards the small bunch of braves, unaware that the remaining troopers of the burial detail ran behind him. He dropped in the grass behind a limestone rock fence built by a shepherd to contain his flock, and commenced firing at the Dakota who faced him. He fired round after round, reloading as quickly as he could in between, until he could feel the heat from the barrel of his Hawken, and then he fired some more.

Even so, the Sioux hiding around Birch Coulee hill remained elusive and deadly. They had cover amongst the trees and in the ravine, which the detail did not, and they were skilled fighters on the prairie. They would pop up and fire then duck out of sight again, leaving no sign but a drifting puff of smoke toward which the troopers could return fire. The fighting increased in intensity and continued for several hours with both sides incurring heavy losses. Still they held on, both soldiers and Indians, fighting with all their might. The piercing "Ky-yi-yi!" of Sioux war cries, punctuated by gunfire, filled the air. Bodies began to pile up near the skirmish lines on both sides, only to be dragged back and replaced with other fighters.

Temporarily holding their fire as they regrouped, the Sioux huddled in conference to discuss their next move. This cost them valuable ground, for upon returning to their various ambush positions, they could see that the battle was lost to the setting sun. Honorable warriors that they were, they refused to fight the soldiers except during daylight hours. They took great pride in knowing they had inflicted a severe hardship upon the soldiers, even though their cost was the loss of several of their number in the process. Huddling again as the sun sank below the horizon at Birch Coulee, they plotted what they would do when the morning sun next greeted them.

MAJOR BROWN AND CAPTAIN GRANT moved up beside Ryker along with Assistant Surgeon Moses R. Greeley. "Good work, Ryker," Brown said. "We routed them."

"Not before they killed one of our finest." Ryker motioned toward the lifeless body of Private Colter.

"It's a misfortune of war," Brown said. "Don't turn soft on me, Ryker."

"But sir, he was just a boy. He had his whole life ahead of him. And he was a good boy too. He supported his mama after his papa died of the consumption."

"How'd you come to know him so intimately?" Brown asked as Greeley and Grant examined the body.

"Knew his whole family, sir," Ryker said. "They were good, honest folks. We used to go coon hunting together. He was just a little squirt then."

"Look at this," Surgeon Greeley said. He grinned at Brown as he stuck his finger into the fatal wound in Colter's chest. "The Indians blew the blood vessels clean away from this man's heart. That was some darn good shooting."

"Oh for cripes sake!" said Ryker, pushing the surgeon away from Colter's remains and standing to face him. "Let the poor lad lie in peace, you morbid sawbones."

"I'm sorry at your loss," Brown said as he and Captain Grant held Ryker fast lest he attack the surgeon. "But like I said, this is one of the misfortunes of war. This is a battle to the death, in case you didn't realize it until now. Little Crow and his followers have nothing to lose.

They don't care if they die in battle. They even count it as an honor if they give their lives trying to protect their way of life."

"I know. I know you're right about that, sir," Ryker said, pulling himself free. "It's just that this is all for naught. There's good people dying on both sides, and for what? We all know us Minnesotans will win in the end. There aren't enough Sioux to reclaim the state."

"Don't think so hard," Brown said. "We got a job to do."

"Yes, we got a job to do, but *how* we do it is what's important." Ryker looked Brown hard in the face. "With your permission, I'd like to powwow with Little Crow again."

"He'll kill you."

"Maybe he will, and maybe he won't. If I can sneak into his camp after dark, and I know where he's camped, by the way, I might be able to talk some sense into him."

Brown studied his scout a moment before looking off toward the darkening horizon, saying nothing. "If it saves even one more life, it's worth the gamble," Ryker added.

"No, I need you here." Brown motioned toward the coulee where the war party had fired upon them. "Not dead over there."

Ryker was silent for a moment then looked to the ground and spit. "I think this is a very big mistake, if you pardon me saying so, sir."

"If it is a mistake, it is my mistake, and I will live with it. I know you have Indian blood in you and are in sympathy with the plight of Little Crow. But Ryker, this is war, and you have to decide right now which side you're on." Brown motioned to the corpse of Private Colter. "I saw you cradling that soldier as he died rather than firing at the enemy the way you were ordered to do."

"There are a hundred and fifty guns here, sir," Ryker replied. "One less made no difference to Little Crow, but it made a whopping big difference to Georgie Colter as he passed over."

"Even so, you need to decide where your loyalties lie." Major Brown stepped back and drew his revolver. "Decide now, Ryker."

"Oh, come on now, you wouldn't shoot me, for cripes sake."

"We're under martial law here, Ryker. I need to know if you're loyal to the Sixth Minnesota and the United States of America, or if you are a spy for Little Crow. The well-being of my troops hangs in the balance."

Ryker glanced around and noticed that Captain Grant, standing behind him now, had also drawn his revolver. The scout adjusted his hat. "Well, sir, when you explain it to me this way, I guess I see your point. I ain't any good to either side if I'm dead here on the ground." He grunted and held out his arm in the gesture of a handshake with Brown. "Until this is settled, I'm the chief scout for the Minnesota Volunteer Regiment, nothing more, nothing less." Gently pushing the barrel of Brown's gun to one side, he added, "Point that thing someplace else, will you, sir? I bleed easy."

Making no effort to return the handshake, Brown leveled his gun on Ryker again and cocked the hammer. "Don't touch my weapon! Quit making jokes! This isn't any funnier than assaulting the surgeon was."

"Assault?" said Ryker, shocked at Brown's aggressive manner.

"Yes, assault! You pull another stunt like this, and we'll settle it out here, frontier style. You hear me?" Tense seconds passed when no one spoke. The officer finally uncocked and holstered his gun, motioning to Grant to do likewise. "Now let's get about our business."

Wide-eyed and feeling chastised, Ryker gulped. "Aye, sir, I'll help the boys tidy up the dead," he said, saluting.

Later that evening, Ryker moved off by himself. The shadows were growing long when he found a rock next to Beaver Creek and sat there, removing his whiskey flask and taking a swig. He heard the scream of an eagle soaring high above the river valley, and glanced into the darkening sky. The moon illuminated the bird, its distinctive white head identifying it as an American bald. "Pappy, if that's your spirit a-soaring around up yonder, I wish you would tell me what to do. You want me to understand Little Crow, and I'm really trying to, Pappy, so help me I am. But I also know innocent Minnesotans who had nothing to do with making the shameful lives of the Indians on the reservations are dying at his hand. What Washington did to the Dakota ain't right, but what Little Crow did here ain't right either." He moved his hat and mopped his forehead sweat onto his arm. "I want to do the right thing, Pappy, but knowing the right thing is mighty hard sometimes. I dang near got my head shot off today trying to do what I thought was right, just because Major Brown's long handles are wedged too tight." He looked at the whiskey flask. "And there ain't enough of this to see me through all this bloodshed. I know you and Mama always told me I should bloom where I was planted and try to make the best of things, but sometimes, I wish I was far away from here, and when this is all over, that's where I aim to go."

5

WA-KAN-TAN-KA, A YOUNG, MUSCULAR, and very fierce Sioux warrior, entered the tipi of Little Crow.

"We made the whites sit up and take notice," Little Crow said.

"Yes, we did. Never again will the Dakota be taken for sheep to be ignored. Sibley knows he has a fight on his hands. I saw the shot you put into that young soldier next to Toby Ryker. One shot only, and you killed him dead. But why didn't you shoot the scout Ryker? He was the bigger target, and certainly more dangerous to us than that baby soldier was."

"That old scout and I have a history, and I don't want him dead, at least not yet. Ryker and I hunted together in better days, and he always knew my kills because they were clean, one shot to the head. He used to comment on it."

"But you did not hit the young soldier boy in the head, Little Crow."

"I know. Maybe my old eyes don't see as well as they once did, or maybe my rifle sights are not centered, but just the same, Ryker got my meaning." Little Crow patted Wa-kan-tan-ka's shoulders in a fatherly gesture. "Prepare for battle. We will return again to that place they call Birch Coulee, and after we kill the rest of that burial detail, we will go east and attack Mankato and St. Peter. Ryker says it is not safe for us to raid downriver, but I think those are just empty words Sibley told him to say."

"I will get my gear and be back directly." With that, Wa-kan-tan-ka left the tipi and, nodding to Cut Nose, who was passing by, headed toward his own lodge.

STANDS TALL, WIFE OF WA-KAN-TAN-KA, watched Cut Nose head toward the tipi where the prisoners were held. She didn't like Cut Nose, considering him a hard and cruel man.

"Wa-kan-tan-ka, please stop him," she said as he entered the tipi, grabbed a bottle of whiskey, and threw down a couple slugs from it.

Wa-kan-tan-ka looked at Stands Tall then at Cut Nose, who was disappearing into the tent. "No one stops Cut Nose," he replied. "He has gained power because he is a fierce warrior, and he is allowed to go wherever he wishes. Be thankful he doesn't cast his eyes upon you."

"You would allow that?" she replied, staring at him.

"I could not stop it," Wa-kan-tan-ka said. "And besides, we are committed to this war with Colonel Sibley's soldiers, and we need him."

"This war will come to nothing," Stands Tall said, "except death and suffering to us all, Dakota and white alike."

"That may be true, but there is more honor in such a death than in watching your people starve, or die of the white man's disease, or grow weak in the mind from his whiskey and do nothing about it." He extended the bottle toward her and laughed.

"Today, Little Crow and others proceed to Mankato. The other women speak of it."

"Yes, and proud I am to ride at his side. We will score a great victory today. The shaman saw it in a vision."

"I see no victory in this war. I see only death."

"Hold your tongue, my woman. If Little Crow hears you, he will kill you himself or laugh while Cut Nose does it."

Stands Tall approached her husband and hugged him. "I too have visions, and mine are not as glorious as the shaman's. I see myself without my man."

"Maybe that is our destiny, but if so, at least the whites will remember us dying as brave warriors trying to save our families." He picked up his knife and readied himself for battle. "I'll bring you a yellow-haired scalp tonight."

"You just come back alive. I don't care to own a white man's scalp." Stands Tall watched Wa-kan-tan-ka walk away from the tipi, put her hands to her mouth, and wept bitterly.

EARLY ON THE MORNING of September 2nd, Colonel Sibley and the rest of the Sixth Regiment now encamped at Fort Ridgely were alarmed to hear gunfire coming from the Minnesota River Valley to the north. Although Birch Coulee was several miles away, the natural acoustics of the valley carried sound for many miles. By listening closely, they could hear the volleys of muskets. "Colonel Crooks, gather the troops into formation," Sibley said.

"Yes, sir," Crooks said, saluting.

When the regulars and the volunteers had gathered, the commander walked among them. He encouraged them to fight today as though their very lives depended upon their performance and, indeed, they did. He also spoke of the law of the land and the need to bring the renegade Dakota to justice but ended again on the personal note that they were fighting for their way of life, just as the Dakota were.

Colonel Sibley was an elegant speaker, and by the time he concluded his remarks, his recruits were fired up with the zeal to go into battle and score a great victory or die trying. "On to Little Crow's camp!" became their battle cry, as 240 infantrymen and a pair of six-pound cannons under the command of Colonel McPhail left the fort to provide relief to Major Brown's detail. Upon his arrival, the ratio of troops to Sioux warriors would be four to five.

BACK AT BIRCH COULEE, Little Crow and 500 well-armed war-riors approached on their way to Mankato. Their assault upon Brown's forces the previous day had left them fearless. As they entered the deep ravine, they looked up to see sentries from Brown's detachment on the plain above them. Quickly taking shelter in the trees, they commenced firing upon the burial detail. At the first sounds of rifle volleys, the bugler sounded the alarm, and Captain Grant hollered, "Fall down!"

His yell was misunderstood as "Fall in!" vastly different under the circumstances, but soon the wagons were pulled into a circle sur-rounding the tents of the troopers, which offered at least some protec-tion. They returned fire toward the rim of the coulee, but they were under-staffed and short on ammunition against such a force as Little Crow commanded.

Ryker, lying under one of the wagons, took careful aim and knocked a Sioux on the perimeter of the ravine backwards and out of sight. He fired off two more rounds, but they went wild. "Geez," he muttered, "I'm too young and handsome to die out here in the dirt. This ain't right. You're pissing me off, Little Crow!" As he spoke, another volley passed overhead, killing three troopers.

"LITTLE CROW," YELLED CUT NOSE, "let's go up there and lift some scalps."

Little Crow, drinking from a whiskey jug taken during the raid at New Ulm, hoisted the jug in a toast to Cut Nose and said, "I will enjoy watching my brave warriors achieve a great coup this day."

Wa-kan-tan-ka, Cut Nose, and several others all shouting, "Ki-yi-yi!" scrambled up the steep coulee and crouched at the perimeter, firing volley after volley at the troops, who were like sitting ducks out on the open prairie ground. The fighting was intense for several hours and favored the Dakota, for they were better armed and better mount-ed than the troops and better hidden from attack in the tall grasses and brush.

Even while the battle grew in intensity, Black Wolf boldly sneaked around behind the beleaguered troops and made his way right into their midst. He killed one trooper with his knife before the man even realized he was there, and captured another, James Cunningham, and dragged him back to his fellow warriors below the bluff. Shoving the blond-haired, slender soldier roughly to the ground, he said, "Look what I found. He's so young and pretty that I don't know if I should kill him or what."

"Carve him up, Black Wolf," said Cut Nose.

"Yes, cut him," said Wa-kan-tan-ka. "I want his yellow-haired scalp."

Black Wolf grinned and withdrew his knife again. "That sounds like a pretty good idea." Bending down to the private, he said, "Let's find out what he knows first. He might have information that is useful."

Cunningham gasped. "Please," he managed to whimper.

"A boy that young doesn't know anything," said Little Crow.

"Maybe not," Black Wolf said. He caressed Cunningham's face, which was so smooth it had no need for a razor. "He'd sure make a pretty squaw man, wouldn't he?" Running his knife blade teasingly over the bulge in Cunningham's pants, he added, "I wonder how big a stallion we have here, anyway?"

Fearing the worst, Cunningham sobbed and began breathing heavily.

While the other warriors surrounded him, Black Wolf slid his hand between the soldier's legs and grabbed him in the groin. As the young man yowled in pain, the warriors nudged each other and pointed at him and laughed, thoroughly enjoying Black Wolf's special brand of torture. "Oops, we're too late, Little Crow," he said. "This mustang's been gelded."

Abruptly, Cut Nose stood, dragging Cunningham to his feet and marching him to the perimeter. He got behind the soldier and held the knife to his throat again. "Hey! Ryker!" he bellowed. "Look what I found. Took him right out from under your nose, you stupid idiot. Tell this to Brown!"

He saw Ryker look up, knowing it was the scout by his buckskin outfit and red hair. Scraping the knife roughly up and down the soldier's throat, he laughed as Cunningham shrieked in terror. "I'm not going to kill you, squaw man," he said. "At least, not until Chief Little Crow gives his approval."

Cut Nose sheathed his knife and shoved the trooper roughly toward warriors Ta-tay-hde-don and A-e-cha-ga. "A-e-cha-ga, take this prize down the ravine and guard him. If he tries to run, put an arrow in his heart."

A-e-cha-ga, a sullen, husky warrior, did as he was told, disappearing from view with Private Cunningham into the thick brush of the coulee.

"THOSE MURDERING BUTCHERS," Ryker exclaimed to Major Brown. "Look at them, sir! They're taunting us."

"I wish there was some way to save Private Cunningham," Brown said. "But how in the world can we do it?"

"Now you know how I felt yesterday when they shot Georgie Colter, sir." Ryker clenched his jaw and stared hard at Brown.

Brown returned the stare, trying to think of a rebuttal to the wisdom of the scout's words. He thought for several seconds but nothing came to his mind. Breaking the gaze, he removed his hat and wiped the sweat off his brow. After clearing his throat, he replaced his hat and looked at Ryker. This time, there was humility in his eyes.

"I see that you were right yesterday, and that I was wrong. I told you if my decision was a mistake, that I would live with it. That is what I must now do, for the rest of my days," the officer said. "I'm sorry, Ryker. I never should have questioned your loyalty, and I should have embraced your compassion for Private Colter. That's what a good officer would have done."

Ryker's glare softened. "That's okay, sir. Although you made a mistake, you made amends. That's what a good officer does, and more

BLOOD ON THE PRIAIRE

importantly, that's what a good man does." He nodded toward the coulee. "As long as Cunningham's alive over there, we have a chance of saving him. Let's think on it and try to figure out how to do that."

Noticing movement in the grass to his left, the scout spied a fat, sluggish bull snake slithering next to a rotting log in an attempt to hide from the activity. Looking again toward the coulee, he snapped his fingers. "I got me an idea. Let me go after Private Cunningham."

"No, it's too risky."

"Not if you can think like an Indian. Now help me catch that granddaddy snake yonder."

"What will that accomplish?"

"Just never you mind, sir," Ryker replied. "I don't have time to explain. Just know that old bull snake can deliver a message to Little Crow more powerful than a bullet. Now grab that gunnysack while I fetch him."

Shaking his head, Brown grabbed the gunnysack and watched as Ryker crept up and placed his boot behind the snake's head, pinning it to the ground. It instinctively began to hiss and writhe and shake its tail in a display of bluff that was as good as any diamondback could do. Donning his leather gloves, the scout reached down and grabbed the serpent behind the head so it couldn't turn and bite him, for he knew that although non-poisonous, a bull snake's sharp teeth could cause a nasty wound. The snake hissed louder and tried to wrap its thick body around Ryker's arm, succeeding to some extent until Brown approached with the sack. Ryker grabbed the tail with his free hand and stretched the five-foot constrictor out, dropping it tail first into the sack and only releasing the head when it was safely tucked inside. Brown quickly tied off the top with rope and set the sack on the ground, which continued to move as the snake hissed and twisted round inside.

"Geez, those snakes are ugly things," Brown said, shuddering.

"You darn tootin' they are, and thanks to us, this one is really pissed off, which makes it even uglier. But they eat a lot of mice and gophers, and that is a service to us all. Now the next thing I got to do is to sneak up to the rim of the coulee." Ryker faced the officer. "That is, with your permission, sir."

Brown paused a moment, thinking. "Okay, I'm sure reinforcements are on the way from Fort Ridgely after all the commotion we're making here. You're an awfully big target, Ryker. Be careful."

"You can count on that, sir. I'm too young and good looking to die. Why, that would deprive too many pretty maiden ladies of the pleasure of my company, and I wouldn't want to go to my grave with that on my conscience." The scout began to creep toward the rear of the detail. "I'd appreciate it if you and the boys were to cover me with your crossfire."

"We'll do that." Brown motioned to the soldiers to get into firing position in the earthwork trenches that had been dug. Ryker, meanwhile, grabbed the sack of angry snake and headed toward the rear of their position.

Ryker ended up taking the same route as Black Wolf had taken to get into the camp. At his signal, Major Brown commanded the troops to fire, and salvo after salvo pierced the air around the perimeter of Birch Coulee. The offensive surprised Little Crow's warriors, and for the first time during the battle, they were driven back from the perimeter to the deeper brush where Cut Nose stood with Private Cunningham.

Ryker crawled toward the rim on his hands and knees, taking what shelter he could in the tall grasses there. When he got to the top of the ravine, he had to crawl over the bodies of several warriors killed in the battle. From this vantage point, he could see to the base of the coulee, and noted the distinctive person of Little Crow with his warriors surrounding him. He thought about shooting the chief but determined it was much too risky for Private Cunningham and would most certainly cause his immediate death. The soldier was now tied to a tree, his arms outstretched and fastened to two boughs as though crucified. Ryker could see his shoulders shake and knew the young man was crying.

"WHY SHOULD WE WAIT?" Little Crow said, eyeing Cunningham wickedly. "Those troopers up there are killing my men right and left. I didn't think they'd do that!" He looked at Cut Nose and nodded.

Cut Nose drew his knife and approached the captive. "Child-man, you are about to become a casualty of war."

James Cunningham, like so many of his comrades, enjoyed the feeling of immortality reserved for the young, and the only reason he signed up with the Sixth Minnesota Volunteers in the first place was for the sense of adventure the war offered. That adventure had worn thin two hours into the battle of Birch Coulee as his buddies fell dead all around him, and now, realizing that death was upon him also, the adventure turned to terror. "Oh, no," he cried between sobs. "Please, no! I'll do anything you say!"

Cut Nose would have none of it. "You'll do nothing, dog." He raised his knife and plunged it deep into Cunningham's chest as the warriors screamed "Ki-yi-yi!" around him. Withdrawing the knife, the Indian then jabbed it into the soldier's abdomen and pulled it upwards in a ripping motion.

Cunningham felt the sting of the knife enter his chest, but was surprised how little pain he felt. The second wound however, although not immediately lethal like the first, hurt like sin itself. The soldier threw his head back, and taking his last lungful of air, he let out a piercing scream of agony that could be heard above the din created by the screaming warriors around him. Mortally wounded, blood pouring out of him in spurts, he grew light-headed just before everything went black.

The warriors weren't finished yet. Like wolves they moved in, scalped him, stripped off his pants, and castrated him. Mercifully, Cunningham bled to death before he had to endure these final indignities. Energized by the sight and smell of blood, the warriors whooped and hollered, did a war dance around the dead soldier, and slashed at him with their knives before charging back up the coulee.

Ryker witnessed the knifing and, shocked at the swiftness of it, knew it was too late to rescue Private Cunningham. "Little Crow, you bastard, you'll pay for this." He stood and fired first the Hawken and then his .44 Remington pistol, killing three warriors at the base of the coulee. He took careful aim at another warrior, who made the mistake of standing next to Little Crow, and killed him with a single shot to the head. Withdrawing the snake from the sack, he held it up and stretched it out over his head. "Here's a fitting mascot for you, Little Crow!"

The chief looked up the ravine and saw Ryker standing giant-like at the rim. His strong legs were planted wide, and he continued to hold the twisting snake over his head. As the warriors watched, he flung the huge serpent down the hillside toward them, and they instinctively recoiled from the hideous reptile. Ryker pointed at them with a sweeping scan, finally focusing his point directly at Little Crow and holding the pose a few seconds. "Sioux!" he hollered. He then yelled, "Ki-yi-yi!" and turned and disappeared from view.

Continuing to stare at the spot where Ryker had stood, Little Crow's eyelids flickered, and he looked offended at the rebuke. As he stared, he clenched his jaw tightly.

Running back to camp, Ryker approached Major Brown and saluted. "I'm afraid I was too late, sir," he said. His face was ashen. "I couldn't save Private Cunningham, and you'll learn soon enough how he died. Know that he'll be remembered as a hero. I can promise you that."

Brown looked from Ryker off into the distance along the valley and blinked away a tear. "First it was George Colter, and now, James Cunningham and all the other brave men who died here. What a senseless waste of life this is."

"When fighters go off to war, reason doesn't always go with them," Ryker said. "Those warriors down in the coulee are fighting with their hearts, not with their heads. Fortunately for us, we're fighting with both our hearts and our minds. Know that while I was up there on the rim just now, I left Little Crow with plenty to think about though."

Major Brown nodded as the distant sound of bugles, drums, and fifes could be heard coming up the valley from the south. "Colonel Sibley!"

"Must be, for sure," Ryker replied.

"I'll tell the men to hold on a while longer. Help is on the way."

Ryker and Brown were only partially correct, for after Bugler Smith sounded the call, it was Colonel McPhail with the infantrymen whom Sibley ordered to assist the burial detail coming to their aid, instead of Sibley himself, who remained at Fort Ridgely with the rest of the Sixth. Onward they came, 240 strong, along with their two six-pound cannon, supplies, and ammunition. As they approached Birch Coulee, however, Little Crow positioned his warriors between McPhail's relief troops and Major Brown's encampment. At his signal, 300 deadly, armed, warrior sharpshooters fired broadside at McPhail, forcing him to halt and secure his position.

McPhail determined it best to hold his position throughout the night of September the second. He sent a messenger back to Fort Ridgely to notify Sibley that he was surrounded and in danger of being overrun. Sibley immediately ordered the long roll to be beaten, and his entire force advanced, quick time, to the scene of the action. After sundown on September 2nd, what would later be immortalized as the "midnight march" was made from Fort Ridgely. At two o'clock in the morning, Sibley's troops arrived at McPhail's detachment three miles from Birch Coulee, beyond which was Brown's detachment. After posting a large detail of guards around the bivouac area, they bedded down for the remainder of the night.

Before dawn, silent, without summon of trumpet or drum, the troops stood in full battle array, ready to move. As they expected, Little Crow moved against them in force and commenced firing at Sibley's troops. They returned fire with such vigor that the Indians were forced to retreat into the timber of the coulee, but not for long.

Ryker heard the cries of wounded and dying men, and looked around the detail from Company A of the Sixth. He recognized Samuel Arbuckle, who lay wounded, Cornelius Cayle, dead, blood oozing from his head and his brains sprayed upon the ground. William Irvine was moaning in pain. Chauncey King, Henry Ralleau, and Henry Whetsler were all dead of gunshot wounds. He looked to his other side at the troops from Company B, and saw even more casualties.

Shelling from Sibley's artillery soon drove the Sioux out of the woods to a distance that their firearms were ineffective, and they were allowed to retreat for lack of an adequate mounted force to pursue them. After suffering a severe loss in warriors both killed and wounded, Little Crow managed to escape the area.

Although Sibley's troops then entered Brown's encampment with great fanfare, what they saw caused them to gag. The stench was unbearable. There were dead and dying men and several wounded being tended to by Surgeon Greeley with help from a half-dozen troopers. Horse carcasses were strewn everywhere, many having been used as fortifications behind which the troopers fired at the Indians. Scores more had dug earthen entrenchments with what tools were at hand and had fired at the Indians from there. Of Brown's original detachment, over ninety horses were killed, thirteen of his men slain, and forty-four more injured, including three staff officers. The tents of the detachment were riddled with bullets, some pierced a hundred times or more. The siege had lasted thirty-one hours, during which time Brown's men were without food or water, and when it was all over, each man walking had but five rounds of ammunition remaining.

As for Sibley's men, the losses were slight. His knowledge of wartime maneuvers was so well advanced that he was able to drive Little Crow from the battleground with little damage sustained to his troops. It was his wise use of artillery that overpowered Little Crow. Had he more cavalry at his command, he would have run Little Crow to ground and ended the hostilities at this time.

"Colonel Sibley, allow me to shake your hand," Ryker said, approaching the commander. "If you hadn't come along when you did, all of us would have died here. We couldn't hold out much longer."

"Too many died as it was," Sibley said. "Remember the Battle of Birch Coulee, September second and third, eighteen hundred and sixty-two, for what it was, the bloodiest and most severe action of the Indian Expedition thus far. But this war isn't over yet, I fear."

"I'm afraid you're right about that, sir," Ryker said. "We can't count Little Crow out yet. He'll make more stands against us. But what we did here the last two days saved the towns of Mankato and St. Peter from the revenge of Little Crow, for the warriors we captured said it was his sworn intent to destroy them."

"Thank you, Ryker," Sibley said. "Not all understand me as well as you do. The press is calling for my resignation. They accuse me of being friendly with Little Crow just because I understand the plight of the Sioux and said so in Washington."

"Be damned the press! Because of the action you took here, the threats of those nincompoops need not concern you. They'll shut their big yaps for good when the state and the nation reward you for what you've done. You got my word on that sir, or by golly, my name ain't Toby Ryker." He stood back and saluted. "Proud I am to serve under you, sir."

Sibley nodded then looked at the battlefield. "Let's clean up this mess."

It took several hours for the burial detail to dig a mass gravesite large enough for their fallen comrades at Birch Coulee, for the victims of the earlier massacre, and for two families killed by the tornado, the bodies of whom they had collected in wagons. No less than eighty-five bodies would be buried in the grave this day.

Ryker helped carry Private George Colter to the site, and then he spoke quietly with four other soldiers, and they all lit out for the base of the coulee where they cut the ropes from James Cummingham, whose body still sagged from the tree. They carried him reverently, silently, back to the gravesite, and as they passed Major Brown, he whispered through his tears the words "Thank you" to Ryker.

After all the corpses were lined up next to the trench, the soldiers joined Colonel Sibley, Major Brown, Captain Grant, and Chaplain Richard Bull for a funeral service. Ryker joined them as they stood at attention and sang the "Battle Hymn of the Republic," just written by Julia Ward Howe, a forty-three-year-old social activist and abolitionist, which was making the rounds of the Union camps and was very popular.

They sang two more verses with the refrain and then stood silently as the bodies of the slain were lowered gently into the earth. When Joseph Young, a fifteen-year-old musician with Company A of the

Sixth, gifted with a pure, sweet tenor voice, began to sing "Just Before the Battle, Mother," Ryker felt the tears stream down his face.

After burying the dead and placing the wounded in wagons with the long grasses of the prairie as their only mattress, Sibley prepared to return to Fort Ridgely. From there he intended to launch another attack against Little Crow's camp. Some fractional companies of the Third Regiment Minnesota Volunteers, 125 strong, who were paroled as prisoners, had returned to the state. Under the command of Major Abraham Walsh, they joined the expeditionary force against the Sioux.

Before leaving Birch Coulee, and knowing that the Indians would revisit the battleground, Sibley left a note for Little Crow, which he attached to a split stake fixed in an upright position in the ground.

If Little Crow has any proposition to make, let him send a half-breed to me and he shall be protected in and out of camp.
H.H. Sibley,
Colonel Commanding Military Expedition

This was the beginning of correspondence between Little Crow and Colonel Sibley. The commander knew that Little Crow held several hostages and that if he attacked the Indian camp, they would be immediately slaughtered. He also knew that any indication given to Little Crow that he would be hunted without mercy would also result in the wholesale slaughter of hostages. In order to save as many of them as he could, he needed to keep alive the hope in Little Crow that he would be dealt with fairly. Once the hostages were rescued, the chieftain would be told of his true fate, but not until then. Sibley also determined that any further engagements with the Indians needed to be made as far away from their camp as possible.

FOUR DAYS LATER, RYKER ENTERED the commander's office at Fort Ridgely with a note in his hand. "Got to see the boss," he said to the staff officer. Upon being admitted to Sibley's office, he said, "Little Crow has replied," and handed over the note. "What's it read, Colonel?"

Sibley opened the correspondence, donned his reading glasses and scanned it. Saying nothing, he handed the paper to Ryker. "Read it yourself."

YELLOW MEDICINE, September 7, 1862

DEAR SIR: For what reason we have commenced this war, I will tell you. It is on account of Major Galbraith. We made a treaty with the government and beg for what little we do get and then can't get it until our children are dying with hunger. It was with the traders who commenced it, Mr. A.J. Myrick told the Indians they could eat grass or dirt. Then Mr. Forbes told the lower Sioux they were not men. Then Robert told his friends how to defraud us of our money. If the young braves have push the white man, I have done this myself. So I want you to let Governor Ramsey know this. I have a great many prisoner women and children. It ain't all our fault. The Winnebagoes were in the engagement, two of them was killed. I want you to give me your answer by bearer all at present.

Yours friend,
LITTLE (his X mark) CROW

"This is going to be touchy, sir," Ryker said, handing back the note.

"Very much so," Sibley replied. "Ryker, you know Little Crow as well as I do and better than most. Now that we have correspondence, I would like you to be my courier to him."

"You got it, sir," Ryker said, "and I'm honored you would ask."

The next day, Sibley penned the following reply:

LITTLE CROW: You have murdered many of our people without any sufficient cause. Return me the prisoners, under a flag of truce, and I will talk to you like a man. I have sent your message to Governor Ramsey.

H.H. Sibley,
Colonel Commanding Military Expedition

Ryker delivered the message the same day.

"Ryker, are you enjoying the war?" Little Crow said as the scout entered his camp holding a flag of truce. When Ryker did not respond, the chief glanced skyward. "This sure is fine weather for a war."

"Yup," Ryker responded, staring coldly at Little Crow. "Since that heavy frost a week or so back, the weather's been holding."

"They call this weather Indian summer."

"I guess they do."

"When do you think we will have our first snowfall?"

"I have no idea."

"As icy as you are today, maybe we have already had it." Little Crow walked toward the campfire. "Come over here and have some puppy stew."

"I prefer government meat."

"Yeah, I suppose you do."

The two men, both sober-faced, studied each other a few minutes. Ryker's stare made Little Crow uncomfortable. "Saw you at Birch Coulee," the Indian said, breaking the silence. "That was some fancy shooting you did from way up there on the ridge. One shot to the head of my warrior."

"One clean shot to the head is what it should always be, Little Crow. Remember?"

"I remember."

"Your shot to Georgie Colter was way off the mark."

"Was that his name?"

"Yup, but he died proud though, even though your shooting was so lousy," Ryker said.

"I know it wasn't a clean kill. Maybe my old eyes are failing me. I apologize for it."

"As well you should. In fact, you need to apologize for a lot of things you've done lately."

"I got your meaning with the bull snake," Little Crow said, looking self-conscious.

73

"Uh-huh, figured you would. Even though you have become evil, Little Crow, I never thought you were stupid."

Little Crow motioned to the paper in Ryker's hand. "What you got there?"

"A message from Colonel Sibley. I'm his courier now."

"You are his courier? Good for you! I guess that means we can't use you for target practice anymore."

"I'm glad of that. You might accidentally hit me, although everybody knows it wouldn't be a clean kill." Ryker gave the communiqué to Little Crow and stood silently as the chieftain gave it to his scribe, who translated it then handed it back.

"Your soldiers beat the daylights out of us at the coulee," Little Crow said, putting the letter down. "Those cannons should be outlawed from the field."

"This war ain't a game, Little Crow. Those cannon you speak of are designed to kill hostiles, and Colonel Sibley is smart as a whip when it comes to battle. He is a fine battle commander and is a force to be reckoned with. This is what war has come to be these days, and Hank Sibley knows how to use the few cannons he has with great effectiveness. There ain't any flies on Hank Sibley, Little Crow."

"Where is this all going to end?"

"Why don't you ask your shaman?"

"He's dead, that's why. A cannonball blew him up."

Choosing his words carefully, Ryker changed the subject so as not to spook Little Crow any more than he already was. "Colonel Sibley is concerned about getting the hostages released unharmed."

"I know. I know. But they are useful to us yet." Little Crow motioned around the camp. "Some of my warriors are dissatisfied with how things went at Birch Coulee and blame me for it." He squinted at Ryker. "I suppose you hate me too."

"You can control your warriors, and as for me, my Indian blood still respects you like a brother, but I hate what you're doing, and I hate what you've become."

"I suppose." The chieftain studied the scout. "I'm getting tired of this war."

"Yup, when you attacked the settlers, you grabbed a skunk by the tail, no doubt about that," Ryker said. "Talk to Colonel Sibley. He'll treat you fairly, and we can end this right now."

"You don't understand. There are expectations, and we have our honor to preserve." The Indian stared hard at Ryker. "And as for Sibley, I know his hands are tied by those in command above him. He can't treat us fairly even if he wanted to, which I don't really think he does."

Ryker ignored this last comment, instead motioning to the hostages and the wounded warriors. "I guess I don't understand you, and I certainly don't envy you."

"Yes, well, I don't have a reply for Sibley just yet," Little Crow said. "You'd best get back to the fort."

"I'm going, but do the right thing for the sake of everyone, Little Crow. And you know as well as I do what the right thing is." With that, Ryker mounted his steed and left the camp.

On September the 12th, Little Crow sent another message to Sibley.

RED IRON VILLAGE, OR WAY-AU-AKAN
To Hon. H. H. Sibley:
We have in ma-wa-kan-ton band one hundred and fifty-five prisoners—not included the Sisitons and Wahpeton prisoners, then we are waiting for the Sisiton what we are going to do with the presoners they are coming down—they are at Lake qui Parle now, the words that I want to the governor I'll want to hear from him also, and I want to know from you as a friend what way that I can make peace for my people—in regard to prisoners they fare with our children or ourself just as well as us.

Your truly friend,
LITTLE CROW

Colonel Sibley responded promptly and gave his reply to the scout.

HEADQUARTERS MILITARY EXPEDITION
September 12, 1862
To Little Crow, Sioux Chief:
I have received your letter today. You have not done as I wished in giving up the prisoners taken by your people. It would be better for you to do so. I told you I had sent your former letter to Governor Ramsey, but I have not yet had time to receive a reply. You have allowed your young men to commit some murders since you wrote your first letter. This is not the way to make peace.

H.H. Sibley,
Colonel Commanding Military Expedition

After Ryker delivered the message to Little Crow, the correspondence between the two leaders came to an end. But a diary, or journal, kept by Sibley during this time period and sent to his wife, his beloved Sarah Jane, explained in detail the war to date that others could not see, and gave reasons for actions others could not understand. Ryker chanced upon it one morning after being admitted to the commander's office, only to find it lying open on his desk while Sibley had gone to the latrine. The scout knew he had no business reading the private diary, but he thought, *What the hell.*

FORT RIDGELY, September 5, 1862—I am well this morning but sorely fatigued after the forced march to the rescue of the companies hemmed in by the savages at Birch Coulee, particulars of which I wrote you yesterday. I have placed my commission at the disposal of Governor Ramsey in view of the complaints about delay, etc. etc., and so, perhaps he may relieve me, and permit me to go home, which I am quite anxious to do. The responsibilities of my position are so great that I am deprived of necessary rest. I can hardly sleep at all. The Indians are in force. They retreated in haste when I reached the beleaguered camp at the coulee, but did not go far, as they knew I had no cavalry and could not overtake them with my infantry. We shall have a battle shortly, when I receive the cartridges and rations indispensable to an advance movement. It is hard, indeed, while we are fighting, and doing our best, to have a "set of ninnies and paltroons" abusing us at home.

SEPTEMBER 7th.—You will have seen the account of the attack on my detachment at Birch Coulee. I was the first man to enter the doomed camp, after driving the savages, and as the survivors emerged from the holes they had dug in the ground, in and around their tents, a more delighted set of mortals I never saw. There lay ninety-one horses, shot dead, others hobbling about wounded. The scene was sickening. I hope the governor will appoint another officer to succeed me in command of the expedition, for I am nearly worn-out with fatigue, night-watching, and the labor necessary to get the raw material I have to work with into a condition fit for a campaign. I get curses because I do not accomplish impossibilities. I cannot safely go ahead without a sufficient supply of ammunition and rations, in both of which essentials we are sadly deficient. It would not do for me, under present circumstances, to resign my commission, peremptorily, for the safety of the state would be jeopardized if one, less experienced in Indian wiles and mode of warfare than I am, should be assigned to the only force which stands between the central portion of the state and desolation.

SEPTEMBER 8th.—I received a letter from Little Crow yesterday, by the bearers of a flag of truce. He writes (his amanuensis is an educated half-breed), that the reason the war commenced was because he could not get the provisions and other supplies due the Indians, that the women and children were starving and he could get no satisfaction from Major Galbraith, the United States agent, that he had many white women and children prisoners, etc. etc. I have sent my trusted scout, Toby Ryker, back to-day with a written reply telling Little Crow to deliver the captives to me, and I would then talk with him like a man. What he will do remains to be seen. The half-breeds, whom I know, say that the mixed-bloods are not permitted to leave the camp and are virtually prisoners, as most of them are believed to sympathize with the whites. They assure me that the Indians are determined to give us battle, at or near the Yellow Medicine, and are sanguine of success. I do sincerely hope they do not change their programme.

Ryker heard a sound by the rear door and heard Sibley's voice mutter, "Dad-burn hemorrhoids! Holy mackerel, do they ever itch!" He moved quickly from behind the desk and took a seat by the main door and looked nonchalantly out the window while he whistled a cheery tune. After reading the journal, his admiration for his commander grew to new heights, and he appreciated the fact that even in the face of great hardship, Sibley remained a brilliant strategist. Minnesota was lucky to have him in command of this expedition. As Sibley entered the room, Ryker stood and saluted and then he briefed the commander on the latest goings on in Little Crow's camp.

Late that evening, Sibley sat in the command tent of the Sixth, and by lantern light, he penned an official correspondence to the Adjutant General expressing his concern for the hostages being held in Little Crow's camp.

HEADQUARTERS IN CAMP, NEAR FORT RIDGLEY
September 5, 1862
Adjutant General O. Malmros, St. Paul,
Sir: I am very anxious to secure the safety of the many prisoners before attacking the camp, as they will doubtless be placed in the most exposed situation. The number of fighting men among the lower bands is 617, acceding the actual enumeration of Wahpatons about 250, and that they have been reinforced by 600 men from the Yankton and Sisseton bands, and that the Eyanktomas or Cut-Heads will be down as soon as they arrive from their hunt. We have therefore to meet, according to Mr. Riggs and Scout Ryker, 2,700 or 2,800 men, and I have, from the beginning, believed and acted upon this conviction, that the Lower bands would not attempt to escape, but would make a determined stand. Their main camp is at Yellow Medicine, and it is said by the Robinsons that the Upper Sioux have refused to allow them to go into the country, but tell them they must fight where they are. From what I can gather, principally from reports of scout Toby Ryker, I am satisfied they will make a desperate fight, and that we must expect night attacks, ambushes, and every species of annoyance in our advance. In view of the great importance of the results of the movements of this column, and the fact that I am without any disposable form of mounted men (there are not more than sixty or seventy left), I must urge the absolute necessity

of having cavalry fully armed and equipped, to the number at least one regiment, and the infantry force increased to 2,000 men.

This expedition, if properly supplied with men and materials, can crush this emeute at a blow, and wipe out the murderers, but should it meet with repulse, or take the field against a vigilant and desperate enemy without sufficient supplies, no one can see the horrible results.

Ryker and the other scouts, as well as the other bearers of the flag of truce, assert that all outlying parties have been called in, in view of the menacing position of our corps, and the latter further state that the party that attacked Major Brown's camp consisted of 349 men, who left the Yellow Medicine with the intention of dividing into two parties at this point, and simultaneously attacking St. Peter and Mankato, and that they had no idea of the force that met and repulsed them being in the neighborhood.

I hope that the Third regiment will be ordered to join this column at once, and that men and cartridges, rations and clothing, will be pressed forward with all expedition. Let us exterminate these vermin while we have them together.

I will report to you in my next the amount and description of the ammunition on hand, and what is still wanting.

In accordance with your suggestion, I have sent to New Ulm eighty-three muskets of different kinds and 2,800 cartridges, which have been turned over to the sheriff of the county for arming the settlers.

I learn from Colonel Flandrau that he would leave for St. Paul to hurry up reinforcements and supplies for the south side of the river.

While I concur in his report of the necessity of adding to his strength, I hope you will not forget that, in all probability, THIS CORPS must meet the main attack, and that the Third regiment, being disciplined, is indispensable as a nucleus and an example to the entirely raw officers and men composing the large majority of the Sixth and Seventh regiments.

H.H. SIBLEY,
Colonel, Commanding Military Expedition.

After re-reading his letter, Sibley removed his spectacles and massaged the bridge of his nose. Exhaustion then overcame him, and he slumped in his chair fast asleep rather than take leave to his private quarters.

6

"OKAY, BOYS, QUIT DREAMING about your sweethearts. Rise and shine!" Reveille was Ryker's favorite time of day. He made his way through the barracks shaking sleeping soldiers awake and sometimes tipping over their cots if they refused to budge. "Come on, boys! We still got a war on, in case you're too stupid to read the papers. Colonel Sibley wants us to head west and catch up with Little Crow."

"What day is it?" said Private Edwin Ross of the Third Minnesota Infantry.

"This is the nineteenth, you lazybones," Ryker growled. "Get up! Have your chow and fall in with your gear. You're marching to Wood Lake today." With that, he rolled the private out of his cot and onto the ground. Had he known that within a few days Private Ross would become another casualty of the Indian war, he might have been easier on him.

"Ouch! I bet you don't do that to Big Faye."

"You're absolutely right about that, Ross. She's too danged heavy. I can't lift her."

"We got to march, but you get to ride a horse."

"Sonny, when you're as old and experienced as me, you'll get to ride a horse too." Moving to the next barracks within the confines of Fort Ridgely, Ryker continued his harangue. His booming voice could be heard throughout the entire fort. "Up and at 'em, boys!" *Thump. Bang. Crash.*

"Ouch! Dang you, Ryker!"

"Quit your lollygagging! Now drop your cocks and grab your socks, you lazy yahoos, you!"

Colonel Sibley, in full battle gear and flanked by Colonel Crooks and his other staff officers, rode to the head of the infantry column and, with much fanfare, bugles blowing and drums rolling, left the fort for the wide open prairie. They marched all day on the 19th of September, and on the 20th and 21st they did likewise, receiving no hostile action from Little Crow or anyone else.

Each day there were several Indians in plain sight of the troops, sometimes alone, sometimes in small groups. Riding up to Ryker, Sibley asked about it. "What do you make of these savages, Ryker? They seem pretty bold out here."

"Reckon they are all scouting for Little Crow," Ryker replied. "His main body is still ahead of us some distance. They are the ones we have to worry about, not these tattletales."

"How far ahead of us do you think Little Crow is?"

"My guess is we'll bump into them maybe yet today or tomorrow for sure. Since they're toting all those prisoners along with them, they ain't moving very fast."

"Well, keep your eyes open."

"Oh shucks, do I have to? I planned to take a little nap here while my horse does all the work."

"I know you better than that." Chuckling, Sibley tipped his hat then returned to the head of the column.

"THERE ARE HUNDREDS OF THEM, but they're mostly on foot," Wa-kan-tan-ka said. He just returned from a reconnaissance ride around Sibley's troops and now sat with the war circle at the campfire. Already seated were Little Crow and warriors Sna-ma-ni, Baptiste Campbell, a half-breed, Ha-pan, Plan-doo-ta, also called Tazoo, and Cut Nose.

"We should attack tonight," Little Crow said. "The darkness will be our friend. We can steal upon them before they even know we are there."

"You expect us to fight like women?" Cut Nose spat into the fire. "That was fine during the raids, but now that we've attacked Sibley's army, they know where we are, and we know where they are. Under these circumstances, true warriors face their enemy head-on, like courageous men."

"You have to be smart besides being courageous," Tazoo said. "I question whether Little Crow has either the brains or the courage to lead us in this fight."

"That's right," Baptiste Campbell said, jabbing a finger toward Little Crow. "Your planning at Birch Coulee cost the lives of many men."

Little Crow scoffed. "You make too much of Sibley's infantry. We could ride in there tonight and kill those soldier babies with no interference, just like we did to that boy soldier back at the coulee. It's almost a shame to waste good Confederate bullets on them."

"A true war chief would not consider such a thing," Cut Nose said.

"During the daylight hours they have the advantage, especially with their big howitzers," Little Crow explained. "And the last time I looked, we have not even one cannon in camp to help even things out. It is only sensible to use the cover of darkness as our ally."

Cut Nose arose. "I think we need a new leader. I will not ride with you against Sibley at night. I have more pride than that." He sneered at Little Crow as the other warriors shook their heads in agreement.

"All right, even in daylight, they are still babies," Little Crow said, trying to sound unconcerned as he looked around the circle. "They are no match for us. We will move against them at dawn on the twenty-third after they settle in at Lone Tree Lake."

ON THE 22ND AT ONE-THIRTY in the afternoon, Colonel Sibley's force arrived at Lone Tree Lake. Ryker told Sibley they were at Wood Lake, but he was wrong about that. If he hadn't been gawking about and enjoying the fall scenery, and if he hadn't been nipping at his flask full of Old Heaven Hill, he would not have gotten disoriented and told Sibley they were at Wood Lake, but by the time the error was discovered, Sibley had already sent several dispatches to St. Paul identifying their bivouac site as Wood Lake. Ryker later apologized for the error, but by then it was too late to change the official records.

They bivouacked along the shoreline. Their break wasn't meant to last long however, for Sibley intended to cross the Yellow Medicine River, about three miles away, on the morning of the 23rd and there await the arrival of Captain Rogers' company of the Seventh Regiment. The company had been stationed at New Ulm, but with the arrival of another detachment to provide protection there, Sibley had ordered the Seventh to join him by forced march as soon as possible.

Ryker stood with Sibley sipping coffee out of a tin cup early in the morning of the 23rd. "After mess this morning, we'll head out for the river," Sibley said, checking his timepiece. "It's seven o'clock now."

"Sounds like a good plan," Ryker replied. "The weather has been holding, so it should only take an hour to reach the shoreline."

"I'm hopeful Captain Rogers will—" He was interrupted by the sound of shooting.

"Well now, will you look at that," Ryker said. "I'd guess that's about three hundred of Little Crow's fighters now, and I doubt they're riding over here to have coffee and doughnuts with us."

"Don't you think so?" Sibley said, dumping his coffee. "Our cooks are known far and wide for baking a mean Danish roll. Colonel Crooks! Fall the men in!" He glanced at Ryker. "Come on. Let's kill some savages."

The Indians, whooping and hollering in their usual fashion, attacked the camp. They fired rapidly into the bivouac area, doing little damage, but they did manage to catch Private Edwin Ross smack-dab in the noggin with a miniball and drop him to the ground. The other soldiers had to move around him as the medics rushed to his side and moved him to the surgical tent where he died shortly thereafter.

Ryker headed out into the thick of the fighting, using not only his Hawken, but also his revolver and even his Bowie knife to shoot and stab the savages. He brought down six of them in short order, then moved back within the perimeter of the camp to get more ammunition. Bullets whizzed, horses fell, and men died on both sides. Principle Musician Aaron H. Dayton, a cadence drummer, began the familiar beat while Bugler Smith kept busy signaling to the troops with the various calls they all knew how to respond to by heart. A half hour into the battle, Dayton's drum fell silent as he took a slug to the chest and slumped dead over the instrument.

"PLEASE DO NOT PARTAKE in this slaughter," Stands Tall said as she watched Wa-kan-tan-ka prepare for battle.

"Little Crow needs all his warriors now," Wa-kan-tan-ka said. "We're making a stand at Lone Tree Lake and intend to show those soldier boys who the better fighters are once and for all."

"All you will show them is how a Dakota warrior dies," Stands Tall said, crying. "I don't want to lose you, Wa-kan-tan-ka. I need you, and so does our son."

"You worry for nothing," Wa-kan-tan-ka said, caressing his wife. "We will not be defeated. The Great Spirit after whom I am named is on our side." With that, he departed the tipi to join the other warriors.
Stands Tall sat at the fire ring with her son, and as the sound of hoof beats and the "Ki-yi-yi!" scream of the warriors reached her ears, she covered her face and wept bitterly.

"*Takuwe niye ceye*, Mama?" (Why you cry, mother?), said five-year-old Louis in the Dakota dialect. Not only was he a bright child, he was also fun-loving and enjoyed practicing both the English and Dakota dialects when conversing with others. This playfulness attested to his heritage as a Dakota.

Wiping away her tears, Stands Tall hugged him and played the game along with him. *"Miye hca tuwe ceye niyate kin a kici ukitawa oyote"* (I cry for your father and for our people.) she said, also in dialect. *"Tka econ snikakije cuke un mitawa istamnihapi, kici lena iyukca niyeteca el okahinge"* (But do not suffer at my tears, for these are things of which you are too young to understand.) She hugged him again and kissed him. *"Hemaca topa akigle nitawa waniyetu, na mis eya econ hiya okahnige iye uma"* (I am four times your age, and I do not understand the sense to it either.)

RYKER, LYING FLAT ON THE GROUND in a shallow trench that had been dug to protect the troops from Little Crow's flying lead, fired round after round at the Indians, who charged the encampment and then pulled back, only to charge again.

"Jumpin' G. Hosiphat, Pappy," he muttered as he reloaded his Remington revolver, a task he'd done so many times that he could do it automatically. He used the ramrod attached to the underside of the barrel to push the residue from the cylinders, then used it again as he reloaded. Powder, tamp, wad, tamp, shot, tamp, wad, tamp. The entire process took him less than sixty seconds, not counting the placement of the primers over the nipples on the cylinder. Holstering the revolver, he grabbed the single-shot Hawken and also reloaded it. "What is the sense to this? All this killing, and for what? When it's all over, a bunch of us soldier boys will be dead if we're lucky, or crippled and singing soprano and hurting so danged bad we'd wish we were dead if we ain't, and it will be the same in Little Crow's camp. And us Minnesotans will still be in charge, this will still be our state, the Indians will still be starving and diseased and drunk, and nothing will have gotten any better." He glanced skyward. "Can't you do something? Put in a word with the Almighty to end all this nonsense? This is so stupid!"

A volley of bullets flew over his head so he again commenced firing. "Big Faye, I need some loving. Where the dickens are you when I need you, you old heifer."

Another volley of bullets whizzed overhead and ripped into the tents behind him. He heard the scream of a horse and looked around to see another of the all too few mounts of the regiment fall to the ground, its blood pouring from a dozen bullet holes.

"For cripes sake, when I signed on to be a scout for the Sixth, nobody ever said I'd have to work this hard." He fired another deadly round and knocked a warrior to the blood-soaked sod surrounding Lone Tree Lake. "Take that, Little Crow! Oops, sorry, Dancing Bear. It was nice knowing you."

Colonel Sibley crawled up alongside Ryker and studied the enemy through his binoculars. "Holy cow, look at those fighting savages!"

"Yessireebob, they're in fine form today."

The two men watched as the Renville Guard under command of Lieutenant Gorman moved to the front to check Little Crow's advance. They fired in waves with ten men in a line, crouching, aiming, and firing, and while the gun smoke still hung in the air and hid them from the enemy, they cleared out to the side while another column took their place. It was an effective maneuver, and the Indians soon began to fall back toward a ravine. Meanwhile, the Third Regiment under Major Walsh moved in to provide cover for the Renville Guard.

The Indians waged a counterattack against the Third and attempted to cut them off from the Renville Guard. The fighting was intense with many casualties on both sides, but Little Crow's warriors were definitely getting the worst of it.

"Oh-oh," said Sibley, his binoculars fixed on the fighting. "Little Crow is pulling his men into the ravine." He looked at Ryker. "They're trying to get behind the Third!"

"And we're vulnerable there," Ryker said.

"Let's fix this right now." Sibley returned to the troops. "Lieutenant Colonel Marshall?"

"Aye, sir?"

"Take five companies of the Seventh Regiment and double-time them over toward the Third to bolster Major Walsh. Little Crow aims to cause him harm."

"Aye, sir." Marshall hollered commands to his staff to have the troops line up in formation.

"Also, take Captain Hendricks and his six-pounder with you."

"Yes, sir," Marshall said, "and thank you, sir. That six-pounder will come in mighty handy. We can blow the Indians sky-high with it."

"You'll need all the firepower you can get," Sibley said.

Lieutenant Colonel Marshall advanced his troops quickly amid a shower of miniballs from the enemy, which fortunately did little damage. As Sibley watched, the Seventh returned a few volleys until Marshall got into position and personally led his men in a charge toward the ravine. "Down with Little Crow!" his men began to chant. "On to Little Crow's Camp!"

The drummer, bugler, and fife player struck up a lively battlefield march as the Seventh charged toward the ravine, laying a wall of lead in the air ahead of them. The fighting was fierce, with the Indians low in the ravine as the men of the Seventh poured over the crest.

"Blast the ornery savages!" Marshall hollered above the din, and his troops were only too happy to oblige. Turning the heavy artillery on the ravine, they shot several cannonballs into the trees and scattered Little Crow's fighting force. After another hour of fierce fighting that oftentimes had both sides engaged in hand-to-hand combat, the ravine was cleared of Indians.

LITTLE CROW DID NOT LIKE what he saw. He knew a frontal assault on Sibley's troops was now impossible. "Get behind the main camp!" he yelled. "We'll attack them from behind! They're unprotected there, and we can do grave damage!"

ALTHOUGH THE INDIANS MADE a scramble toward the rear, Major McLaren with Captain Wilson's company took a stand on the extreme left side of the camp and intercepted them. With the aid of the six-pounder and a mountain howitzer, which were used with great effectiveness, the Indian toll began to rise, proving the wisdom of Little Crow's expressed concern of the previous evening. The battle raged fiercely for over two hours when finally the Indians, suffering a heavy toll, backed away from the battle. Over thirty warriors had been killed outright during the fight and several more were seriously wounded. Although the fighting was bloodier with more loss of life at Birch Coulee, it was the Battle of Wood Lake that broke the ranks among Little Crow's men and ended further major hostile action for the year. The press quoted Sibley as saying that if the Battle of Birch Coulee saved the towns of Mankato and St. Peter, the Battle of Wood Lake saved Minnesota.

While the troops cleaned up the battlefield and buried several of the dead from both sides, the Indians returned to camp with their wounded, and after tending them, they began to debate the wisdom of either surrendering their white hostages or killing them outright as retribution.

"Damn that Colonel Sibley!" Cut Nose roared as he paced around Little Crow's camp. "Those cannon are monsters! No one can succeed against them. Sibley isn't fighting fair!"

"I told you that," Little Crow said calmly as he puffed on a pipe. "We sat around this very circle last night, and I told you that. You, Cut Nose, and you . . ." he pointed to the others at the circle, "you were all so fired up with false courage that you let it overtake your reason. It makes me wonder if you drank too much whisky before we had our powwow last night rather than behaving like the seasoned warriors I thought you were."

Cut Nose, his hand resting on his hatchet, marched up to the seated Little Crow and hovered over him threateningly. "You should have done a better job of convincing us," he snarled. "We listened, but you talked in circles like a crazy man."

Little Crow stood. The chief towered over Cut Nose and glared at him. "Sit down, you stupid idiot, or I'll give you something to remember me by." The two went eyeball to eyeball in a silent standoff, but when Cut Nose saw Little Crow move his hand toward his scalping knife, he raised his hands in a conciliatory gesture.

"You are the chief, Little Crow. I honor your position."

"Don't you try making coup on me ever again," Little Crow said. He pointed around the circle. "Or any of the rest of you either. My mistake was listening to you poor excuses for warriors last night rather than following my heart and doing as the Great Spirit guided me."

"It's over," Baptiste Campbell said. "Whether right or wrong, it's over and done with. What we must concern ourselves with now is what we are to do next."

"We'll keep fighting," Little Crow replied. "We aren't defeated yet."

"Let's kill all the prisoners and dump them in Sibley's lap," said Hypolite Auge, another half-breed.

"That would make just as much sense as if we handed over all our ammunition to Sibley," said Little Crow. "The prisoners are valuable to us alive, but they're certainly worthless to us dead. Don't you know anything about war? Only if they attack our camp should the prisoners be slaughtered."

"We are all as good as dead anyway," Cut Nose said. "I don't know about the rest of you, but I'm going to take my pleasure on as many of the white women hostages as I want to right now. At least, I will die satisfied." With that, he stomped off toward the prison compound as Ryker, under flag of truce, entered the camp.

"Little Crow, I have a message from Colonel Sibley," Ryker said.

"Oh, I suppose," Little Crow said crossly. "What does the great white Colonel Sibley want now?"

Reaching into the pocket of his buckskins, the scout removed a letter and held it out.

"You read it," the chieftain said. "I trust you will give an accurate account of what it says."

"Well, all right, if you say so," Ryker replied, opening the letter. With only a brief hesitation, he donned his spectacles and read aloud.

WOOD LAKE, September 23, 1862

When you bring up the prisoners and deliver them to me under the flag of truce carried by Toby Ryker, now in your camp, I will be ready to talk of peace. The bodies of the Indians that have been killed will be buried like white people and the wounded will be tended to as our own; but none will be given until the prisoners are brought in. I will wait here a reasonable time for the delivery of the prisoners; if you send me word through Toby Ryker that they will be given up.
A flag of truce in the daytime will always be protected in and out of my camp if one or two come with it.

H. H. SIBLEY
Colonel, Commanding

Removing his reading glasses, Ryker squinted solemnly at Little Crow and handed him the letter in front of the Indians who had congregated around them. Those among them who understood English translated Ryker's words to the others. Warriors from several of the other tribes, who until this time were allies with the Dakota chief, determined to take their leave after hearing Ryker's reading. Standing Buffalo and the Upper Sissetons immediately became the enemies of Little Crow, and any dream he had of initiating another massacre like the one in August was dashed. Even several of the warriors who remained within Little Crow's camp turned traitor and betrayed him, bargaining instead with Sibley, and pledging their allegiance to the victorious troops.

Little Crow retreated with the captives and his remaining supporters to a site across from the headwaters of the Chippewa River near Lac qui Parle and again set up camp. It was the beginning of the end for Little Crow, and he was able to sense it. Meanwhile, Sibley prepared two more messages, this time to the Indians who had turned against Little Crow, and gave them to Ryker for delivery.

Upon his return to Sibley's camp, Ryker noticed a large group of soldiers standing at attention next to a freshly dug grave.

"Oh no, not another one." He groaned as he approached the group. Even from a distance he recognized the body of Erastus Guard, an orphan who became a Principal Musician and drummer with the Seventh Regiment Minnesota Volunteer Infantry. Erastus was just fourteen years of age when he joined the volunteers, although he lied about that. Ryker recalled that the boy had been injured at Birch Coulee. Unfortunately, largely because of the lack of sanitary conditions on the battlefield, his amputation had taken on gangrene, and that was what ended his life. Ryker removed his hat as a sign of respect, ran his fingers through his hair, and joined the troops at the funeral service. After a eulogy by Chaplain Oliver T. Light, just twenty years old himself, Oscar Webster, another musician who had drummed alongside the deceased, sang "The Drummer Boy of Shiloh."

There was a long moment of silence, a pregnant pause, after Oscar Webster concluded the song. The only sound on the burying ground was that of the breeze blowing over the prairie. Ryker saw several soldiers with tears on their eyes, and felt the salty wet sting on his cheeks as well. A twenty-one-gun salute followed, and after that, musician Henry Rogers blew "Taps."

As Ryker made his way back to his tent, a weariness bordering on depression overcame him. It was the death all around him that caused it. He planned to drain the whiskey flask again tonight.

7

RYKER, AS SOON AS WE BREAK CAMP here, I want you to lead us across the Yellow Medicine River," Colonel Sibley said. "Find a spot on the open prairie within sight of Little Crow's camp. We'll bivouac there."

"Yes, sir," Ryker replied. "I'll scout it out directly, and be back here within two hours."

The commander withdrew his watch. "It is half past nine. I'll make sure we're ready to travel by noon."

By this time, Ryker was astride his horse, a big bay quarter horse gelding he named Wino because the horse liked to share a nip with him now and again. The animal, a cavalry mount, was young, just four years old, and stood nearly sixteen hands tall. That was good because, as hefty as Ryker was, he needed a sturdy horse to ride. He tipped his hat to Sibley and headed toward the river.

Five miles beyond the waters of the Yellow Medicine, he came upon an area of the prairie that would serve well as a bivouac site. From here he could smell the smoke from Little Crow's campfires, and when the wind blew towards him, he could even hear the sound of voices emanating from the lodges. He squinted towards the camp then glanced at the blazing sun above. Removing his hat, he ran his bandanna around the rim of his Stetson and sopped the sweat from his forehead. "Well, Wino, I got the feeling in my bones that before long this campaign will be over. What do you think? Huh?"

Wino nickered and bobbed his head, which made Ryker smile. "Yes, you want to get back to green pastures too, don't you? The dried-up crap that passes for grass out here won't keep a big gelding like you alive for long. Well, in a little while you'll be back at Fort Snelling eating fresh-cut brome hay with a side of oats, I promise you that." He glanced in the direction of St. Paul. "You hear that, Big Faye? I'm a-comin' to you, darling. Leave the red light on, so's I don't trip over my feet in the dark. We're going to have a celebration the likes of which St. Paul ain't seen in years!"

Replacing his hat, he neck-reined Wino toward the river and headed at a trot back toward camp. It was half past eleven when he reported to Sibley.

"There's my scout," Sibley said as Ryker reined Wino to a halt in front of the command tent. The commander was in good humor. "Get down here and have some stew."

"Yup, that I will, and I found a good spot for us," Ryker replied. "Decent graze, as decent as it gets out here this time of year, fresh water, and some shelter from the westerly winds."

By the time the scout had dismounted, Sibley had filled a blue graniteware plate with stew, the makings of which was somewhat questionable. "Mmmm, smells delicious," Ryker said, his ample belly starting to rumble.

"What the devil is that noise?" Sibley looked through his binoculars. "Sounds like thunder off to the northwest, or maybe cannon fire."

"Aw, quit it sir," Ryker said, blushing. "It's just my tater basket preparing to take on some food, is all. This ain't as good as the Don't Ask Stew Aloysius Bodine makes, but almost."

His face growing sober, Sibley said softly, "Sergeant Bodine won't be cooking for us anymore. He was killed last week in the battle at Antietam. I just got the post."

Ryker looked at the commander, stunned. "I told him he shouldn't have transferred to the Third."

"Well, you know how he was, you two being friends and all. He wanted to do his duty to the country and see action in the Civil War, and once he made up his mind, there was no stopping him."

Shaking his head, Ryker removed his hat and gazed at the ground a moment. "He was just a young man, sir. Not even thirty yet."

"Yup," Sibley said, also removing his hat.

"You got a couple of glasses in your tent?"

"Sure do."

"Let's put 'em to work."

Once inside the large command tent, just the two of them at the moment, Ryker removed his whiskey flask and poured a generous shot into the two glasses. Picking them up, he handed one to Sibley. "To the memory of Sergeant Aloysius Arbuckle Bodine."

"Amen to that," the commander replied. Clicking their glasses together, they drank the burning liquid in silence. Sibley then rested his hand on Ryker's shoulder. "Can you handle the news about Bodine?"

"I got no choice but to accept it."

"Good. Now finish your stew," Sibley said, setting down his glass. "We got to get moving. There's still a war on."

"I heard that one before. In fact, I said it myself several times," Ryker replied. "I'll be back in the saddle in five minutes."

"Fine, I'll gather the troops."

HEADING DUE WEST, RYKER led the infantry back across the Yellow Medicine River. They made the bivouac site in just over two hours, and there they made camp. Sibley and his officers trained their field glasses on the Indian compound a short distance away, and after much discussion of strategy, they decided to have the troopers dig trenches facing the tipis from which they could fire. He also ordered all the artillery at his command, all the six-pounders and the howitzer cannons, to cover the Indian camp and be prepared to fire.

Amid the hustle and bustle, Ryker moseyed up to the officers. He was chewing on the sweet-tasting stem of a wild oat he had pulled off the prairie. "Gents, I don't think there's much opposition left over there," he said, nodding toward Little Crow's encampment.

"From what I see, you might be correct," Sibley said, surveying the camp through his fieldglasses. "It looks like there are more hostages over there than warriors. Several flags of truce are standing."

"Nevertheless," said Lieutenant Colonel Marshall, "you dare not underestimate them. They can still muster to a fight, and they can still kill hostages."

"I think it is worth the gamble," said Sibley.

"What do you mean, sir?" Marshall replied as the other staff officers looked at the commander.

"I mean that I am going to march right into the center of that camp and take command of it."

"Oh, sir, I don't know how good an idea that is, if you pardon me saying so," Marshall replied. "You could get yourself killed by such a show of bravado. Let the rest of us overrun the site first and quash any remaining rebellion."

"Nope, I've decided," Sibley said. "If this is my day to die, so be it. But I have a gut feeling that we will be celebrating a great victory by tonight, and that we will break the spine of Little Crow's support."

"If you insist," Marshall replied. "But I go with you, and two companies of infantry will back you up." Several other officers also volunteered to join the march with their beloved commander.

Looking at his watch, Sibley said, "Thank you, men. Get ready to march. At two o'clock I intend to enter camp. Ryker, are you ready?"

"Reckon I'm as ready as I'll ever be, sir."

"Good. Let's do it then."

At precisely two o'clock, Ryker, riding at Sibley's side and backed by two companies of infantry in full battle gear with their drummers beating the cadence, marched impressively into the heart of Little Crow's camp. They met no resistance and discovered that Little Crow and some of his supporters had high-tailed it to the west. They heard a scream of pain and found Cut Nose raping one of the hostage women, and they arrested him on the spot and put him in irons.

Although Ryker was a seasoned scout, he still was taken aback at what he saw. The prisoners were mostly women and children. In fact, only one white man, George H. Spencer, badly wounded, was found alive in camp. The women showed the scars and the pain of their captivity. Several of them, women and young girls alike, had been brutalized in the most unthinkable ways. Turning away from the sight, Ryker swallowed hard.

He heard the cry of a child, and looking toward the sound, could make out the figure of a young white girl with blonde hair the color of corn silk, maybe two but certainly less than three years old, holding a doll and sitting alone in a tipi. She wore a dirty gingham dress and sandals and sat on a torn Indian blanket. He moved quickly to her.

"Whew's Mama? I want Mama!" she cried, not yet old enough to talk plainly.

"It's all okay now, honey," Ryker said, sitting down next to the girl. He figured the girl's mother was among the dead, but he couldn't bring himself to tell her that. Terrified, she looked at him and hugged even closer the cloth doll, which appeared to be her sole possession. "My name's Toby, and I'm a scout for Colonel Sibley. You're safe now and don't have to be afraid ever again. Can you tell me your name?"

The girl raised her large blue eyes, eyes filled with tears, to her rescuer. At first she said nothing, simply looked him all over as she fought back her sobs. She studied his buckskins then looked back to his smiling, gentle face. He reached out to touch her but she pulled away. He knew she was traumatized just like young David Stewart had been back at St. Peter.

"It's okay, honey. I'm not going to hurt you, and I'll see to it that nobody else does either." Changing his tactics, he motioned to the doll, which was dirty and torn in two places. "It looks like she's hurt. What is her name?"

96

The girl at first clung more tightly to the doll, but as Ryker gently touched it, she released her grip. "She's Sawy," she said. "My dowy. A Indian man hurt her."

Ryker snapped his fingers. "I got just the thing. You wait here. I'll be right back." With that he arose and, after posting a soldier guard at the entrance to the tipi, he rode the few hundred yards to Sibley's bivouac, ran to the surgeon's tent and asked for some bandages.

"Here you are," Surgeon Alfred Wharton said. "There's more, if you need them."

"I think this is enough."

"What kind of a wound are you treating?"

"A very sick cloth doll."

"A very sick what?" The surgeon raised his finger into the air and prepared to say more, but by this time, Ryker was already in the saddle and heading back to Little Crow's camp at a gallop.

Running up to the tipi, Ryker dismissed the guard and ducked inside. "I'm back, honey," he said, plopping down at her side and sitting cross-legged on the grass. He held up the bandages. "These will fix up Sally just fine."

The little girl smiled briefly, the first such smile he had seen, and then she looked into his face. Saying nothing, she handed the doll to the scout then began to suck her thumb, curling her index finger over her nose and studying the goings-on with great interest.

Ryker took the time to carefully wrap the badly injured doll where it had been torn, and tucked the bandages in around the wounds as well as any surgeon could have done. "There, honey," he said, handing the doll back to the girl. "Sally's gonna be fine now."

Taking the doll, the girl studied it and then hugged it to her chest. "Sawy says *danke* vewy much."

"No thanks needed," Ryker replied, recognizing the girl's German word. "This ain't the first doll I've nursed back to health. One time Big Faye, she's my dolly, when she got a case of the cupid's itch, I tended to her. You know what she had?" He smiled at the girl and she smiled back.

"Crabs!"

"Cwabs?" She giggled and clapped her hands.

Ryker's smile disappeared. It dawned on him that he was telling this child much more than she needed to hear, or that she could possibly understand. After all, she was not much more than a baby. *What kind of a dunce am I? This is a little girl, for cripes sake!* Before his flapping gums got him backed into a corner, he blushed and said, "Yeah, it made her real sick, but enough about Big Faye. She's much better now."

Still clinging to the doll, the girl stuck her thumb in her mouth again.

"Can you tell me your name, honey?"

"Maywy," the girl replied around her thumb.

"Molly?"

She removed her thumb from her mouth. "No, MAYWY."

"Oh! Mary! Well, Mary, I'm Toby Ryker, but my friends call me Toby. I'd be obliged if you called me that."

Standing, Mary crawled into Ryker's lap then ran her fingers over his beard. "Yow face is bweeding, but it is dwy."

"No, it isn't bleeding, honey. I just got red hair, that's all."

She leaned up and kissed him. "Thank you, Toby, fow hewping me. You my fwiend."

Feeling the emotion swell within him, Ryker blinked away a tear and kissed the girl back. Thinking about what she must have endured in the last several weeks made him shudder. "Do you know your family name, Mary?"

"No," came the reply. "It too wong."

"Too long, huh?"

"Yeah." She placed her arms around his neck. "I'm hungwy, and I want Mama."

Again, Ryker had to force back his emotions. He sniffed then looked deeply into Mary's eyes. "You know something? I'm hungry too. Let's get us some food."

"Okay."

Rising with the little girl, who weighed all of about twenty-five pounds, Ryker left the tipi and approached Wino. "This here's my horse," he said, holding her up to the gelding's head. "His name's Wino."

"Hi, Wino," Mary said, holding out her hand and running it flat against the horse's muzzle. The horse sniffed the girl, then nickered. "Good howsie."

"Let's go over to my camp and eat," Ryker said.

"Put me down. I walk."

Ryker ambled toward Camp Release, as the bivouac site came to be known, passing the hostages and troops and Indians who had surrendered to Sibley. As he walked past the commander with the girl, who walked at his side holding his hand and clutching her dolly, his eyes met those of the commander and the two winked at each other.

Continuing over to camp, they entered the cook tent where he and Mary had some oatmeal. The way the girl ate, it was obvious she was half-starved.

SIBLEY SENT A DETAIL OF INFANTRY after Little Crow, but he knew they couldn't cover much ground. Still lacking an adequate cavalry, which was the hand he was dealt, the Indians quickly outdistanced the foot soldiers and made good their escape to the James River in Dakota Territory.

Much time was spent with the hostages, feeding them, clothing them with what little they had, and trying to make them as comfortable as possible. There were several dead hostages and Indians, and a burial detail cleaned up after them.

Late that evening, Sibley penned his notes of the Camp Release liberation for his records. As he demonstrated every day, even on the battlefield, there was paperwork. It was difficult work to describe the condition of the hostages. Without much clothing, painfully thin and emotionally traumatized, he carefully detailed what he had seen. Then, rereading his report before assigning it to the courier for delivery to St. Paul, he cried at the memories that this tragic day at Camp Release stirred within him.

STANDS TALL PACED THE FLOOR of the lodge she shared with Wa-kan-tan-ka and Louis. Her heart went out to the captive women and children in camp, and she and a few other woman who had the courage to do so provided them with what aid they could. They knew they may incur the wrath of the warriors, but they were driven by conscience to ignore this danger. They shared what little food and clothing they had and tended to the sick.

"Wa-kan-tan-ka, my husband, it is over, and we lost as I knew we would," she said as the warrior entered their lodge holding a bottle and very drunk on whiskey. He was in a foul mood since the defeat at Wood Lake and slapped her in the face hard.

"Shut up, woman!" he hissed. "First the soldiers beat us into the ground then Little Crow runs off and hides, and now my own wife speaks ill of me. I do not need to hear this!" He ran his fingers through his long hair, shook his head and looked at her again as she cringed in terror at the monster her man had become. Leering, he snatched her and threw her to the ground then fell upon her and took her forcibly.

When it was over and they were clothed, she searched his eyes for some clue as to why it had come to this. She saw only hate in this man who had become a stranger to her. "War has made you into an animal. War, and that firewater," she said, then clung to their son, Louis, as he entered the tipi. She was grateful that at least he did not witness the assault.

Glaring back, Wa-kan-tan-ka took another gulp of the whiskey and wiped his mouth on the back of his hand. Stands Tall didn't like the look in his eyes; there was something violent in them and lustful, and that frightened her, but she tried not to show it. Then the alcohol seemed to take over, and the look passed. "You never did love me as a dutiful woman should," he said, and he staggered as if the alcohol was making him dizzy. She, however, was furious. She slapped his face so hard that, in his already dazed condition, she knocked him over.

"How dare you speak of me that way!" Stands Tall said. "I loved you and honored you much more than you have me."

"I guess it doesn't matter, anyway," Wa-kan-tan-ka replied, crawling to his feet. "Sibley won't let this pass. Soon I'll be dead, and you'll be free to marry another more to your liking." He gulped some more liquid courage then snorted at her and stumbled out of the lodge.

Stands Tall watched him go out into the night and join some other warriors around the campfire. She saw him stagger and fall to the ground and heard the other warriors, equally drunk, laugh at him, and she began to cry.

"What is wrong with my father?" said Louis, now using the excellent English taught him by the missionaries.

"Your father is very sick," Stands Tall replied, hugging him and bending down to his eye level. "But he is still your father, and he loves you very much. You must remember that always."

"He does not look sick."

"His sickness is not in his body. It is in his soul. You go now and lie on your robe. It is time for you to sleep." As Louis hugged her and moved over to the edge of the lodge, she looked after him. Then she returned her gaze to Wa-kan-tan-ka and cried bitterly

THE NEXT FEW DAYS WERE taken up with tending to the hostages now in the camp of the soldiers. Now that the fighting was over, Sibley wanted to be relieved of his command so he could return to his personal affairs and formally made this request of his superiors. The response he received surprised him and was applauded by all. A courier delivered it to his command tent where he and Ryker were taking a breather and chatting.

Ryker, as he liked to do, was leaning back in his chair and just finished scraping the dirt from under his fingernails with his jackknife when the courier arrived. He pointed the blade at Sibley and shook it for emphasis. "So, I says to Big Faye, I says, Faye, you old heifer . . ." Ryker looked up at the courier who was holding an open dispatch and grinning from ear to ear. "What're you so tickled about, soldier?"

The courier said nothing, simply waved the dispatch.

"Let me see that." Ryker took the paper and read it slowly then looked up at Sibley and smiled also as the courier saluted, did an about-face, and departed.

"Well? Don't keep it to yourself," said Sibley. "What does it say?"

"I think I'll let you read it, sir," Ryker said, standing and handing over the correspondence. Then he stepped back one pace and, still smiling, saluted the commander.

"Oh for Pete's sake, let's see that. I suppose it's another order from Washington that is impossible to fulfill." As he read the correspondence, his eyebrows went up and his mouth hung open in disbelief.

WASHINGTON, D.C., September 29, 1862
Major General Pope, St. Paul, Minnesota:
Colonel Henry Hastings Sibley is made brigadier general for his judicious fight at Yellow Medicine. He should be kept in command of that column, and every possible assistance sent to him.
H.W. Halleck,
General-in-Chief

"Well chop down my mizzen mast and call me a toothpick. I don't know what to say."

"You don't have to say anything, Brigadier General Henry Hastings Sibley, sir. Brigadier General Henry Hastings Sibley—that title has a nice ring to it, and you earned this promotion the hard way, on the battlefield. You deserve it, and proud I am to serve under you." Ryker saluted his commander again and pulled out his flask. "Where are them two water glasses of yor'n? We need to celebrate this."

The U.S. Senate confirmed this promotion, and Colonel Sibley of the State of Minnesota, now brigadier general in the service of the United States, accepted the appointment and decided to remain at his post even though his private interests were to suffer. The next point of business was to round up the Indians, separate the guilty from the innocent, and schedule military trials of the murderers. The day previous to this appointment, Sibley had issued the following order:

SPECIAL ORDER, No. 55.
HEADQUARTERS, CAMP RELEASE
September 28, 1862

A military commission composed of Colonel William Crooks of the Sixth Regiment, Lieutenant Colonel Marshall of the Seventh Regiment, Captains Grant and Bailey of the Sixth Regiment, and Lieutenant Olin of the Third Regiment, will convene at some convenient place in camp at ten o'clock this morning, to try, summarily, the Indians and mixed-bloods, now prisoners, who may be brought before them by direction of the colonel commanding, and pass judgment upon them if found guilty of murder or other outrages upon the whites during the present state of hostilities. The proceedings of the commission to be returned to these headquarters immediately after their conclusion for the consideration of the colonel commanding. The commission will be governed in their proceedings by military laws and usages. Lieutenant Heard, Adjutant Cullen Guards, will act as recorder to the military commission.

By order of Colonel H.H. Sibley, Commanding, Military Expedition.

S.H. Fowler,
Lieutenant Colonel, S.M., A.A. Adjutant General

Based upon the testimony of the hostages and those Indians who were friendly to the army, Sibley's men prepared to take prisoners of their own. Colonel Crooks, on the night of the 30th of September, quietly entered the Indian camp with his troops and arrested all warriors suspected of participation in the massacre. They were imprisoned in a log jail built for the occasion at Camp Release. At the same time, Captain

Whitney executed the movement at Yellow Medicine. In total, 425 Indians and half-breeds were charged with robbery, rape, and murder, and scheduled to stand trial before Sibley's military commission. Although the Great Sioux Massacre of 1862 was now history, there was still much work to do.

8

"HEWO, TOBY," MARY EISENREICH SAID, as Ryker entered the hospital tent. She sat alone on a cot, still hugging her doll.

"Hi, honey, how are you feeling today?"

"I want Mama."

Ryker sat next to the girl and hugged her. "I know you want your mama, honey, and I wish I could help. Maybe she will come soon." He knew she would never come because he found out that Mrs. Eisenreich and her husband had been killed during the August raids.

"Hi, Ryker," hospital steward John Gillig said, as he entered the ward and waved at Mary. "Hi, Mary."

"Hi, Johnny."

"I see she's charmed you too," Ryker said.

"It's hard not to be affected by this little sweetheart," Gillig said, smiling. "I've got one about this same age back home in St. Peter."

"I didn't know you were from St. Peter."

"Sure am, near where the Traverse de Sioux treaty was signed."

"That treaty is what caused this mess," Ryker said.

"That's what some folks think, but I don't know much about that treaty one way or the other. I wasn't living around here back in fifty-one."

"St. Peter, huh? Do you know any of the Seitzers who live around there?"

"Big dairy farmers, I think. Don't they raise purebred Holsteins?"

"The big black and white ones? That they do," Ryker replied. "I met them during my trappin' days along the river, and bunked with them for a spell."

"Really?"

"Uh-huh, that was back in, what, 1839, I reckon it was. Let's see here, I was nineteen then and I'm forty-two now, this is sixty-two . . . yup, thirty-nine, it was. I was just a young pup then, not any older than a lot of the boys we got fighting with us here."

"Did you trap for Hudson's Bay?"

Ryker chuckled. "Ain't nobody trap for the Bay for nigh on a century now. No, but there's still a few buyers about. Still, I found out I didn't cotton to trapping much. One time I was checking my lines and came across a trap with nothing but a fox foot in it. The critter had chewed his foot off to escape. Limped off and died, I'm sure, because he couldn't hunt no more. That's when I put my trapping days behind me."

"You have a tender heart for animals, don't you?" Gillig said.

"I guess you could say that," Ryker said.

"Well, the next time I bump into a Seitzer, I'll say howdy for you."

"Much obliged. They're mighty nice folks."

Mary started to fidget, so the orderly began to bounce the girl up and down on his knee gently. Soon the thumb went into the mouth and she started to snooze. "I'd love to keep her here in the infirmary with me forever, but I need the cot."

"I know you do, and I've been studying on that. I'd take her, but she needs more attention than I can give her at her tender years."

"Maybe I can help."

The two men turned and saw Stands Tall by the entry flap of the tent. "I don't know about that," Ryker said.

Stands Tall approached the men and rubbed a gentle hand across Mary's sleeping face where a wisp of golden hair had fallen out of place. "I know her. She stayed with me and my husband and son after the raid at St. James."

"Who's your husband?" Ryker asked.

"Wa-kan-tan-ka."

"I know of him," Ryker said, glaring at the squaw. "He's over in the stockade right now. He's got a lot to answer for."

"He was such a gentle man," Stands Tall said, not meaning to defend his actions, but trying to explain them. "The war, disease, the broken treaties, and the whiskey damaged him. He is not the man I married five years ago, and now, he will have to pay with his life for making war against the Minnesota settlers."

"He must be tried before the military commission first. That'll take several weeks."

"Ryker," Gillig said, putting his arm around the woman protectively, "this woman is Stands Tall. She's been here before to soothe little Mary. The child trusts her."

"It was my lodge where you found her," Stands Tall said. "I left her a moment when my son and I went to get some food."

At the sound of talking, Mary woke up. She looked at Stands Tall and smiled and held out her arms. "Mama!"

Ryker looked at the child, surprised. "Will wonders never cease? She has adopted you, for cripes sake!"

Gillig handed Mary to Stands Tall, and the two embraced and spoke to each other in short phrases in the Dakota dialect. "Well, I declare," Ryker said. "Will you listen to that? When I heard her asking for her mama, I thought she was talking about her real one, but she's talking about you. She's even picked up some of your lingo, and she knows German, too. She's multilinear, by golly."

"Multilingual."

"Huh?"

"Multilingual. Mary's multilingual, not multilinear, Mister Ryker."

107

"Multi . . . yeah, what you just said. Mary is a smart little tot, she is."

"Mister Ryker, she knows me. Let me care for her until she can be returned to her family. I hope, as a good man, you can understand I only want to help."

"Well, I try to do what's right."

"I saw you in camp several times, when you acted as courier and brought messages from Colonel Sibley to Little Crow."

"Oh? I didn't see you. As pretty as you are, I would have remembered." He smiled.

"I stayed out of your sight. In normal times, it is our way. But these are not normal times."

"No, they sure ain't." Ryker embraced the woman and child. "I'm going over to headquarters now to see about what we spoke of."

"Thank you, Mister Ryker," Stands Tall said.

"*Danke*, Toby," Mary said.

"You are very welcome, both of you."

This domestic scene was interrupted by a scream of pain from a young soldier lying on a cot across from the group. Breathing heavily, with sweat beading on his forehead, he clutched at his chest as Gillig rushed to his side. "My God, help me!" the young soldier cried, gasping and in panic.

"Easy, Alonzo," Gillig said. "Just take it easy." He glanced at Ryker and shook his head. "This is Alonzo Birch. He's twenty-one years old. He got gut shot at Wood Lake, and now, he's delirious with fever. The surgeons removed the bullet but not the infection."

Alonzo cried out again then arched his back, went rigid, and slumped upon the cot. The orderly reached over to check his vital signs.

"What wong that man?" Mary asked.

"I'd best take her," Stands Tall said.

"Good idea," Ryker replied. When they were alone, he removed his hat and sniffed back a tear. "The poor boy." He looked at Gillig through sad eyes. "Twenty-one years old. What a waste."

"Yes, it's a shame," Gillig replied. "Gangrene maybe. There'll be another funeral tonight." He pulled the sheet over Alonzo Birch's face.

Ryker dragged himself to his feet and reset his hat. "Seems like all I do lately is go to funerals."

Two hours later, Ryker and a small group of men from Company B of the Sixth Regiment Minnesota Volunteers stood around the body of Alonzo Birch, now in repose next to an open grave on the prairie. General Sibley also made it a point to attend. Chaplain Daniel Cobb read from the good book and spoke of this gentle but courageous young soldier who, like so many in the Indian Expedition and in Mister Lincoln's war, died within a few months of enlistment. Miles Allen, age twenty-two, another trooper with Company B, eulogized Birch's bravery at New Ulm, Birch Coolie, and Wood Lake, and told of how many lives of his fellow soldiers he saved. In the end, Miles said, he could not save his own. Chaplain Cobb then commended his spirit to the bosom of the Lord and began to sing the mournful dirge, "The Vacant Chair." Ryker and all present were again driven to tears at the words.

Overcome with grief, Chaplain Cobb's voice cracked, and he fell silent. It appeared the dirge would end there for lack of voice. Such was not the case however, as Ryker, soft at first then growing louder until his voice was booming, continued with the second verse. He was pleasantly surprised to hear the rest of the mourners join him in singing the dirge. Even General Sibley joined in.

After the body of Alonzo Birch was committed to the grave, the men sang the song again while his comrades buried him deep so that the coyotes couldn't disturb his rest.

RYKER WANDERED NERVOUSLY BACK and forth in front of Sibley's command tent at Camp Release. He had taken to doing that for the past few days now. The commander finally set his pen aside and watched the pacing scout. "Oh, for Pete's sake, Ryker, sit down. You make me so nervous I could just fly."

"I'm sorry, sir, but since last June when I went up north because my Pappy Oliver was dying, everything's been changing around me faster than a whore's underwear on a busy Saturday night. I've been shot at by my friends, shot at friends myself, and buried way too many fine families and soldier boys. I led you through battles, scouted out your bivouac sites, and served as courier to Little Crow. I'm not complaining sir, because I was proud to do it, but now I need to take a breather. I need to get away from all this death and pain, to enjoy life and forget about this war, at least for a little while, and I reckon I've figured out just how I can do that. Right now, I'm anxious to get back to St. Paul and play a few games of checkers with Big Faye."

"Checkers, huh?" Sibley said, raising an eyebrow.

Ryker scratched his whiskers, trying unsuccessfully to hide his grin. "Why sure! What else?"

"You're a lousy liar, Ryker. But I guess I can spare you for a couple weeks or so. These trials will continue to take up our time here, but your testimony has already been entered into the record. I need to have someone lead an ambulance detail of our wounded to Fort Snelling for proper care, and you fit the ticket. After you arrive at the fort, you'll still have a few weeks to, ah, play checkers with Big Faye." He pulled out an official paper and wrote on it. "Here's a pass. Report to me in Mankato no later than the first of December. That's where we'll be bivouacked."

"Why, thank you, sir," Ryker replied. "This is very generous."

"Yes, it is. Just remember what a wonderful commander I am when it comes time for my federal evaluation. Now draw your pay and get on out of here."

"Count on it," Ryker said, saluting. "I'll leave directly."

"I hope you improve your checker playing skills."

"Um, yeah, I'm sure I will." With that, he was gone.

FIVE DAYS LATER, AFTER ESCORTING the ambulance detail to the hospital at Fort Snelling, Ryker rode Wino down Wabasha Avenue in St. Paul, grinning at all the folks he saw on the street. To see them, the women dressed in their finery and the men walking briskly into the shops, one would never know there was a war on, let alone two of them. This was the atmosphere Ryker craved. He'd seen enough war in the last several weeks and just wanted to relax. He reined Wino to a halt before a large brick building with a sign on the front that said METROPOLITAN HOTEL, and under that in smaller letters: ROOMS FOR RENT BY THE HOUR, DAY, AND WEEK—FAYE KNUTSON, HOSTESS.

Ryker tied Wino to the hitching rail and hung a feedbag full of oats off his muzzle, then studied the three-story building. "Faye, my dear, dear lady, you don't know how long I've looked forward to this." Dusting off his buckskins, which were so filthy that he accomplished absolutely nothing from the effort, he ambled up to the front door.

It was quiet inside. Of course, it was also three o'clock in the afternoon. Ryker approached the big bar in the lobby just as an older man, still stout of frame, entered from a back room toting a small beer keg on his shoulder.

"Howdy, Stubby."

Stubby Swartzentruber looked up. "Why, Toby Ryker, you ugly old goat, how the devil you been?"

"Just fine, Stubby. I've been fighting the Indians with Colonel Sibley down south on the prairie. Did you hear the latest word about him?"

"You mean that Colonel Sibley is General Sibley now?"

"Yeah! How in the dickens did you know that?"

"It was written up in the St. Paul newspaper a few days back. Made the front page, which is about all I have time to read anyway."

"Oh, sure, I should have known that."

"How about a fresh draught beer?"

"Sounds hunky-dory to me. What you have?"

"Schell's from New Ulm."

"Schells? Wonderful! The Metropolitan is coming up in the world."

"Not only that, but with the Indian war on, our suppliers are having a tough time getting their products through. If it weren't for Schells, we'd all be reduced to drinking dandelion wine and sarsaparilla. But for some strange reason, the Indians never bother the Schells beer wagons."

Ryker smiled at the bartender's comment, but rather than reply, he simply drummed his fingers on the bartop and watched Stubby set the keg on the back bar.

"What you doing in town?" Stubby asked.

"On leave for a few weeks, but I got to be back down south to Mankato by the first of December. They'll hang a bunch of the murderers there, I suspect."

"As well they should. Those gull-danged redskins ruffle my feathers. Sibley ought to konk all of them in the head."

Ryker also felt his feathers getting ruffled at Stubby's remarks, but he forced himself to remain calm about it. The man was obviously ignorant, and this was obviously bar talk. "Say, Stubby, is the lovely Miss Faye about?"

"She's in the back room, doing the books."

"Thanks. I'll just go in then."

Pulling out a single wild rose blossom on a short stem that he spotted alongside the trail on the way into town, Ryker held it proudly as he knocked on Faye's door. "Come on in, the door's open."

"Howdy, Faye honey, you're a sight for sore eyes." He held out the rose. "A rose for a rose, but this rose pales in comparison to your beauty."

"Aw, Toby," Faye replied. "You dear, sweet man. Where've you been keeping yourself?"

"In the middle of the Indian war with Little Crow, that's where I've been keeping myself."

"That devil! You killed him, I hope?"

"Nope, he got clean away." Again, Ryker felt a bit riled at Faye's bigotry, but he reasoned that since she knew very little about his personal background and the fact that he was half Indian himself, he had to forgive her. After placing the rose in a stem vase, he sunk down into Faye's plush red velvet chair. "But enough about me. How you been, Faye?"

112

"Just fine, I guess, although I had a bout of the gout last week. My big toe swelled up to the size of my ear. I got to start watching what I eat, so they tell me."

Ryker got down to what was really on his mind. "Um, Faye honey, I been living out of the saddle for several weeks, and now I want two things. First, I'd like a nice bath, and second, I want to take you upstairs and poke you 'til we're both blue in the face"

"Toby, you sure know how to charm the panties off a lady," Faye said, chuckling. "Let's draw you a bath first. We'll negotiate about the other later, after you smell better than lathered horse."

TWO HOURS AND A BATHTUB FULL of trail dust later, Ryker emerged from Faye's personal toilette dressed in a crimson robe that she had bought him as a gift the previous Christmas. She sat with him as he bathed, scrubbed his back, and added sweet smelling toilet water to the tub. He came out not only clean, but also smelling like a refined gentleman rather than horse manure and saddle leather.

Ryker scratched his whiskers. "You know, a fellow could get used to this."

"Hell, just up and quit the army and move in here. There's sure plenty of work to do, and I can use the help."

"Naw, reckon I wouldn't make a gentleman of leisure. But I thank you for offering to marry me."

"Who said anything about marriage?" Faye replied. "I don't want to marry you. I just want you to live with me."

"Oh, Faye, you want me to be your love slave. Now, admit it."

"I have to admit that for not being a Swede, you're pretty good in the sack."

"Thanks. It runs in the family. Have you had any excitement up here lately?"

"Not much, just those two idiots that rode down the street last week."

"Who's that?"

"Well, Ethel and me, see, we were sitting on the front steps airing ourselves out when these two guys come up Wabasha Avenue riding a Missouri mule. They looked kind of stupid, so after they rode past, I says to Ethel, I says, 'Look at those two assholes on that mule!' I must have said it kind of loud, because they heard me say it too."

"You? Talking loud? Go on, Faye. I don't believe it."

"Oh, shut up," Faye said, slapping him playfully on the arm. "So anyway, after I said that, those two morons climbed off that mule and backed it up so its butt was facing us, and then they lifted its tail and looked and said, 'Naw, he only has one asshole. See?' Well, that mule didn't like us gawking at its bung, I guess, so it up and kicked at those two fellows, and when they fell back, the danged critter up and ran away."

Ryker stared at Faye a second then started to laugh so hard he turned red in the face. "Stop, Faye. You'll give me the apoplexy!"

Faye chuckled. "I ain't seen you laugh this hard since the time I tied you to my bed and tickled you with that feather."

"It's good to laugh, Faye. This takes the knots out of my guts."

"Yes, that's what this trip is all about for you, isn't it? Well, anyway, the story about those two dimwits on the mule is true. That's no joke. It really happened."

"No! You got to be kidding me!"

"If I'm lying, I'm dying."

Breaking into hysterical laughter again, Ryker slapped his knee. "Well, if that don't beat all, for cripes sake." He shook his head and wiped tears of mirth from his eyes. "So what did you do then?"

"We didn't do nothing. We just went back inside the house and watched them wander up the street."

"Did they ever catch their mule?"

"Oh, sure, sure, it didn't wander very far. They climbed back on the dumb thing, and after the critter dumped a load of crap on my sidewalk, all three of them continued on down Wabasha Avenue."

"I wonder who in the dickens they were."

"Haven't the foggiest idea, except that the first one called the second one Steve and the second one called the first one Mike. But they were obviously a few bricks shy of a load."

Ryker started laughing again. "I guess it takes all kinds to make a world, so they say."

"I suppose."

"Well, anyway, I'm willing to be your love slave, Faye. And it won't cost you even one doggone cent."

"Aw, Toby, you are so considerate."

"Thanks, Faye. And speaking of dumbbells, did you hear the story about Hans and Hannah's wedding?"

"Oh, I suppose," she said, drawing a deep breath. "Another Hans and Hannah joke? You do need to get more material."

"Oh, maybe someday," Ryker said.

"Okay, I'm listening."

"Well, Hans marries Hannah, see, and the two start off in the buggy on their honeymoon. They got married in Glueck, out west by Montevideo, and were going to spend their honeymoon in Granite Falls, but by the time they got half way there, Hans was so dang smitten with passion over Hannah's beauty that he pulled the buggy off the trail and started hugging and kissing her all over. Well, after a while, Hannah, she gets passionate, too. She starts wheezing, and breathing heavy, and squirming around, and then she farts a couple times, you know, just like you do to signal when you are really excited, and she says, 'Uff-da, Hans,' she says, 'you shure do-on't have tah stop.' So Hans, he says, 'Yes, my dearest,' and clucks to the horse and drives the buggy clear into Granite Falls." Ryker paused and looked at Big Faye, who looked back at him with a blank expression on her face.

"Yeah? So?"

"So, that's it," Ryker replied. "That's the joke."

"That's it?"

"Yeah."

"Well, what's so danged funny about that?"

"You see, Faye, when Hannah told Hans he didn't have to stop, she meant he didn't have to just kiss her, but that he could go all the way and let the stallion out of the corral and put the blocks to her. But Hans, he thought she was talkin' about the horse." Ryker chuckled as he said it.

"What about the horse?" Faye said.

"Huh?"

"What about the horse then? Why would Hans think Hannah was talking about the horse?"

"Because he stopped the horse before he started kissin' Hannah, that's why."

"Oh." Faye thought a moment. "Oh, I get it! Hans thought Hannah meant he shouldn't have stopped the horse!"

"Yup, you got it, Faye."

"But if he hadn't stopped the horse, how could he start kissing Hannah? With all that bouncing around, the buggy would have tipped over."

"Well . . ."

"Or, if he hadn't stopped the horse, he would have had to put the reins down when he went to kiss Lena . . ."

"Faye."

". . . and the horse would have run away."

"Faye."

"That would have been just awful."

"Close your pretty mouth, Faye. It's a joke, that's all. Don't bust your brain trying to figure it out."

"Well, okay, but it's kind of a stupid joke, if you should ask me."

"That's what I love about you, Faye. You're so danged dense."

"Aw . . ." Faye snuggled up to him, "that's what I love about you too, my lard-ass soldier boy. Come on over here to mama and give me some loving."

He kissed her. "Do you want to do the dance of love?"

"No, I want you to put the blocks to me, like Lena wanted Ole to do."

"You sure have a way with words, Faye."

"I know. It's a Swedish thing."

SOMETIME LATER, they lay in bed awhile and smoked a couple cheroots that Ryker had purchased on the way into town. He normally wasn't a smoker, but enjoyed one after being intimate with Faye.

"Toby?"

"Hmmm?" He blew a smoke ring.

"Toby, did you bring me a Indian scalp to hang on the wall?"

"No! Faye, why would you say such a thing! I'm more civilized than that, for cripes sake!"

"Well, those Indians aren't very civilized from what I hear."

"Actually, Faye, they're very civilized. They're just different from us. But this war business ain't all their doings, you know. The government didn't honor the treaties the way they swore they would, so finally, Little Crow and his warriors got desperate."

"Turned into savages, you mean."

"War ain't pretty. They killed and wounded near a thousand Minnesotans, though." He rolled over toward her and kissed her breasts. "But let's not talk about them, Faye. I rode all the way to St. Paul so I could forget about them."

"You want to come to mama again?"

"You can read my mind, Faye."

After another bout of lovemaking and two more cigars, they decided to go out on the town for a sumptuous meal and then to go dancing. They danced until the early hours then returned to the hotel and took a leisurely bath together, which led to another bout of lovemaking. Finally, exhausted, they cuddled together and slept until the sun was high the next day.

9

FTER A BIG BREAKFAST OF HAM, eggs, and fried spuds, Ryker wiled away the rest of the day with Faye. They visited, joked, and chased each other around Faye's boudoir like a couple of young lovers. Ryker then tackled her, threw her on the bed, and tickled her feet until she grew hysterical with laughter. That collapsed the bed, for a quarter ton of humanity thrashing around on a bed will tend to do that. After replacing the slats, Ryker went out to the Pig's Eye Tavern and bought a bottle of local shine for Faye, and several jugs of decent whiskey for himself. While there, he felt a tap on his shoulder and turned to see a familiar face grinning at him. "Why, Herman Wolf, you big tub of guts, what in the dickens are you doing here?"

"On a leave of absence from the fort," Herman replied. "They let me out for a while because Penelope is due to have a baby."

"Oh, you big devil, you got her in a motherly way, huh?"

"Yup, as you recall, it was mighty cold last February."

Ryker laughed. "Well, this is plumb great. How about letting me buy you a beer?"

"Sure thing," Herman replied. "Obliged to you, Toby."

The two sat at a table and chatted about the Indian campaign, about how great a commander General Sibley was, and how nice it was he got a battlefield promotion, and how sad it was that their favorite cook, Aloysius Bodine, was killed in action down south.

"I ain't et a decent piece of pie since he left," Herman said. "Penny ain't much of a baker."

"It sounds like you're the baker, Herman," Ryker said. "You put the muffin in the oven. Penny maybe ain't much of a baker, but she sure is a right good looking woman."

"That she is, and that's the other reason I snuggled up to her last February."

Laughing, the two visited several more minutes then Ryker decided he'd best get back to the hotel. "When do you have to be back at the fort?" Ryker asked.

"Not until December."

"I probably won't see you again until sometime after the first of the year then," Ryker answered. "As I recall, you are ahead of me at cribbage. I want a chance to get even."

"You'll get your chance," Herman said.

A little later, Ryker returned to the hotel. As for Herman Wolf, it was the last Ryker saw of him. Wolf deserted Company B on the 15th of December, 1862, and, it was said, fled with his family to Canada.

BY THE THIRD DAY, RYKER felt himself growing restless. He didn't visit as much with Faye, and he began to pace the boudoir. Knowing him as she did, Faye recognized the signs.

"My lard-ass soldier boy's got the wanderlust again, doesn't he?"

"Huh? No, no, it's just . . . I'm just . . . ah, oh shucks, I can't fool you, Faye. You know me too good."

"It comes with loving you for all these years."

"I suppose so. It's just that I want to get out to Fort Snelling and check on some of the troops recovering there, and see what the news is from Mankato. Maybe I even have a post or two waiting for me."

"Who would write to a tumbleweed like you, Toby?"

"Probably just my Mama is all. Never got any letters from anybody else, except for that hanky you sent me that time."

"Oh, I'd almost forgotten about that. It was so long ago."

"I still have it tucked away in my gear, Faye."

"You do?"

"Yes, I do, and I take it out and sniff it once in a while, and I think of you."

"Then it's serving its purpose." Faye came over to Ryker, and the two, arm in arm, looked out the window together over the city of St. Paul. They could see the steamboats docked on the Mississippi, a raft of logs drifting downstream from the big woods to the north, and a steam engine as it chugged along the line, and they commented to each other what a busy place St. Paul had become. They then fell silent, each lost in solitary thoughts, until Faye stood on her tiptoes and kissed him. "But I know you. You're a wanderer. You'd best be moving on now." She slapped him on his ample butt. "Away with you!"

He removed his hat and bowed. "Yes, dearest, I'll be going directly." He returned her kiss. "It's always good seeing you, Faye."

"You too. When will I see you again?"

"I don't really know. I'm not sure how long everything will take in Mankato, with the Indians and all."

"Will the army hang them?"

"I suspect so," Ryker said. "They did some horrible things, Faye. General Sibley has to set an example, and the victims demand retribution."

"Well, I'll see you again when I see you, Toby."

He kissed her again. "That's a good way to leave it, my lovely Faye."

A FEW HOURS LATER, RYKER rode Wino into Fort Snelling. He reported in at headquarters, showed the Officer of the Day his furlough papers from Colonel Sibley, and told him he planned to bunk at the fort for a few weeks until he had to report back for duty in Mankato. These details taken care of, he next checked for any mail. As expected, there was none. He then headed to the infirmary, but before entering, he braced himself for what he was sure he would see. As it turned out, he was glad he did.

There were over two hundred wounded soldiers in the infirmary, some from the Indian campaign, and several more from Mister Lincoln's war. The stench of rotting flesh and blood reached his nose, along with the smell of urine from those incontinent because of spinal injuries. Amidst the groans of the injured, he heard the pleasant sound of a harmonica playing "Aura Lee," and saw that the young soldier playing it had lost a leg. The soldier looked at Ryker and waved him over. Ryker approached the bed as the fellow put down the instrument and held out his hand for a shake. He had lost a leg, but had not lost his big, infectious grin.

"Howdy son, my name's Toby Ryker, scout for the Sixth. And who might you be?"

"Private Edwin Balch, Minnesota Infantry, at your service, but folks just calls me Eddy."

"Howdy, Eddy," Ryker said, shaking hands with the young man. "How old are you?"

"Turned twenty last month. I was at Flint Hill with the First Volunteers. That's where I lost my leg."

"How did it happen, son?"

"Miniball. Got in the way of a rebel miniball."

Ryker swallowed hard. Yet another young man maimed for life. "Miniball, huh? Yeah, those things are wicked, I'm afraid."

"I got in my licks in though. In fact, I shot back and hit the reb in the shoulder and knocked him down, and then sent him to perdition with my bayonet before I went down myself." Eddy looked at his stump. "Damn rebs, I'd kill a passel more if I could."

"You did your duty." Ryker saw the ooze from the amputation site and knew that gangrene had set in, and that Edwin Balch wouldn't see Christmas. "Where you from, Eddy?"

"Glencoe," Eddy replied. "They're sending me back home in a few days."

Sending you home to die, you mean. "Eddy, I'm heading that way myself about that time. I'd be honored to accompany you." He marveled not only at this young man's courage, but also at his pain threshold. That amputation had to hurt like the devil.

"Great! I'll look forward to it. Mama and Papa are waiting for me, and so is my girl, Becky. The army's getting me one of them there wheelchair things."

"They're really handy," Ryker said. "They even got cane seats in them."

"Cane seats? That's fancy."

"Yeah, those big air holes woven between the cane strips keep your butt from getting sweaty, you know, just like a fancy dining room chair."

"That's good," Eddy said. "It's sure no fun to have a sweaty butt."

Ryker laughed. "Take care of yourself, Eddy. I'll see you later. Best mosey on and jaw with a couple other fellows in here."

"Sure thing, but just remember that you're coming home with me. My mama makes a great pot roast."

"She does? Well then for sure I'm going home with you." Ryker chuckled, shook Eddy's hand and tipped his hat to the young man.

Moving on through the ward, he saw several other soldiers in various stages of either healing or dying, but they weren't nearly as animated as Eddy was. Hearing a groan, he moved to the bedside of another young man. "Easy, son. Would you like some water?"

"I'd like some whiskey instead to dull this pain in my gut."

"I'm sorry, son," Ryker said. "You take a miniball too?"

"No, I got hit with shrapnel when we dynamited a munitions factory down Arkansas way." He groaned again. "It tore my insides up."

"What's your name, boy?"

"James F. Boss, with Company C of the Sixth."

Ryker inspected the bandages covering the soldier's abdomen. "Uh-huh, and how old are you?"

"Twenty-one, sir."

"You don't have to call me sir," Ryker said, propping the young man to a seated position and offering him a glass of water. "I'm Toby Ryker, scout for the Sixth, but you just calling me Toby is fine."

"You look kind of old to be a scout."

"I'm but forty-two," Ryker said. "Just hitting my prime."

Boss laughed and coughed up some blood. "I have to agree, you look plenty tough." He gripped his abdomen and groaned again. "Oh lordy, but this hurts."

Ryker glanced around and, not seeing a surgeon or hospital orderly anywhere, he pulled out his flask and offered the boy a drink. "Take a little bit of this. I hope it helps ease the pain."

The young man sipped some of the whiskey and coughed at the stoutness of it. "It makes me feel warm, and that feels good."

"At least for a while, it will. Is there anything else I can do for you while I'm here?"

"Yeah, could you take a letter for me? Write down what I say? I want to send a note to my wife, but I never learned writing and such."

"Sure, son." Ryker got a piece of paper and a pencil and sat down again by Boss's side. "I'm ready when you are. I got six whole years of schooling from my mama behind me."

"Can I have another snort of that whiskey?"

"Hell, yes," Ryker said, handing over the flask. "Keep it. It's yours. I'll get another one at the Pig's Eye Tavern."

"The Pigs Eye, down by the caves." Boss took another swig of whiskey and mustered a smile. "I went in there a few times with my buddies."

"It's a lively place."

"Sure is." He looked at Ryker. "I think I'm ready now."

"Okay, son, you say the words, and I'll write them down just like my Mama taught me."

Dearest Rachel,

I'm here at Fort Snelling with a hole in my guts. They probably didn't tell you that. I know it is a long way to Litchfield from here, but I'd sure like to see you again. That probably isn't possible, though. I hope little Daniel is doing well, and Caleb, too.

What I really want to say, Rachel, is how much I love you. I always have, ever since we first met in the schoolhouse all those many years ago. You have been a fine wife to me, and a wonderful mother to our boys. I could never have wanted for more. I fear I shall not survive much longer and feel bad about that. It's not the dying so much that bothers me, but not seeing you and the boys again tugs at my heart.

I told them here where our farm is, and told them that is where I want to be buried. Please put me in the family plot next to our baby, Lydia Marie. That way, I will be with you always.

Don't cry for me when I'm gone, Rachel, for I am in a better place. You have my permission to go courting again and marry a nice man, so our boys will have a father and you will have a companion. I consider you doing so an honor. The way I see it, if our love as man and wife is so wonderful that you desire to renew it with another after I'm gone, that is a testimony to the power of our love.

Good-bye, my dear, sweet wife. Lydia Marie and I will await you beyond the clouds.

Your loving husband, James

Ryker put the pencil down and placed the letter on the bedside table. He looked out through the window a moment then back at the pained face of James Boss. "You're a very brave man, Mister Boss." He stood and saluted the fallen soldier. "You're an inspiration to me. I salute you, and I hope when my time comes, I can die half as bravely as you."

"Thank you, Toby. I have a feeling that you will."

James Boss died of sepsis on February 23rd, 1863, at Fort Snelling and now rests in the family plot outside Litchfield, Minnesota.

MOVING ON, RYKER STOPPED at the foot of another bed and stared at the sleeping man there. He seemed so at peace that it was easy to overlook the wounds on his chest, the amputated arm, and the massive head bandage. He snored gently, but suddenly snorted himself awake. With the wakefulness came the look of pain to his face.

"Hello, son, my name's Toby—why as I live and breathe, if it ain't William Burroughs!" He was shocked at the condition of the eighteen-year-old soldier before him, whose folks lived on a homestead situated near where his mother lived on Lake Mille Lacs. The boy's left arm was missing, amputated above the elbow, and both his stump and his head were wrapped in cotton bandages. Blood and pus had leaked through the bandages and crusted on the fabric. "I ain't seen you in three years!"

"Toby Ryker? Is that you? It sounds like you, though I haven't heard that booming voice in a long while."

"It's me, all right, you young whipper-snapper." He bent over and patted the boy gently, then noticed that the patient was gazing at the wall beyond him. "Can you see me?"

"Nope. I'm blind as a bat."

"How'd it happen, Billy Boy?"

"Billy Boy . . . . it's been a while since I've been called that." Private Burroughs motioned towards the sound of Ryker's voice. "This happened at Birch Coulee."

"I was at Birch Coulee."

"Yeah, there were a lot of us. What did you do?"

"I'm the chief scout for the Sixth."

"Was that you out front, in buckskins?"

"Yup."

"I wondered who that big guy with all the red hair was! When did you start wearing a beard?"

125

"Several years back, Billy. I had a lot of pimples on my face when I was a young man that left some scars, and also have a fair number of pox marks there too. The beard covers them up."

"Well I'll be danged. How are your folks, Toby?"

"Pap died a few months back. Ma's alone now. She's doing fine."

"Oliver died?"

"He was sixty."

"Sixty! Oh, well then, that old, he can't live forever."

"Your folks come over to the burying. Your mama made up a big batch of German potato salad. I recollect they said you was in the infantry."

"I ain't seen Ma and Pa in close to a year." He gazed out at nothing. "Now I'll never see them again."

Ryker sat on the edge of the bed and rested his hand on the soldier's shoulder. "How'd this happen, Billy?"

"I'm not real sure. One minute I was fighting Injuns there at the coulee along with Charlie Prince from back home. We enlisted together and were both in Company C. Did you know Charlie?"

"Sure did." Ryker chuckled. "I knew his older sister Marlene even better though."

"Oh, she was a lot older, but quite a looker."

"Yeah, she was the oldest of the Prince kids. I used to call her 'Marlene Prince, my little princess' when we was a-courting."

"You always were a romantic devil, Toby."

"Yeah, I come by it natural. Pappy Oliver had a way with the ladies too. He was a real charmer."

"Yeah, he was, and a good, honest man."

Both men were silent a moment, each lost in their private reflections. "So, anyway, you were at Birch Coulee with Charlie Prince, and there was an explosion," Ryker said. "Then what happened?"

"Well, then the next thing I knew, the lamp went out. I remember there was a big explosion, and I got hit with stuff. Then I fainted, I guess. When I woke up, I was like this. They say Charlie picked me up, and carried me off the battlefield to the surgeon's tent. Saved my life.

He'll probably get promoted for it. He's gone south now to fight the rebs, the lucky bastard."

"Is there anything they can do about your sight?"

"Nope, something happened inside my head."

"I see, Mister Burroughs."

"I wish I could see too," the soldier said, chuckling. "You called me Mister Burroughs just now instead of Billy. How come, Toby?"

Ryker leaned over and squinted into the sightless eyes. "Because you're too brave to be called Billy. You're a man, and a fine one at that, Mister Burroughs, and proud I am to be your friend."

"Thank you, Toby," Burroughs said, beaming. "I do have to admit it doesn't hurt much. But I can't do anything but sit here."

"Well, they can maybe retrain you when these wars are all over," Ryker said.

"I hope so," Burroughs replied, yawning. "Kind of tired now, Toby."

"You rest then," Ryker said, getting up from the bed. "I'll look in on you about chow time."

"You know what I'd like?"

"What?"

"A nice thick juicy steak."

"A beef steak, huh? Well, now, let's see what we can do about that."

"There's something else I'd like too."

"And what is that, pray tell?"

"I'd like to go home."

Taking a deep, halting breath that he hoped the boy would not hear, Ryker replied, "I have a feeling you will be granted that wish too, Mister Burroughs."

William H. Burroughs lived nearly three more years of hell on earth—surgeries, pain, and suffering—before dying at Fort Snelling on August 14th, 1865, at the age of twenty-one. Charlie Prince transferred

127

to the Union army and was promoted to corporal on September 1st, 1864. It was a short-lived promotion. After an attack of dysentary claimed his life on February 15, 1865, he actually beat Burroughs to the grave. The two childhood pals, reunited in death, rest side by side in a small cemetery in northern Minnesota.

10

WHILE RYKER SPENT MUCH OF HIS LEAVE time trying to comfort his sick and dying comrades at Fort Snelling, General Sibley was busy on the western frontier. Between tending to the victims, searching for Indian renegades from the massacres, and trying to separate the innocent from the guilty, his time was more than taxed. His report to General John Pope summarizes his activities during this time period.

HEADQUARTERS, MILITARY EXPEDITION,
CAMP RELEASE, Oct. 21, 1862
Maj. General JOHN POPE, Commanding,
Dept. of the Northwest, St. Paul, Minn.

GENERAL: Your dispatch of 17th instant reached me to-day through Lieutenant Shelley. I shall of course change my plans so as to accord with your orders. The commission is proceeding with the trials of prisoners as rapidly possible. More than 120 cases have been disposed of, the greater part of whom have been found guilty of murder and other atrocious crimes, and there remain still nearly 300 to be tried. I shall report to you the names of all when the commission has ended its labors and I have had time to review its proceedings, and I shall suspend the executions until the pleasure of the President is known. To-morrow or the following day I shall move my camp to the lower agency, where I shall organize the cavalry expedition and then proceed with the prisoners to South Bend or Mankato and await orders, as you direct. It is very desirable that 50 or 60 mule teams be sent me to Fort Ridgely, laden with forage, so as to prevent the delay incident to procuring corn, etc., at the lower agency, for the purposes of the expedition against the western bands of Sioux. Forage in abundance must be furnished or the experiment will be a total failure at this late season of the year, and involve a great expenditure in horses, if not in men, without any result. I pray you to have this attended to, and have the mule teams, complete with their loads, pushed forward from Fort Snelling with the least practicable delay.

Warm clothing and a good supply of blankets for the men are also indispensable. The horse teams I have with me are nearly worn-out by incessant labor, and the greater part are utterly unfit for an expedition like the one contemplated.

I cannot but regret that you propose to deprive me of the Sixth and Seventh regiments, for they have become somewhat accustomed to Indian fighting and cannot readily be replaced by others. Toby Ryker, my scout, of whom I have written previously, is the only other enlisted man who has the knowledge of Indian ways required in this endeavor. I would respectfully request that these regiments be retained on this frontier, if consistent with the public advantage, and the other and later regiments be sent South in their stead.

I have made no mention of your expressed intentions to any one, nor shall I do so until I have further instructions from you. I have ordered the mounted force to concentrate on the lower agency, where forage can be had for the horses. They will act as escort and guard in the transfer of the prisoners to that point.

Lieutenant Colonel Marshall has just arrived with his detachment and 39 men and about 100 women and children prisoners. Among the former are known to be several murderers and rascals, who will of course be made to pay the penalty of their crimes. I have now about 400 Indian men in irons and between 60 and 70 under surveillance here and at Yellow Medicine.

Lieutenant Colonel Marshall proceeded to within 35 miles of the James River and he passed within 26 miles of Big Stone Lake. He took captive all the Indians to be found in the district of country visited by him, and the prisoners report the Sissetons and Eastern Yanktonnais to be several days' march further west. When his report is received it will be transmit-

ted to your headquarters. He was ably assisted by Major Brown, of my staff, who accompanied him, as well as by Captain Valentine of the Sixth and Curtis of the Seventh regiments, and Lieutenant Swan, (of the Third Regiment) in immediate command of the mounted men, whose companies, with a mounted howitzer, under the charge of Sergeant O'Shea, composed his force.

I am, general, very respectfully, your obedient servant,

H.H. SIBLEY,
Brigadier General, Commanding.

The Winnebagoes referred to by you will be tried by the military commission when it convenes at South Bend or Mankato. Some of the Sioux prisoners will serve as evidence against those of them who are implicated in the late massacres. Regarding Chief Scout Toby Ryker, of whom I wrote earlier, although he grouses about the military service a lot, there isn't a finer soldier anywhere. I suspect that right now, although he is on a leave of absence approved by me, he is back at Fort Snelling giving aid and comfort to our stricken troops. I believe he warrants an increase in rank and a raise in pay. I recommend you commission him a First Lieutenant in the regular army corps.

"How are you feeling today?" Ryker said to Edwin Balch as he entered the infirmary at Fort Snelling. The surgeon was changing the young man's bandages and inspecting his wounds.

"Pretty good, considering," Eddy replied.

"Well, young man," the surgeon said, trying to sound cheerful, "I think you're ready to go home today." He looked at Ryker so the boy couldn't see, and shook his head sadly.

"How will I get there?" Eddy asked. "I can't sit a horse."

"Don't fret about that," the surgeon said. "You'll ride home in style in one of our fancy new ambulance wagons."

"That's good," the private said, grinning. "Toby Ryker here is coming with me."

"He is?"

"Yup, I promised him one of my Mama's delicious pot roast dinners."

131

"What I know of Ryker, he'll ride a hundred miles out of his way for a dinner like that."

"You got that right, sir," Ryker replied. "An army travels on its stomach, you know."

"That it does. Well, Private Balch, let's get you into the ambulance, so you can be on your way."

While the physician and the hospital stewards assisted Private Balch, Ryker headed to his quarters in the barracks and readied himself for the trip. Once he had his clothing and weapons and all his other truck packed, he went to the stable and saddled Wino. The big gelding seemed happy to be heading back to the trail. Like its rider, it never liked standing around doing nothing for very long.

Arriving back at the infirmary, he saw that Eddy was tucked comfortably into the ambulance wagon, and was busy eating a sandwich. The driver, Henry Henrick, a teamster and wagoneer with Company E of the Sixth, sat up front in the wagon seat. He read the St. Paul Pioneer Press newspaper until they were ready to roll.

"Hey Eddy, I see you're anxious to get to Glencoe," Ryker said.

"Sure am," Eddy said. "I can hardly wait. I wonder how long it will take."

"We got to go slowly," Henrick said. "I don't want to jostle you around on these rutted trails on account of your injuries. Probably four or five days, I'd guess."

"Then I'm glad you're coming along, Toby. You can keep me company."

"Sure thing," Ryker said. "I got my cribbage board along, and some cards, and some pennies to play poker with."

"Cribbage?" said Eddy, smiling. "I love to play cribbage! When Becky, she's my girl, and I used to get together on a date, we'd sometimes play cribbage for hours."

"The heck you say."

"Yeah!"

"Didn't you do any courting?"

"Well," Eddy said, blushing, "we did some of that too."

"Well, I should hope so. Tell you what," Ryker added as he tied Wino to the back of the ambulance, "I'll ride with you in the wagon so we can play cribbage while we ride. It'll sharpen your skills so much that by the time we get to Glencoe, you'll be so danged handy with this cribbage board that you'll beat Becky every time."

"Oh, I can't beat her every time," Eddy said seriously. "That would hurt her feelings, and it would get her steamed up too. I have to let her win most of the time."

"I think that's what they called being chivalrous back in the olden days, Eddy."

"Well, I don't know what it's called, but I know I have to do it."

ONCE RYKER WAS SETTLED in the wagon, Henrick clucked to the horses, and the caravan of one headed southwest from Fort Snelling. Eddy's cheerful voice could heard by passersby as he moved his pegs up and down the board and counted, "Fifteen two, fifteen, four, fifteen six, and a pair is eight," when the pegging was done.

Ryker didn't let the boy win the games easily. He played it straight, but quickly realized he was no match for the skill of this soldier when it came to playing cribbage. They covered sixteen miles that day, which took them beyond the southwest side of Minneapolis. There they made camp for the evening and helped Eddy with his slops and changed his bandages. Henrick, a quiet man, proved to be not only an able teamster but a good orderly and cook as well. He prepared a tasty hot dish of potatoes, corn, and ground beef, with some dried, sponge-like morel mushrooms simmered in. Ryker figured no Swede, not even Big Faye, could have prepared a meal any better.

That night, they built a campfire, and moved Eddy's cot out and set it next to the flames. They visited and joked and even Henrick joined in. Both Ryker and Eddy were pleasantly surprised when the teamster brought out a banjo from under the wagon seat and began to play some lively tunes.

Ryker dug out his jew's harp and twanged along with Henrick, and Eddy laughed with glee. For a little while he was Eddy Balch, a normal twenty-one-year-old man from Glencoe, rather than Private Edwin Balch, wounded war veteran, making the last long trip home. Ryker glanced at him several times, and was amazed at the spirit of this fellow. "Hey, Henrick, do you know 'Oh, Susanna?'" Eddy said excitedly. "The boys down south sing it a lot, and it sounds real snappy with a banjo." "You mean, like this?" Henrick immediately launched into a lively version of the popular civil war ballad. Eddie picked up the beat and began to sing the words to the Stephen Foster song, but with his own twist to it.

I came from Alabama
With my banjo on my knee
I'm going to Minnesota
My true love for to see
It rained all night the day I left
The weather it was dry
The sun so hot, I froze to death
My Becky don't you cry
Oh! My Becky,
Oh don't you cry for me
I've come from Alabama
With my banjo on my knee

I had a dream the other night
When everything was still
I thought I saw my Becky
A-coming down the hill
The buckwheat cake was in her mouth
The tear was in her eye
Says I, I'm going to the North
My Becky don't you cry

Oh! My Becky,
Oh don't you cry for me
I've come from Alabama
With my banjo on my knee

I soon will be in Glencoe town
And then I'll look around
And when I find my Becky
I'll fall upon the ground.
But if I do not find her
This man will surely die
And when I'm dead and buried
My Becky, don't you cry
Oh! My Becky,
Oh, don't you cry for me
I've come from Alabama
With my banjo on my knee

"That was a good version, Eddy," Ryker said. "You have a quick wit."

"That you surely do," Henrick agreed.

"Thanks, gentlemen," said Eddy.

Ryker glanced at Henrick then looked behind them and raised his hand to shade his eyes. "Who's he talking to, Henrick?"

Henrick also looked around. "I don't have the foggiest idea. The only other people around here are you and me, Ryker, and we're both rascals, not gentlemen."

Eddy shook his head and laughed. But he soon grew apprehensive, and the smile faded from his face, and he stared grimly into the blazing campfire. Without looking up, he said, "That part about me dying scares me a little bit."

"Don't fret about that," Ryker replied. "You'll probably outlive us all."

"Do you think so?" he looked at Henrick.

"I knew a soldier who lost a leg just like you did, and he lived to be fifty-six years old," Henrick said. "They made a wooden leg for him like they did for Captain Ahab. He got around better than most men with two legs."

"Sure," Eddy said, mustering a smile. "I'll probably live to be a hundred." He pulled out his harmonica and the three men played several melodies including *Tramp! Tramp! Tramp! The Boys are Marching*, and *John Brown's Body*. Later, as the embers burned down to a red glow in the campfire, Eddie again grew pensive. In his deep, resonant bass voice, he sang the Stephen Foster favorite, *I Would Not Die in Summer Time*.

> I would not die in summer time
> When hearts are light and free
> And joy is borne from every clime
> O'er mountain, stream, and lea
> I would not leave the friends I know
> Beguiled of hope and cheer
> To lose in burning tears of woe
> The glad time of the year
>
> Oh no, I would not pass away
> When from the leafy grove
> The red bird carols all the day
> Its song of joy and love
> When merry warblers trill their notes
> From every bush and tree
> And on the breeze an anthem floats
> Of heaven-borne melody
>
> I would not die in summer time
> And lie within the tomb
> When blushing fruits are in their prime

And fields are in their bloom.
For I would reap the yellow grain
And bind it in the sheaves
Then die when autumn winds complain
Among the blighted leaves

Eddy's voice began to fade toward the end of the last verse until it was barely audible. He looked at Ryker and Henrick, who had both fallen silent, the jews harp and banjo still in their hands. He stared into the embers, and in the fading rose hue of the firelight, Ryker could see the young soldier's jaws clench and his chin tremble as he unsuccessfully tried to fight back his tears. He stepped over to the man and rubbed his shoulders gently. "I think maybe it's time we settle in for the night, Eddy."

Sniffing and rubbing his eyes, Eddy said, "This is so stupid! I apologize for feeling sorry for myself and for crying in front of you all."

"Think nothing of it, and no apologies needed," Ryker said. "You are walking a lonely path and fear the dark, and there is no shame in that. We all must walk that path one day."

"Yeah, I suppose so." Eddy wiped his eyes and blew his nose. "Lift me into the ambulance, will you, fellows? I want to be by myself now."

THE FOLLOWING MORNING, Ryker and Henrick broke camp, and by seven o'clock were headed back down the road toward Glencoe. They made steady progress all day, and by the time they stopped for the night, they knew one more day would do it. The last day was more difficult on Eddy, for the road was filled with ruts, and despite Henrick's attempts to drive the team easy, the soldier's wounds broke open. He cried out in pain whenever the iron-clad wagon wheels hit a bump, and finally, they had to stop to clean and rewrap his wounds. By the time they arrived in Glencoe, he was considerably weakened, and had fallen into a light slumber.

"Hey, soldier, wake up! You're home!"

At the sound of Ryker's voice, Eddy opened his eyes and smiled. There before him were his parents, Becky and her parents, and a minister. Becky was dressed in a beautiful white wedding gown with a long veil, and held a bouquet of flowers. He looked at Ryker questioningly.

"Do you know anything about this?"

"Yup, I know all about it. Eddy, we're going to clean you up now and dress you in a spiffy two dollar suit. This is your wedding day!"

"Becky? Ma? Pa? Is this a joke?"

"It most certainly is not!" Becky said, bending over the cot and kissing him. "You are my shining knight, and I've waited too long to make you my husband. I should have done this before you left last June, like you wanted to."

"Becky, oh, Becky," Eddy cried. "You have made this the happiest day of my life!"

Two hours later, after Ryker and Henrick had Eddy all tidied up, and dressed in a fancy black suit and vest complete with a gold watch on a fob, the wedding party moved indoors at the Balch residence. Becky and Eddy, both looking fine in their wedding clothes, were married. They posed for several pictures that the local photographer took with his big camera, and everyone then sat down to a sumptuous feast. It was pot roast with all the trimmings, just like Eddy told Ryker it would be. Later that night, the couple shared the bridal bedchamber, and they consummated their love.

The next morning, after Ryker bid the family farewell, he untied Wino from the rear of the ambulance. He mounted up and neck-reined the big gelding back toward the river, which would eventually take him to Mankato. The sky was blue and the weather was mild, even though it was November. He looked over the fields as he rode along, noticing the corn now in shocks, the stalks now dried and brown, and the words of Eddy's song came back to him:

For I would reap the yellow grain
And bind it in the sheaves
Then die when autumn winds complain
Among the blighted leaves

He reined Wino to a halt, and sat there a moment, resting his hands on the saddle pommel. He felt the old weariness coming back, the weariness of war, and the weariness of burials and loss of life, and the weariness of severing of friendships. It bothered him, for he knew he still had several grisly days ahead before this tour of war duty was over. Glancing toward the sun, he said, "Pappy, what are these times all about? What's the wisdom to all this? I have half a notion to desert this war, and go where there are but few people, and live out my life there." Of course, he wouldn't do that, but it felt kind of good to say it anyway. Clucking to Wino, he spurred him gently and trotted off toward Mankato.

Private Edwin Balch died on November 27, 1862 on the family farm outside of Glencoe, Minnesota. His wife Becky never remarried, for she never found another man she loved as much as Eddy. Before he died, he and Becky played several games of cribbage in their bedchamber. He made sure she won most of them. Sixty-five years later, Becky joined Eddy under the sod in the windrow behind the house, never to be parted from him again.

11

WHEN RYKER RODE INTO CAMP LINCOLN six days later, which was located between Mankato and South Bend, the latter named after a large bend in the Minnesota River, he reported to Colonel Stephen Miller, showing him his leave papers signed by General Sibley, and telling him the commander had instructed him to report here. He learned that the condemned Indians, escorted by Sibley's troops, were making their way from the lower agency to their location even as they spoke.

"When they arrived at New Ulm, or rather, what is left of it, the settlers were outraged," Miller said.

"I'm sure they were," Ryker replied. "The folks down there lost a lot of kin to the Sioux."

"They prefer to be called Dakotas."

"I know they do, but the Ojibwe refer to them as Sioux. It is a less honorable term."

"There was a riot. One woman split an Indian's jaw, and another one fractured an Indian's skull," Miller said. "Several others stoned the procession, and I hear tell a wounded soldier named Elisha Peck shot one of them from his sickbed window."

"Elisha Peck . . . was he wounded at Birch Coulee, by any chance?"

"That he was," Miller replied. "He was in bad shape, but still mustered to a fight."

"I remember him. He was one of the young fellers I helped carry off the battlefield."

"General Sibley finally routed the prisoners around the main part of the town."

"That was the prudent thing to do, I'm sure," Ryker said. "When you expect them in camp?"

"Tomorrow. They are due in about noon. When the wind is just right, you can hear the drum cadence coming from up the valley."

"This is something I want to see. Where do you want me to bunk?"

"I've set up a field of tents for the incoming troops, and built a compound to contain the prisoners here at Camp Lincoln," Miller said, pointing to a large, open area spotted with tents surrounding a log building on the bivouac grounds. "Take your pick."

Ryker saluted. "Thank you, sir. I'll tend to Wino here, and see you at mess tonight."

"Wino?"

"Yeah, my quarter horse gelding here," said Ryker, pointing to the horse tied to the rail outside.

"That's one big quarter horse."

"Yup, big and sassy, just like me."

"How come you call it Wino?" Miller wondered aloud.

"Cuz he likes hard cider," Ryker said. "He and I share a nip now and again."

"But . . ."

"Yeah, I know. Shoulda called him cider. Seemed too girly."

"Well I'll be danged! So, you're telling me this horse here drinks alcohol?"

"Just hard cider, but not so much that he gets tipsy, cuz I take care of the gettin' tipsy part for both of us, but yeah, he likes a little bit once in a while."

Miller adjusted his hat. "Well for Pete's sake, a hard cider-drink-ing horse! That's a new one on me." He pointed to an adjacent area. "You can tether him along with ours on the picket line over to the east of the tents. We have plenty of forage for him, but I'm afraid we're fresh out of horse wine."

"On behalf of Wino, I thank you, sir," Ryker said, chuckling. "Ah, by the way, what's for supper?"

"Just beans and corn tonight."

"Geez, I'll be loose as a goose."

"Unless you like sour kraut. Got lots of that."

"Geez, I'll be even looser than a goose."

"The latrines are beyond the picket line."

"I'm sure I'll find them."

"Save your big appetite until tomorrow," Miller said. "With Sibley's troops coming in, we're going to have a barbecue. We butchered six big steers this morning and a couple hogs that were donated to us by several grateful families around Mankato. The mess sergeant is baking bread this afternoon, maybe some pies later."

"Yum," Ryker said, feeling his stomach rumble. "Those are tasty words to me."

BY TEN O'CLOCK THE FOLLOWING MORNING, after camping at Minneopa Falls, Sibley's troops made their way the last few miles to Camp Lincoln. Ryker stood near the front gate of the stockade and took a sip from his flask as he listened to the drum cadence and watched the troopers come into view. Small moving blue flecks at first, they grew taller and taller.

The procession was an impressive sight. Twenty drummers and five fife players marched immediately behind General Sibley, who led the procession in full dress uniform astride Hercules, his big sorrel gelding. They played "When Johnny Comes Marching Home" as the cadence for the soldiers, and immediately behind them, 400 manacled Sioux, con-demned and non-condemned alike, were chained in pairs together and crowded into wagons, ten per wagon. They were guarded by a military escort of 1,500 troops, all but a few of whom marched in perfect step with the drumbeats.

That evening after the prisoners were settled, the accompanying victims of the massacre tended to, and the troops quartered in the bivouac area, Ryker stood holding a tin cup full of coffee as he visited with the commander.

"Mike and Steve and a Missouri mule, huh?" said Sibley. "It sounds to me like Big Faye had three jackasses out front of her hotel instead of just one."

"No, Big Faye swore on her daddy's grave it was the truth."

"Say, by the way, how is Big Faye getting along these days?"

"Fine, just fine, she's just hunky-dory."

"How many games of checkers did you two play?"

"Oh, a few, when we weren't busy doing other things." Ryker grinned.

"Begging your pardon, General Sibley, sir." Both men turned to see Lieutenant James Shoemaker of Captain Bierbauer's Company of Riflemen standing at attention. "We are ready to begin working on the gallows tomorrow, but we don't know how big you want us to build it."

"I'm not certain of that either," Sibley said. "We have several hundred condemned here and several others yet to be tried before the military commission. President Lincoln himself has demanded to see the evidence against the convicted savages, so I don't know what the final tally for execution will be."

"What's Lincoln got to do with this?" Shoemaker said. "We went to all the trouble of fighting these Indians and capturing them and hauling them clear down here off the prairie. This is our business, and it ought to be up to us to decide how many get hanged."

"That is not true," Sibley replied. "I'm a federal officer now, and these savages are federal prisoners. President Lincoln is my Commander-in-Chief. If he wishes to personally review these matters, that is his privilege, and it is also consistent with federal military protocol. Besides that, I'm glad President Lincoln is making the final decision and issuing the death warrants rather than me. This is one job I'm more than happy to pass up the line to the top."

"I heard down in the tavern that Little Crow's getting help from the British," Ryker said.

"I heard that too, but I don't know if it is true or not. I also heard that the Confederate Army provided aid to Little Crow, because they counted on the Indians creating a diversion here in Minnesota, which would disrupt the activities of the Union Army."

"I wouldn't doubt it," Ryker said. "In fact, Little Crow told me that himself."

Returning his attention to Lieutenant Shoemaker, Sibley said, "Build the gallows to support the execution of forty men, ten to a side. We'll hang the condemned in shifts if we have to. Also dig a mass burial trench down by the river. Make it thirty feet by twelve."

"Aye, sir." Shoemaker saluted and walked away.

"This is going to be quite a spectacle," Ryker said.

"You are correct about that, Ryker, and that's the intent. We must make examples of these Indians who committed such atrocities against the state and the nation so that all will see that rebellion will not be tolerated. Even if President Lincoln pardons many of the condemned, I suspect this will still be the largest mass hanging in our history."

"The press has already condemned every last one of them."

"The press just wants to sell newspapers, that's all there is to that. They sensationalize everything. Remember that not over a month ago, they called me a traitor and a friend of the savages and called for my removal from command. And now, those same newspapers are singing my praises and calling me a hero."

"The press is fickle. I'm glad it's you they're focusing on, sir, and not me."

"It goes with being the commander of the expedition," Sibley said. "Even when I go to the latrine, it's news. I'm surprised they don't ask to take a picture of my hemorrhoids."

"That'd look interesting on the front page of *Harpers Weekly*," Ryker said, chuckling. He tipped out the rest of his coffee. "I'm hungry. Let's mosey on over to the mess tent and get us some barbecue or maybe a slab of side pork, if they have it."

"Sounds like a fine idea," Sibley replied as the two wandered in that direction.

OVER THE COURSE OF THE NEXT several weeks, the remaining untried Indians appeared before the military commission. With those previously convicted, a total of 303 Indians and half-breeds were sentenced to death by the halter. Their names were sent to Major General Pope accompanied by a complete list of the charges, the evidence gathered, and the testimony in each case. On November the 10th, Pope fixed the execution order and forwarded all records to President Lincoln in the White House.

ON NOVEMBER 7TH, SIBLEY ORDERED Lieutenant Colonel Marshall, still at Camp Release, to transfer the remaining 1800 captive Indians to Fort Snelling under heavy guard. Most of the prisoners were women and children. The entire detail, four miles in length, reached Fort Snelling on November 13th, and shortly thereafter, General Pope issued a bounty of five hundred dollars for Little Crow, dead or alive. Pope also sent notice to Major General Halleck in Washington that "The Sioux War is at an end." This would later prove not to be the end of the Indian problem, however.

Pressure continued to build at the encampment in Mankato while President Lincoln reviewed the evidence against the Indians. Popular sentiment was to kill them all. Fueled by the press, by a petition from St. Paul signed by 300 Minnesotans, by memorials in the valley towns and by protests and appeals from state senators and representatives, a band of 200 armed men attacked Camp Lincoln. They were determined to massacre all Indians under sentence of death and to take vengeance into their own hands. Although Sibley was inclined to share their sentiment, he issued an order for the arrest of anyone attempting to invade the camp or to conspire to commit illegal activities in connection with the condemned men. While everyone awaited President Lincoln's decision, Colonel Miller implemented this order and insured its compliance.

"GENERAL, MAYBE A FEW OF US boys should mosey on into Mankato there, and give those hotheads what for," Ryker said. "What the devil's the matter with them? We got the Indians under guard. They ain't going anywhere. They can't do any more harm."

"I know," Sibley said. "But what we're dealing with here is passion. The citizens are just as inflamed as the Sioux were three months ago when the massacre started."

"I suppose," Ryker replied. "But they ought to leave this to us to take care of. Don't they even trust their own troops, for cripes sake?"

"Yes they trust us, but they're still grieving the loss of their loved ones, and that bitterness tends to fester. There's no logic to what they did. When cooler heads prevail, they'll understand that."

"What do we do in the meantime?"

"We try to protect the Indians from them, and we try to protect them from themselves."

Ryker looked out the window at the chained prisoners. "I guess I can see that. Well put, sir. But I still think if a bunch of us boys went on into town there and accidentally on purpose rearranged some of their faces a little bit, we'd end this foolishness right now."

"Ryker, now admit it, you just enjoy a fist fight."

The scout grinned and sipped from his flask. "Can't argue that, sir."

"But that isn't how we do things in the United States Army. If we yielded to the popular pressure, we would be no more civilized than the savages we're going to put to death."

Ryker continued to stare out the window at the chained Indians, and beyond the Camp Lincoln stockade, at several citizens who were patrolling in front of the gate. "I just have a feeling in my bones that this is going to get worse before it gets better."

As he spoke, a courier burst into the room with a communiqué. Sibley read it hastily then dismissed the courier and glanced at Ryker. "Doggone it. Sounds like you're right. I got to get another letter off to General Elliott. I also have to move on to my new command post at St. Paul yet today, but before I go, I want to give you this."

Taking the folded order, Ryker opened it. Not having his reading spectacles with him, he had to squint at the words.

HEADQUARTERS, CAMP LINCOLN, MANKATO,
December 2, 1862
Major General Pope, St. Paul, Minnesota:
Per our earlier correspondence, I have promoted Mr. Tobias "Toby" Ryker, Chief Scout for the Sixth Minnesota Regiment, to the rank of Second Lieutenant due to his demonstrated bravery and leadership in battle during the duration of the Dakota Conflict. This promotion is effective immediately.

H.H. Sibley
General, Commanding

Ryker's jaw dropped as he read the order. He glanced up at Sibley and then read the order again. "General, you mean . . ."

"Why Toby Ryker, for the first time in my memory, I've caught you speechless."

Ryker motioned to the order, waved it toward the commander, but said nothing.

"You deserve it," Sibley said, filling the silence. "Your dedication to duty, your intervention with Little Crow, your courier service, your attention to our sick and dying, your compassion for the victims of the massacre, especially that little girl—none of that has gone unnoticed. Congratulations, Lieutenant Ryker." The commander held out his hand.

"Th-thank you, sir," Ryker stammered as he shook Sibley's hand. "This is a great honor."

"I will expect you to remain here and assist Colonel Miller. He needs a steady man with knowledge of Indian ways."

"Aye, sir, you can count on me."

"Good-bye for now. The next time you are in St. Paul for a checker tournament with Faye, stop in at headquarters, and we'll share a nip out of that flask of yours."

"Yes, sir, and have a safe trip," Ryker replied, saluting.

"General! General, come quick! It's the citizens again!" Colonel Miller's large frame appeared in the doorway.

"Ryker, here is your first assignment as an officer," Sibley replied. "Colonel Miller, I'm sure between your able command and the leadership of Lieutenant Ryker here, you can quash any rebellion of the citizens."

"Thank you, sir," Miller said. "Lieutenant Ryker, let's talk to them."

"I'm right beside you, sir."

The two men, accompanied by a small detail of soldiers, marched toward the stockade gates. As they approached, Ryker spotted a man at the head of a group of locals who gestured to them and pointed at the stockade. Something about the man seemed familiar.

"Let's go in there and take them," the man said. "They're all condemned and will be killed anyway. Let's do the government a favor and speed up the process, courtesy of the citizens of Minnesota."

"Now just hold on there, buster," Ryker said, walking through the gate to stand face to face with the man. "We do things lawfully here, not by mob rule."

"But," the man gestured to the shackled Indians, "they're murderers! They killed my whole family over to New Ulm." The man's face grew red with rage.

Ryker now realized why this man seemed familiar. He was the grief-stricken U.S. Marshal whose family was massacred while he was away on duty.

"What is your name, sir?" Ryker said, resting a large arm on the man's shoulders.

"I'm John McQuiston, and those bastards killed my family! My wife, Libby, my kids, Josh and Rebecca, they cut them down! Showed them no mercy! I have no one now." He broke down into tears, the adrenaline drained from him.

"There now, I fully understand your feelings, believe me, I do," Ryker said. "But this isn't the way. Let us handle it all legal and proper like. They'll be just as dead and won't be able to hurt anyone again."

"But, my family . . ." McQuiston looked into Ryker's eyes pleadingly.

"Killing these men won't bring your family back," Ryker said. "If it would, I'd go in there with you right now and help you throttle them all."

Totally played out, McQuiston sobbed and looked at the ground, shaking his head. "Libby, Libby."

"But if you go in there and kill them or try to do them harm, you will become a criminal yourself. That'll accomplish nothing." He patted McQuiston's shoulders. "These savages have destroyed too many lives already. I have an idea, though, how you can get vengeance. It will take some talking, so you must trust me." He glanced at the crowd. "Don't give them the satisfaction of turning you into murderers too. Go on, now. Go on back to your homes and get on about your business." He slapped his hands together and waved them away. "Go on, go on, shush!"

The crowd murmured amongst themselves and glared at Ryker, but then they slowly began to disburse. The scout stood outside the gate until they were gone then returned to the stockade.

"Well done, Lieutenant Ryker," Colonel Miller said. "That was impressive."

"Thank you sir," Ryker said. "I don't blame them for being angry, but more violence ain't the answer. General Sibley convinced me of that. I talked them down this time, but I'm afraid this isn't over. Not by a long shot."

"Let's hope General Sibley can get reinforcements here pronto."

"I'm sure he will do everything in his power to assist us, sir."

IN A HUGE WHITE MANSION in Washington, D.C., a tall, gaunt man with only a lone lamp to illuminate his face stared out a bedroom window onto Pennsylvania Avenue. It was not a handsome face. It was pocked and the eyes were sunken. The man had tears in his eyes as he returned his gaze to the bed in the room. "Willy, my dear son, Willy, I miss you so."

A woman entered the bedchamber. "Willy is gone. You must accept that."

The man turned at the sound. "You miss him too, Mary. You've barely left the mansion since he died in February. Now admit it."

Mary Todd Lincoln, dressed in her nightgown and cap, approached the president.

"I know." She waved a fan in front of her face. "But just the thought of facing the public gives me the vapors. It makes me too sad. But you must. You are a statesman."

Lincoln scoffed. "Some statesman! I can't abide slavery, so now the entire country is at war." He turned his sad gray eyes at Mary. "I'm not even a good father. I bring my two sons into this...this..." he motioned around, "this tomb, and tell them to make it their home, and what happens?" He looked at the bed again and began weeping anew. "I killed my Willy boy."

"The boys got into some contaminated water. It was the typhoid fever that killed William, not you. You are not responsible for his death."

Lincoln mustered a faint smile. "Remember when we came to Washington on the train? Willy and Tad, they were so frisky. Remember how they approached those passengers and asked them if they wanted to see Old Abe, and then they pointed to that other tall fellow?" He chuckled. "They were playful boys."

"Tad still is."

"Yes he is, but our poor Willy will never play in this house again." He kissed Mary. "But you, my love, must not closet yourself in this mausoleum for the rest of your life either. If you do, you are just as dead as Willy."

"Let us make a deal. Let us invite the Custice's over for supper next week."

"That's a start. We must fend off this depression."

"Now please come to bed, Mister President."

"Mary, how many times must I tell you that I am your husband first, and President Abraham Lincoln second. Just call me Abe."

"I know, but I like the sound of it," she said, approaching her husband. "You need your rest though. Come to bed."

"I can't. There is too much work to do."

"It will wait until morning."

"I'm afraid it will not. This situation in Minnesota with the condemned Indians is frightening. I fear there will be more bloodshed, and the citizens and General Pope are demanding retribution."

"Why don't you let them handle it?" she said. "You got the civil war to worry about."

"Like Pontius Pilot? Wash my hands of the whole affair?"

"Yes."

"I wish I could, Mary, but I can't. It is my duty as Commander-in-Chief to review this matter and render a decision. The troops are waiting, the citizens of Minnesota are waiting, and even the condemned Sioux warriors are waiting." He sighed. "It is up to me to see that justice is done."

Mary approached him and hugged him. "You think too much, Abraham."

"That is what I was elected to do."

"Come to bed."

"No, I think I shall review the evidence one more time. Do you know what really bothers me about this Sioux massacre, Mary?"

"What?"

"The fact that Henry Sibley warned the nation this was coming many years ago, back when he was a congressman and Minnesota was still just a territory. The federal government signed treaties with the Sioux bands which put them on reservations, and we promised them food and protection and money. But we failed to fulfill our obligations under the treaties. Not the Indians, us! The Indians did as they agreed to, but we, the people of the United States, reneged on the agreement. We are as much responsible for what happened in Minnesota as the condemned Sioux are."

"You weren't the president then."

"No, I wasn't, but my point is that we failed the Sioux. Had we fulfilled our promises, this massacre, this Dakota Conflict, may never have happened."

"Don't blame yourself for a failing you inherited from others."

"But I must! Good or bad, I am responsible."

"If you insist on stewing over it, I guess that is up to you. As for me, I'm going to bed."

He kissed her. "All right, Mary. I will be along in a while."

"I know what that means. You'll sit up most of the night until you fall asleep from exhaustion."

"Don't fret, my dear. I will do what I must."

"Good night, Abe."

"Good night, Mary." He looked to the heavens. "Good night, William Wallace Lincoln."

Lincoln went to his big desk in the study, now stacked with files. He turned up the lamp before sitting down and then looked at the volumes before him. He picked up the first file, opened it, and squinted at the words, but all he saw were blurred images. Pulling a white handkerchief from his pocket, he wiped away the tears that still stung his face then pulled out his gold-rimmed spectacles and put them in place, careful to wrap the flexible bows around his ears. Adjusting them, he picked up the file again and, taking a deep breath, began reading it, again comparing the words to the notes he had taken from previous readings. He did this for file after file, better than 300 of them, until the pink of dawn began to show through the east window. He then stood, stretched, yawned, and cranked his left shoulder as he massaged away the ache. Sitting again, he took up his pen, and wrote out in longhand the order for the largest mass execution in United States history, and sent it to General Sibley.

Upon receiving the order, Sibley immediately drew up Special Order Number 59 with a copy of the correspondence from the president, and directed the execution to be carried out at Mankato on December the 19th.

COLONEL MILLER RECEIVED THE ORDER on the 16th of December, and immediately conferred with General Sibley, saying that three days' notice was not sufficient time to complete the gallows and carry out the executions. Sibley telegraphed Lincoln, who responded by saying the executions should take place at whatever time the General suggested. The time was set at one week later as confirmed by the president's return wire.

WITH EVERYTHING NOW LEGALLY in place for the executions, it was time to wait until the appointed day to carry them out. The soldiers went about their duties of guarding and protecting the condemned and of readying the huge scaffold for the hangings. They placed it by the river near the center of town and also dug the burial trench, thirty feet long and twelve feet wide as instructed, in a sandbar in the Minnesota River.

12

WORD SPREAD QUICKLY, BOTH through the press and by word of mouth. Citizens began pouring into Mankato to witness the execution. Somewhat of a carnival atmosphere began to emerge. Gypsies arrived, selling items that they stole from burned-out homesteads as souvenirs. They also sold lengths of hemp rope, which they claimed came from the rolls that would be used to hang the Indians, performed tricks, other amusements and danced while their associates deftly picked the pockets of distracted passersby. Photographers made some money shooting portraits of families standing by the gallows, which were taking shape under the skill of the soldiers-turned-carpenters.

All the hotels and boarding houses were filled to capacity. They all did a rousing business for several days as their rooms filled with military officers, families of the victims of the massacre, and the morbidly curious. Over at the Union House, Mathias Ulman couldn't be happier about the huge influx of people. This would be a good December for him. He had just served Ryker a shot of whiskey, when another man came in.

"Howdy, young man," Ulman said from behind his large bar. "What's your pleasure?"

"Give me a whiskey, and keep them coming," the man replied.

Ryker regarded him, then asked, "You're John McQuiston, aren't you?"

"Yes, how did you know that?"

"We met a few days back out at Camp Lincoln, and you're staying here at the Union House like I am. Remember you from when you checked in here the other day. I was standing right behind you."

"Well bully for you," McQuiston said. Having not slept well last night, he was feeling ornery today and acted like he didn't recognize Ryker.

"Here for the hanging?" Ulman asked conversationally.

"I got a few days off from my lawman's duties, and I came down here to watch these murdering bastards swing," McQuiston said bitterly, nodding toward the gallows. "In fact, I'm going to lend a helping hand to the whole affair."

"Oh?"

"The army's given me the honor of cutting the rope."

Ryker grunted. It was he who arranged with the army for McQuiston to cut the rope along with a man from Lake Shetek, because he had lost his family to the Sioux during the massacre. Obviously, McQuiston didn't remember that, either.

"Congratulations! They are pure evil," Ulman said. "I was captain of the Mankato Militia up until last year. Now I'm a corporal in the Home Guard."

"That's quite a demotion," McQuiston said. "Rank-wise, you're going in the wrong direction."

The bartender chuckled as he set a bottle and a shot glass in front of McQuiston. "I guess we disbanded too soon. Of course, there wasn't anything going on with the Sioux upriver in sixty-one, and now, this fiasco."

Ryker thought about chipping in that the Dakota had been treated badly, but he knew this environment would not hear anything that put the Indian in a righteous light.

"No, all hell didn't break loose until this past August," McQuiston replied. "August the nineteenth, 1862, I'll never forget that day as long as I live." He tossed down the drink and gritted his teeth at the bite of it. "That's the day they massacred my whole family."

"Oh, no! You too?"

"We lived over to New Ulm. I was on duty that day, but it wouldn't have mattered. I couldn't save my wife and kids from that bastard, Little Crow."

Again Ryker had to bite his tongue.

"I'm sorry for your loss," Ulman said.

"You've had a tough time," Ryker said.

"Sorry doesn't help. They're still dead."

Ulman shook his head sadly. "And you know the irony to of all this? Little Crow started this whole ruckus, and he got clean away! High-tailed it into Dakota Territory, so they say."

"Well, after this is all over and these butchers are in the ground, I plan to light out after Little Crow myself."

Ulman wiped out a beer mug. "The army is already ahead of you. They plan to relocate every Indian out of Minnesota."

"The army!" McQuiston scoffed. "They're fettered by that Indian lover, Lincoln! They can't do any more than old Abe says they can! They'll never catch Little Crow."

"Take it easy, John," said Ryker. "You aren't talking like a lawman."

"No. I'm talking like a widower." McQuiston downed another drink.

"Your feelings run high, and that's understandable," the bartender said. "If those savages hadn't been stopped at Birch Coulee, they would have made it to Mankato, and if that happened, you wouldn't be standing here talking to me either. I'd be dead in the ground, and my hotel would be nothing but smoldering ashes."

"Most likely." McQuiston motioned to the back bar. "Would you give me another snort, please?"

"Sure. Sure." Ulman poured another shot of bourbon. "And this drink's on me."

"Thanks Mister Ulman, you're a gentleman and a scholar. Ulman, your name, are you from New Ulm originally, by any chance?"

"New Ulm, Madelia, Mankato, some back in Wisconsin, Ulmans are all over the place. As for me personally, my wife and I came over on the boat from Niederzissen, in Rhineland, Germany, with my father, Peter, and my brothers, John and Michael, back in 1847. Since then, some of my kin spell their name Ulman, and some spell it Ulmen."

"Your kin don't know how to spell very well, do they?"

Ulman chuckled. "I guess not. Anyway, in a few days, this execution will all be over with, and things will get back to normal."

"Maybe here in Mankato, if you're lucky. But even with the hanging of these butchers, the Indian problem isn't over. Mark my words. It's not over yet."

"I hate to say it, but I'm afraid you may be right," said Ryker.

"How long do you want to keep the room?" Ulman asked.

McQuiston dug out his money pouch. "I'll pay through the twenty-sixth and then see. Okay?"

"Fine," Ulman said, pulling a general ledger and a cigar box from under the bar and running his finger down the ledger page. "McQuiston-n-n," he mumbled, "here you are. Two dollars a night for four nights, that's eight bucks."

Counting out the fee in silver dollars, the deputy slid them across the bar. Almost as an afterthought, he asked, "You affiliated with any good clean whores?"

"As a matter of fact, a few do frequent the saloon here," Ulman said, depositing the cash in the cigar box, entering the payment in the ledger, and sliding both of them back under the bar. "See that young filly over there at the table?"

"That looker over there?"

"Yeah, that's the one. Her name's Clara. She charges five dollars. There are some cheaper ones out at the Frontier Tavern if you haven't got much money, and if you aren't particular."

McQuiston eyed Ulman. "Is she any good?"

"Wouldn't know how good she is. Us Catholics don't pair up with women of the night."

Ryker smiled to himself.

"You Catholic?"

"Um-hum, Saint Phillips, out on the edge of town."

"The mission church out on Agency Road?"

"That's the one, the log cabin. Michael Hund donated it to us back in fifty-two."

"I don't know how you do it, keeping chaste and all."

"Well, we German men like to entertain our German wives. They enjoy having babies."

Ryker couldn't resist chuckling at Ulman's comment. When he was scouting down this way a few months back, he stopped at the hotel and enjoyed the pleasure of Clara's company himself. He remembered seeing a goodly number of Germans hanging around her door that night. Ulman scowled at him.

"Now I just bet they do. I've heard that about German women. The ones I know from New Ulm tend toward the chubby side, though. I like my women skinny as a rail."

"That's from all the potatoes and the hot dishes we eat. And of course, the beer puts on the pounds too."

"So, Ulman, you lady's man you, how many kids you got?" McQuiston said, grinning now that the whiskey had loosened him up.

"My dear wife, Elizabeth, has presented me with seven young Ulmans so far."

Ryker slapped the bar. "Seven? Wow, you do stay busy."

"Yup, and I'm proud of every one of them. There's . . ." he began to count them off on his fingers, "Michael, John, Elizabeth, Clara, John B., Caroline, and Mary. Mary's just a tot. Not even a year old yet."

"Mary, huh?" McQuston nudged Ryker under the bar top, so Ulman couldn't see it. "Geez, I'd think with seven kids already, you'd have called her Quits."

"No, no," Ulman said. "Good Lord willing, Lizzie and I will have a few more yet."

McQuiston pulled out a handful of coins and paid for his drinks. "Well Ulman, you keep to your home hearth, but I think I'll wander over and introduce myself to Clara now. She's a lot prettier than you are. "

"Yeah, and she's scrawny, since that's the way you like them. Not like the round woman I got. Go ahead. Be my guest."

"I am your guest anyway."

"Yeah, I guess you are, at that," Ulman said, laughing. As McQuiston moved over to Clara's table, the bartender replaced the whiskey bottle on the back bar shelf, but rather than depositing the payment in the cigar box, he pocketed it. This done, he mopped up the bar where McQuiston set his shot glass and turned to listen a moment to the minstrel, who was strumming for pennies in the saloon. The fellow soon began the familiar melody of "The Streets of Laredo":

> *As I walked out in the streets of Mankato*
> *As I walked out in Mankato today*
> *I spied a dead Indian who still was a-danglin'*
> *Was still a-danglin' and cold as the clay.*

The saloon patrons laughed, and Mathias Ulman did likewise as he applauded and, digging into his pocket again, tossed a seated liberty dime on the floor by the minstrel.

ON MONDAY, THE 22ND OF DECEMBER, the condemned were removed from the log jail constructed for the purpose of confining them at Camp Lincoln and incarcerated in a stone building closer to the execution site. They remained chained and secured so that any hope of escape from the ultimate penalty was dashed. Reverend Riggs entered the guardhouse and read the following statement prepared by Colonel Miller to them in their native tongue.

The Great Father at Washington, after carefully reading what the witnesses testified to in their several trials, has come to the conclusion that they have each been guilty of wantonly and wickedly murdering his white children. And for this reason he has directed that they each be hanged by the neck until dead, on next Friday, and that order shall be carried into effect that day, at ten o'clock in the forenoon.

The good ministers are here, both Catholic and Protestant, from amongst whom each one can select a spiritual advisor, who will be permitted to commune with them constantly during the few days that they have yet to live.

Say to them now that they have so sinned against their fellow men, that there is no hope for clemency except in the mercy of God, through the merits of the blessed Redeemer and that I earnestly exhort them to apply to that, as their only remaining source of comfort and consolation.

The Reverend Dr. Williamson and Father Ravoux, missionaries who had worked among the Dakota, were allowed to move among them and give them counsel. "My children, a merciful God awaits you," said Father Ravoux. "Fear not the death of the flesh. Repent and you will yet be saved."

"Goose shit!" said Cut Nose, as several of the other condemned muttered in agreement. "We're martyrs! We're expendable! The army wants to get us out of their great state of Minne-so-ta!" He spat the word defiantly. "The government tried to starve us to death and that didn't work. They stuck us on wasteland they call a reservation, where nothing grows or survives, and that didn't work. In the treaties they said we'd be paid handsomely for our land, but where's the money? A-e-cha-ga, do you have it?"

A-e-cha-ga shook his head.

"Ha-pink-pa, have you seen it?"

Ha-pink-pa shook his head.

"Ah," Cut Nose said, sarcastically, "Wa-he-hua, surely you have it!"

"I had it, but it must have fallen out of this hole in my pocket," Wa-he-hua said as the others laughed.

After Cut Nose stopped laughing, he said, "Then the settlers gave us their diseases and got us stupid on their whiskey, and that didn't work either. So now, the government has no recourse but to kill us."

Black Wolf looked at the spiritual leaders. "What Cut Nose says is correct. There is no honor to the word of the white man. They speak with *ehani nigetakiya*."

"Forked tongue? Black Wolf, you know how I hate that cliché." Cut Nose smirked as others among the condemned chuckled bitterly.

"Black Wolf, Cut Nose, all of you, listen to me," Father Ravoux replied. "I know that the government has not honored its commitments under the treaties. But there are legal ways to remedy that. Going forth and killing innocent settlers who had nothing to do with the treaties is morally wrong."

"Morally wrong, padre?" Black Wolf said. "Until you watch your children die, don't you dare come among us and talk about morality."

"You are my children, and I have watched you die."

Black Wolf looked at Cut Nose, and Cut Nose returned the look, and for a moment, neither spoke.

"Father Ravoux is right."

They looked at the speaker, Wa-kan-tan-ka.

"What are you saying, Wa-kan-tan-ka?" Cut Nose said. "You fought bravely at my side, but now, you are in cahoots with them?"

"I fought bravely at your side because I was full of whiskey. Now that my head is clear, I see that our actions were not justified. Father Ravoux is right."

"Ha!" Black Wolf said. "You are just afraid to die."

"I admit, I do not want to die," Wa-kan-tan-ka looked at Father Ravoux pleadingly. "Maybe the holy men can save all of us."

"If it is any consolation to you, Bishop Whipple has interceded in your behalf with General Sibley," Reverend Williamson said. "And so have Reverend Riggs and Father Ravoux and myself."

"Bah!" Black Wolf snorted. "That means nothing."

"Wa-kan-tan-ka," Father Ravoux said, "Black Wolf speaks only of your mortal body. We are more concerned with saving your immortal souls."

"Chow time!" The ministers were interrupted by soldiers entering with food for the prisoners.

"By all means," Black Wolf said. "You don't want to hang a starving Indian. Make us plump and well fed, so when we drop on the twenty-sixth, the rope will rapidly loose its slack."

"Look, I'm just doing my job," said Private Coleman Hawkins. "If it was up to me, I'd let you all starve, you heathens! You understand that?"

Black Wolf and Cut Nose and several of the others began to mutter and rattle their chains.

"Go to hell," Black Wolf snarled.

"Maybe I will," Hawkins replied, leaning down toward Black Wolf. "But you want to know something? You'll get there first!" He kicked the Indian in the ribs. "You killed my ma!"

"Oh, yes, so I did," Black Wolf replied. "I remember that dark woman now. If she hadn't been so damned ugly, I would used her first."

"You bastard!"

"Now, now!" said Reverend Ravoux, intervening and holding back the soldier's fist. "There is no call for this. Serve the rations and get out of here, or I'll report you to Colonel Miller."

The soldier glared at Black Wolf then shifted his angry eyes to Father Ravoux. "Let go of me!"

"Apologize to Black Wolf. He is about to die and does not deserve your grief in his last days."

"When hell freezes over, that's when I'll apologize," the soldier said, jerking his arm away. He threw the plate at Black Wolf. "Eat it off the ground, you filthy swine!"

"Guard!" At Father Ravoux's yell, Ryker entered the building armed with a rifle fixed with a bayonet. "Get this man out of here and put him on report. He is in no mental condition for this duty."

"Yes, sir." Ryker grabbed the soldier's collar and walked him toward the door.

"But, but . . ."

"But nothing. I heard your carryings on in here. You ought to be ashamed of yourself." Ryker shoved him through the doorway and quickly followed him outside, where he pushed him up against the wall. "Look, I had to say that to make it look good in there. Believe me, I'm no friend of Black Wolf, but we must maintain order. I assure you that in a few days he will be deader than a doornail, so please don't stoop to his level. That's no way to honor your mama's memory."

"Suppose so," said Hawkins, his breathing returning to normal. He adjusted his cap and started walking toward the camp kitchen then paused and looked back at Ryker with a pained expression on his face. "I apologize for my outburst. It's just that when I saw him in there, I lost control of myself. It's probably best I'm going south with Company E in a little while. I got to get away from these memories."

"I fully understand your hurt."

As Hawkins nodded and headed to the mess tent, Ryker watched him go, shook his head, and sauntered back inside the prison compound.

"TOBY RYKER, GREAT SCOUT for the Sixth Minnesota and Sibley's errand boy," Black Wolf said, smirking. "What are you doing here? Did you come, like so many others, to watch us choke to death on the scaffold?"

Ryker approached Black Wolf, who was sitting on the floor, and pushed his boot into the Indian's face. "Oops, sorry." Before Black Wolf could react, he kicked the Indian in the groin. Neither blow was hard enough to cause pain, just hard enough to cause humiliation. "I'm so sorry, Black Wolf. It's my game leg acting up again. When it spasms, I just can't control it. You ought to have seen what it did to a Lutheran minister a few months back."

"You rotten coyote!" yelled Black Wolf. "You're a real tough man when your enemy is shackled and cannot fight back."

"Ryker!" said Father Ravoux. "This is uncalled for!"

"Begging your pardon, but you see, there are some things about Black Wolf that you ministers don't understand. He is a big bully. I have simply communicated with him in a way he understands." Ryker looked back at the Indian leader. "Embarrassing, ain't it? Downright disgusting, ain't it? Not an honorable attack at all. How does it feel, Black Wolf?"

"What are you trying to say to me, Mister Scout Lieutenant for the mighty Sixth?" Black Wolf said, rubbing his cheek.

"I'm saying that I just gave you a taste of your own medicine, that's what I'm saying." Ryker glared at the captives. "Your fight with the white settlers was as dishonorable as what I just did to Black Wolf. I shouldn't even call it a fight, because it was nothing less than a slaughter of innocents. It was not the action of true Dakota warriors. It was the behavior of cowardly Sioux."

"Leave us alone Ryker," Baptiste Campbell said. "You're like all the rest. What do you know of our pain? What do you know of growing up a half-breed and being spurned by everyone?"

"Quite a bit, you knothead. I'm more of a half-breed than you are!"

The Indians looked at him, shocked. "You?" Campbell replied. "Who ever heard of a red-headed Indian?"

"The red hair comes from my father's side," Ryker said. "He was full-blooded British, but the rest of the blood flowing in my veins is pure Ojibwe. I'm more Indian than you are, you watered-down whelp!"

"Ojibwe? Are you trying to make us believe you are half Ojibwe?"

"Yes, Ojibwe, and I don't give a diddly-squat if you believe it or not, it's still the truth. You Dakotas whupped our butts up north, but at least you did it honorably. What you did here to the settlers is hideous! Fighting farmers who have nothing to fight back with, killing them, mutilating them, scalping them, raping their women—need I say more? Where is there any honor to that?"

The Indians fell silent, looking first at Black Wolf then at Baptiste Campbell and then down at the floor.

"See here, Ryker," Ravoux said as Williamson, who had gone on to counsel others in the compound, approached them again, "this is accomplishing nothing. Thank you for your intervention, but I think you best leave now."

"It is Lieutenant Ryker to you, gents, and I'll leave when I'm darn good and ready, and I ain't ready yet. There is something more I have to say to these savages."

Both spiritual leaders, surprised that Ryker pulled rank on them, stepped back in deference to him. "As you wish," Reverend Williamson said.

"Thank you." Ryker pulled out his watch. In his best diction, he said, "Gentlemen, in less than a hundred hours you will no longer breathe the air of this earth. The Reverends Ravoux and Williamson are here to offer you counsel and to help you redeem your souls. You are not going to escape the noose, nor should you. Even though the United States government failed in its promises through the treaties, this is no justification for what you did to innocent bystanders. You may feel this is all unfair, but no one ever promised you that life would be fair. Now repent your evil and at least die as honorable warriors rather than as snakes crawling in the dirt."

"I fear the noose," Wa-kan-tan-ka said, weeping.

"Wa-kan-tan-ka, you were once a brave warrior, but you strayed from the path. At least you can die as an honorable man." He leaned down to the Indian. "And believe me when I tell you that dying by the rope is much quicker and less painful than dying with a miniball in your gut or with your scalp cut off. Do it for Stands Tall, if not for yourself."

"You know of my wife?"

"Yes, while you were out killin' the whites, she cared for the survivors and saved the life of the small girl you stole from St. James."

"That blonde girl with the long German name? I remember her."

"That blonde girl, yes, she's the one. Had it not been for Stands Tall, she would not have survived. Your wife did the Christian thing, the right thing." He motioned to the ministers. "Now it is your turn to do the right thing. This is the last chance you will have." He glanced around at the rest of the prisoners. "I challenge any of you to say my words are not true."

There was no response of any kind in the compound. Only the labored breathing of the Indians broke the silence. The ministers nodded at each other and smiled at Ryker.

"Reverend Williamson, Father Ravoux, I think they are ready to be serious now, and listen to what you have to say." He turned and headed for the door.

"Thank you, Lieutenant Ryker, and may God's peace go with you." Reverend Williamson opened the Good Book. "As you approach the day of your final accounting, I hope you take comfort in the twenty-third psalm." And Father Ravoux translated the passage into Dakota.

Many of the Dakota warriors wept, impressed by Ryker's words as well as by those of the ministers. Several of the savages were baptized over the next few days as they prepared for their journey to meet the Great Spirit. Black Wolf and Cut Nose and Baptiste Campbell, however, remained stoic, bitter to the very end.

13

S TEP THIS WAY, FOLKS," RYKER SAID. "Don't trip on the doorsill here, or bump your noggins on these low beams." He escorted several visitors, mostly women and children of the condemned, into the jail compound. Several armed troopers were stationed within the enclosure, watching closely as a group of prisoners performed a sun dance. The "Ki-yi-yi!" of their war chants had always been hair-raising to Ryker because the first time he heard it as a young child, the Dakota were attacking his mother's band of Ojibwe.

The dancing continued for several hours with the Indians dressed in their finest ceremonial garb. Every hair, every feather, all the war paint was in place. Outside the compound, several townspeople had gathered and were listening to the commotion, and among them was John McQuiston, who still harbored the idea of getting revenge against the Dakota. "The butchers are lively today, aren't they?"

"We ought to burn that building to the ground with them in it," said Henry Jackson, an older fellow. "It makes me sick to have heathens like that dirtying up my town."

"*Your* town?" said McQuiston. "What do you mean, *your* town? You own this dump full of river rats?"

"No, of course not, and this town isn't a dump," Jackson replied, eyeing McQuiston up and down indignantly. "My partner Parsons Johnson and I staked the original claims here back in fifty-two, and folks have been moving in ever since."

Realizing his big mouth had once again caused offense, McQuiston smiled condescendingly, trying to make amends for raising the ire of this man who was a total stranger to him. "Don't get touchy, old timer. I'm just pulling your leg."

"Yeah, I just bet you are," Jackson said, glaring at the deputy.

"Mankato. That's a pretty name." McQuiston's cheesy smile widened until he no longer looked antagonistic, but rather, like a simpleton eager to learn. "Say, where'd the name come from anyway?"

"It's the Indian word *Mahkato*, but it was misspelled Mankato, and never changed," Jackson replied, relaxing his guard.

"Oh, geez, you even named the town after these red devils?"

"*I* didn't," Jackson replied quickly, "but yeah, it comes from a Dakota Indian word meaning greenish-blue earth because of all the blue clay down by the river. Even Blue Earth County got its name that way."

"Dakota Indians, you say?"

"Yeah, the Sioux, but they don't like the handle of Sioux. The Ojibwe gave them that name. It means 'snake-like enemy.'"

"The Ojibwe sure have them pegged," McQuiston said. "Blue Dirt County, huh?"

"Blue *earth*, not blue *dirt*, and yes, that's what the word *Makkato* means." Jackson chuckled, the insult of a few moments ago forgotten. "You want to know something else? When Pierre Charles LeSueur explored this area for the French back in about seventeen hundred or thereabouts, he thought he found copper when he saw all that blue clay. The idiot loaded up a whole boat full of it and hauled it back to France and ended up sinking the boat."

"What a moron," McQuiston said.

"Yeah, the Frenchies are kind of dumb, but he was smart enough to get LeSueur County and LeSueur Center to the north of us named after him. He even built a fort downriver a ways and called it Fort LeHuillier. He did some fur trading from there way back in the early days."

"You know something? This is way more than I want to know about this area," McQuiston said. "After we hang these butchers, I'm heading out of here just as fast as the stagecoach can carry me."

"You were the one who asked," Jackson said.

"So this is where they're holding the condemned Indians, huh?" Othmar Huettl approached the two men and interrupted the conversation. "You know, those Dakota warriors who are going to be hanged by the military troops in charge here, the ones President Lincoln signed the death warrants on."

Jackson and McQuiston turned to look at the young man, who was dressed in a heavy winter coat with a sheepskin lining and a fur cap also lined with fleece.

"That's right," McQuiston said. "But there's a lot more of them here in town than these that we're going to hang. Camp Lincoln has a ton of them out there." He shook hands with Mister Huettl. "I'm one of the lucky men who gets to cut the rope and drop the scaffold out from under the red devils."

"I'm glad it's you and not me," Huettl said as he looked toward McQuiston through closed eyelids, a nervous mannerism of his. "As cruel as those Indians are, I still wouldn't want to be the one to put them to death."

"It doesn't bother me a bit," McQuiston said. "They killed my whole family, my wife and kids, over to New Ulm."

"Thou shalt not kill, the Good Book says."

"Tell them that," McQuiston said. "Not that they'd listen to a farmer like you."

Changing the subject, Huettl shaded his eyes and squinted toward the jail. "They sure are making a lot of racket in there."

"It's their war cry," McQuiston said.

"I thought that was what it was. I heard that yelling and screaming a lot in the past few months."

"They won't be screaming for long. They swing on the twenty-sixth."

"This is all so sad," Huettl said. "Why can't we all live in peace? There's plenty of room for all of us here in the great state of Minnesota."

"You can't live in peace with these butchers," McQuiston said. "They carry a grudge against all whites. They want to see every last one of our scalps hanging on their lodge poles, and us dead in the ground."

"Washington didn't honor the treaty. I heard that the agent out at the agency was starving them."

"He didn't starve them soon enough, as far as I'm concerned," McQuiston replied.

"Not only that, they weren't getting paid their reparations, and what decent food there was, Galbraith sold to the settlers. That isn't right."

"I don't know anything about that, and I don't give a damn about it either. They're killers, I can tell you that. And they've been doing it for generations. Long before us whites were here, they were killing other Indians." McQuiston spit on the ground. "They call themselves warriors, but they are just sons-a-bitchin' butchers, if you should ask me."

Tired of arguing, Huettl pulled out three cigars and offered one to each man. "Cigar?"

"Don't mind if I do," McQuiston said.

"No thank you," Jackson said.

The two men lit up with a bit of broom straw touched to the lantern fire and looked at the jailhouse again, the sound of the drums within causing a rhythmic beat.

Othmar took a puff and blew a smoke ring. "I wonder how many square feet there are in this prison anyway."

Sensing an opportunity to get into the prison compound, McQuiston said, "Maybe we could pace it off."

"Yeah, maybe we could." Huettl signaled to the guard. "Say soldier, will you come over here to the gate a minute?"

"State your business," replied the eighteen-year-old guard, Chauncey R. Sackett, who mustered into the Seventh in August. The farm boy swaggered toward the gate, puffed up with his own importance. "This is a restricted area."

"We were wondering how many square feet are in that jail house?"

Sackett looked at the dwelling. "I don't know, a couple thousand maybe, I suppose. Why?"

"Well, I was studying it and counting the limestone blocks, and I figure they're about . . ." he held out both hands, fingers extended, "I'd say, ten inches long, and I can figure the length that way, but I can't see the width."

"What difference does it make?"

"None, I guess. I'm just curious, that's all."

The guard grumbled something inaudible. "Well, you look harmless enough. Maybe . . ."

Huettl pulled out another cigar and offered it to the guard, smiling. The guard's eyes lit up as he reached out for it, but Huettl drew it away.

"Only if I can come in and measure off the jailhouse. Then this . . ." he said and ran the cigar under his nose and sniffed it, "then this here fresh cigar is yours, soldier."

The soldier glanced around for any sign of an officer. Seeing none, he said, "Oh, all right! But just you and not that other guy there." He thumbed at McQuiston. "He's trouble. How about you, Mister Jackson?"

"Don't think so. I built that darn thing and almost broke my back toting those limestone blocks. I got to get going anyway," he said, walking away.

"All right, Mister..."

"Huettl, Othmar Huettl."

"All right, Mister Huettl, you can come on in, but make it snappy."

"Thank you," Huettl said, sporting a wide grin. "Here's your cigar."

"You got a light?"

"Sure. You can light it off of mine."

The soldier drew a long inhale on the cigar then coughed. "Wow! This is strong."

"Yup, I rolled it myself just this morning. Got the tobacco leaves from a store in the fort."

The guard took a smaller puff and inhaled. "Not so bad when you get used to it. I ran out of smoking tobacco couple of days ago, and I'm mighty jittery."

"Enjoy it," Othmar said. He moved over to the guardhouse, withdrew a bit of measured string tied to two nails, and stuck them in the ground along the foundation as he paced off the building. Then he disappeared around the other side. After ten minutes of this, he returned to the guard with a stub of graphite pencil and a square of rough paper in his hand. "It's fifty by sixty. That works out to three thousand square feet exactly."

"I told you so ten minutes ago," Sackett said, flicking the ash from his cigar. He figured he'd come ahead in this deal.

"No, you said a couple thousand, but you were just guessing." He held up the paper. "Now there's proof. It's three thousand."

"So, what are you going to do with all this valuable information?" McQuiston said.

"Nothing, I was just curious, was all. I want to build a barn, and now that I know the size, I know how many trees I have to chop down."

"That'll make a darn big barn," Sackett said.

"Oh, I'm not going to build it that large. Mine is going to be fifteen by fifteen. I only got one cow and a couple horses, you know."

"Well, if you already knew that then why in blazes did you measure off the jailhouse?" Sackett said.

"Yeah, why?" said McQuiston, switching the cigar from one cheek to the other.

"I'm just curious, that's all." Huettl smiled and leaned toward the men. "And now I can tell folks I got right up to the jailhouse and saw the Indians inside. While I was on the back side, I drew a sketch of them, too." He turned over the piece of paper he'd written the dimensions of the guardhouse on, revealing well-drawn sketches of several of the condemned. "See? And all it cost me was a few cigars."

"Well, aren't you the foxy one." Sackett laughed. "It's probably a good idea you got those sketches because by this time next week, folks will have forgotten all about the hanging."

"I highly doubt that." Huettl glanced toward the gallows, held up his thumb and fingers like a square, and looked through them. "Will you look at that? That scaffold you're building for the execution isn't even plumb, for crying out loud."

The guard glanced toward the gallows. "It looks level to me."

"Well, it doesn't to me." Huettl wandered in that direction as McQuiston and the guard watched him. "Say, soldier," he said to the trooper nailing on the floor of the scaffold, "this floor isn't level." He held a plum bob against the side post. "You're off plumb vertically and probably horizontally too."

"What of it?" said seventeen-year-old Wyman Folsom of Company C of the Seventh, irritation evident in his voice. "It's close enough for government work."

"It isn't going to drop right. You'll have trouble with the ropes, and you'll knock out your footings." He reached inside his sheepskin coat and pulled a spirit level out of the pocket of his overalls. "Yup, look at where that bubble is. You're off plumb horizontally too."

By this time Captain Burt, thirty-five, from Stillwater, who was in charge of the scaffold construction, approached the two men. "What seems to be the problem here?"

"This floor isn't plumb," Huettl said, his eyes fluttering.

"Plumb?"

"Level. It isn't level. See?" He pointed at the bubble again. "When you go to drop this, the floor will fall sideways, and the whole danged contraption will collapse in a cloud of sawdust. Then what?"

"Well, I—"

"And look at those ropes. Those are granny knots, not hang-man's knots. They can slip on you, or snap the rope, and some of this rope doesn't look very good to begin with." He reached up and grabbed one of the ropes and tied a perfect hangman's knot. "There. That's a hangman's knot. It won't slip, and if you know how to place it, it'll put the executed into eternity in a split second."

Captain Burt removed his cap. "Ah, Mister . . ."

"Huettl. Othmar Huettl."

"Mister Huettl, would you mind helping me supervise while my men fix this contraption? You know a lot more about carpentry than we do, and I'd hate to botch the executions. That wouldn't look good at all in my federal report."

Huettl smiled, reached into his pocket, and handed Captain Burt a cigar. "Want a cigar? It's fresh. I rolled it myself just this morning."

Three hours later, the gallows were braced and leveled and the ropes were all retied with perfect hangman's knots to Huettl's satisfac-tion. "There. That's pretty good." He removed his pocket watch and clicked open the cover. "It's getting on towards supper time. Julia and the kids will be waiting for me. I'd best get going. See you fellows."

"Obliged to you, Mister Huettl," Captain Burt said. "I appreci-ate you helping us."

"Oh, I didn't do this for you. I did it for those poor Indians back there in the jailhouse. Since you're bound and determined to kill them, I want to insure they die quickly and painlessly." Othmar raised a finger to Captain Burt, closing his eyes as he began to speak. "Judge not oth-ers, lest you be judged, the Good Book says." Opening his eyes, he con-tinued, "Vengeance is mine alone sayeth the Lord. You're murdering them in the name of the law, but you're committing murder just the same." He shook his finger at the officer. "Stew on that for a while, Captain." With that, he began walking toward the north end of town.

"He's quite a character, isn't he?" Captain Burt said, watching the departing man pick up speed.

"That he is," Folsom replied.

"Did you see that beak on him?"

"Yeah, he's got quite a honker there. I bet he's German."

"With a name like Huettl, that's a safe bet."

RYKER LEANED AGAINST A SUPPORT POST in the prison enclosure, keeping a close eye on the prisoners but trying not to interfere in their conversations with their friends and family. He noticed Stands Tall in a corner talking quietly with Wa-kan-tan-ka. When she arose to leave, he tipped his hat to her and opened the door. "Hello again, Stands Tall."

The woman looked up at him a moment before it registered who he was, for she was preoccupied with sad thoughts of Wa-kan-tan-ka. "Aren't you Ryker, the scout for Colonel Sibley? I'm sorry. I did not recognize you."

"That's me, ma'am." Ryker glanced around the enclosure and saw that all was quiet. "Let's step outside a moment and get some air."

When they were alone, Ryker put his hands on Stands Tall's shoulders. "Are you all right?" he said softly.

For a second it looked like she would break down, but she refrained as she looked back into his eyes. "Yes, I'm fine. Have you heard anything about Mary?"

"Mary Eisenreich? Yes, I saw a dispatch that her relatives claimed her in New Ulm when Colonel Sibley's caravan came through. She's living with an aunt and uncle."

"I know that part," Stands Tall said. "Louis and I were with her when they came. It about broke my heart."

"But it was the right thing to do. She's with her kinfolk now."

"Yes, I know, but I still miss that poor, dear child."

"Where is Louis?"

"We're camped with relatives under the large elm tree in town. The soldiers have already been there and given their approval. I came in alone today, but on Christmas I will bring Louis to see his father for the last time."

"Shucks, that's right!" Ryker said. "With everything that's going on around here, I forgot that Christmas is just two days off."

"Yes, the day the savior was born who died for our sins, and the day before Wa-kan-tan-ka and the others will die for their sins against the settlers."

Ryker nodded. "I think Wa-kan-tan-ka is a good man again. I think he will die with honor and make you proud."

"It was the whiskey," Stands Tall said. "If he hadn't been drinking, I don't think he would have been involved in any of this."

"I want to tell you again how much I admire what you did," Ryker said. "You would have been forgiven for not helping little Mary. You took on a large risk to yourself when you did that."

"I know. I thought of that, but then I saw her and knew she was at more risk than I was." She shuddered. "I saw Little Crow's warriors kill children that age just for sport during the massacre."

"Can't even imagine that," Ryker said, glancing at the prison.

"Again, it was the whiskey. Some of the men did things that they didn't remember doing afterwards."

"How about Wa-kan-tan-ka?"

"Yes, he was a terrible beast." She cried briefly, but quickly regained control of her emotions. "He's been . . . rough with me in our lodge and didn't remember afterwards. I can only imagine what he did out on the prairie during the massacre."

"I wonder if he even knows what all he did."

"I asked him about those days when he was drinking heavily. They are all a blur to him now."

"Maybe he should be excused for what he did. If he was out of his mind, how can he be held responsible for his actions?"

"No! He drank of his own free will. No one forced him to do it. I told him and told him many times that he was not himself when he drank. He chose to do so anyway." Stands Tall crossed her arms. "No! He did the bad things they say he did, and now he must face the consequences."

"At least he will die proud, as a warrior."

"Even better than that, Reverend Riggs talked to him, and he is to be baptized into the church this day."

"This is wonderful," Ryker said, smiling.

"Yes, he will die not only as a warrior, but as a Christian."

"What will you do?"

"Louis and I will return to the reservation, for that is the only life we know. I intend to raise crops, and we can hunt deer. There are lots of them in the river bottom lands."

"You will be alone," Ryker said. "You're still a young woman. Don't you want a man?"

"Maybe, in time," she replied. "But for now, no."

"Understandable," Ryker said. "We're so concerned about the settlers that we tend to forget that the Indian women and children are victims of this war too."

"You understand, but few others do," Stands Tall said.

"It's the Indian blood in me," Ryker replied. "I carry the pain of both the Indian and the white settler because by blood I'm half Ojibwe."

"The Ojibwe were Dakota enemies in the old days. Those were simpler times." She looked at Ryker. "My mother was Ojibwe."

"She was?"

"Yes, in what is now Wisconsin. She was taken as a young girl in a Dakota raid and was raised Dakota. She married a Dakota brave."

"So Ojibwe blood flows in you also?"

"Yes."

"Well ain't that just peachy! We're kin!" Ryker hugged her. "Did you know my Pappy Oliver? He was a fisherman at Mille Lacs many years."

"Oliver Ryker?" Stands Tall rubbed her tongue against her cheek for a moment. "Yes, I remember my mother speaking of him. Let me see. There's something else. Did the Ojibwe call your mother Waawaashkeshi?"

"Yup, that means 'deer' in Ojibwe, but she is my Mama, all right. She still lives up north in the Ryker cabin. She's alone now, because Oliver died this year."

"I'm sorry," Stands Tall said, looking at Ryker with sympathy.

"He had a rich, full life," Ryker said. "But we all got to go some-time."

"Yes, that's true. As a child, I remember meeting your mother once or twice at the wild rice harvest during the times when we were not at war with the Ojibwe."

"It sure is a small world."

"That it is, Mister Ryker." She snugged her wrap more tightly around herself. "It grows cold. I must get back to the great elm. Tomorrow I will bring the paint and feathers for my man. Maybe I will see you then."

"I'll be here," Ryker said. "I'll be working the prison shift tomor-row also. In fact, I'll be with these warriors right up to the very end."

"That would be good," Stands Tall said. She shook Ryker's hand. "Good-bye for now."

"Good-bye." Ryker watched her go through the snowfall that had begun. She looked like a spirit as she walked under the street lamps, ramrod straight as her name implied, gliding silently over the ground. He blew into his hands to warm them and continued to watch until she disappeared into the white haze, leaving only her footprints to show she had passed by. Turning, he re-entered the guardhouse.

14

O N THE 24TH OF DECEMBER, the day before Christmas, Ryker arrived at the prison door in time to help serve the morning meal of beans, corn, and a small ration of meat. He walked slowly among the prisoners, who were considerably more subdued than the day before. They were in good spirits though, having received wise counsel from the Reverends Williamson and Ravoux. Several had begun their sad, mournful death chant the previous evening, and several more picked it up today. Others practiced the prayer taught them in both Dakota and English by the ministers, "Jesus Christ, *Nituwashti Kin*." It was a rehearsal for the 26th, the day they vowed to die proudly as true Dakota warriors.

> Jesus Christ, *nitowashti kin,*
> *Woptecashna mayaqu.*
> Jesus Christ, thy loving kindness
> Boundlessly thou gavest me.

"It is indeed a sad situation," Ryker said to Father Ravoux. "Look at them now, how serene they are. They look like nobility."

"Most of them are noble," the priest said. "Only Black Wolf and Cut Nose, and Baptiste Campbell, the half-breed, remain belligerent."

"They will die belligerent, I suspect," Ryker said. "They are the most evil of the lot."

"I fear you are right," the priest replied. "I think we saved the other souls in here, but I don't think we saved those three. They're doomed to eternity in hellfire."

"It's their choice," Ryker said.

"A very poor choice, but yes, we all have free will."

Stands Tall entered the compound with her son, Louis, in tow. She carried several articles of finery with her for the preparation of Wa-kan-tan-ka's long walk to the scaffold.

"Hello, Mister Ryker, or rather, scout Ryker, I should say."

"I'd be obliged if you just called me Toby because my friends call me that. We called my Pappy Oliver 'Mister Ryker,' not me."

"As you wish," Stands Tall said. "Louis, say hello to Toby."

The boy complied, then added, "Are you the man who will kill my father?"

Ryker whitened then swallowed. "No, son, I am not. That will be done by the other soldiers, and two survivors of the war will actually cut the rope." It pained him to say this, but he knew the boy was entitled to a straight answer.

"I wish you would do it," Louis said. "You have always been a friend to the Dakota. It is best to die with a gentle friend."

"He will have a hood over his face."

"But he will know you are there."

Ryker hugged the boy and was amazed at his comprehension of the situation. "I will be there with your father and with all of them. Anything I can do to ease their passage, I will do it, Louis." He looked at Stands Tall. "I see you have new buckskins with all the finery for Wa-kan-tan-ka."

"Yes, I brought paint and feathers and beads and special food to celebrate his life, and I intend to fix his hair."

"He asked about you at chow," Ryker said. "I told him you would be here, and he awaits you."

"Thank you, Toby," Stands Tall said. "Louis and I wish to spend some time alone with him."

"I'll see to it that you are not disturbed. In fact," Ryker picked up two large blankets, "we can hang these up to create a screen."

"Hello, Lieutenant Ryker," Wa-kan-tan-ka said as the trio approached. "I'm glad you found my woman and son."

Ryker noted that Wa-kan-tan-ka's eyes were red from weeping, but he wore a smile. "They weren't lost, Wa-kan-tan-ka. They've been waiting since shortly after dawn. You have a fine family, and I invite you to call me Toby, like my friends do."

"As you wish, Toby," the warrior replied. "And, yes, I do have a fine family, much better than I deserve. I thank the Great Spirit for that."

"I'll leave you in peace," Ryker said after hanging up the blankets.

That afternoon, Ryker approached Stands Tall and Louis as they were preparing to leave. "I hope your visit went well."

"Very well," Stands Tall said.

"I knew those blanket screens would come in handy," Ryker said, smiling.

"I'll be left with good memories," she replied.

"My father gave me this to remember him by," Louis said, holding up an owl's feather.

"That's a wonderful token," Ryker said. "The owl is wise."

"So is my father."

Ryker patted the boy on the head then glanced up and saw Wa-kan-tan-ka in his ceremonial attire. Dressed as he was with full war paint, feathers and plumes, he was a handsome man and looked to be resigned to his impending death. "He looks grand, Stands Tall."

"He feels fine, as fine as he can feel under the circumstances. We will be back early tomorrow to celebrate his last Christmas with him."

"I will be here to greet you."

"Thank you, Toby."

After they left, Ryker wandered around the compound, visiting with the other guards and with some of the Indians. When he got to where Cut Nose was standing, he saw that the warrior still wore a sneer. He still looked like the angry man he had always been.

"Cut Nose, is there something on your mind?"

"Of course there is, you big jackass!"

"If all you want to do is talk guff, you can save it for Beelzebub."

"I'll tell you something, all right. I'll tell all of you something. You just be sure and listen."

Ryker dismissed the belligerent Sioux with a wave of his hand. A short time later, he exited the lockup and ambled over to headquarters where Colonel Miller was seated at his desk. He took off his hat and playfully tossed it onto the floor.

"Oh, Lieutenant Ryker, mosey on in and take a load off. What'd you throw your hat on the floor for?"

"I figured if it came flying back at me, you probably weren't in a very good mood, and this was the wrong time to come visiting."

Miller chuckled. "Naw, naw, you don't have to worry about that." He removed a handkerchief and blew his nose, making a loud honking sound. "This darn wood smoke plugs my nose right up tight."

Ryker removed his flask. "Care for a snort? It loosens the phlegm."

"Sure. Don't mind if I do." Adding to Ryker's rationale so neither of them had to feel guilty about sucking on the jug this early in the day, he said, "It helps to ward off the chilblains, too."

After the two shared a drink, they sat down to talk about the war. "What I want to jaw with you about is what's going to happen to the Sixth after this hanging is all over here in Mankato," Ryker said.

"That will be up to General Pope, but I know he's anxious to get us south to bolster the Union troops."

"I suppose." Ryker took out his jackknife to trim his nails.

"Why? Have you heard something from General Sibley?"

"Nope, nary a word, except for his official reports since he went on to St. Paul."

The men sat without talking a moment with only the sound of the ticking clock to break the silence.

"If you were a betting man, what would you think will happen?"

"Well, I'll bet we'll be seeing more Indian action."

"Are you anxious to go south?"

Ryker looked up. "A few months ago, I was chomping at the bit to go south and mix it up with those rebs in Mister Lincoln's war, but now, I'm not so sure."

"What's changed your mind?"

"Everything that's happened since the seventeenth of August, that's what. Colonel, this execution the day after tomorrow ain't going to be the end of the Indian problem. Not by a long shot."

"I know the federal government wants them relocated out of Minnesota. We all do."

"Yes, they do, and there's a lot more than Dakota Sioux tribes involved. Hell, the Winnebagos ain't but twenty miles from where we're sitting."

"What do you think the big shots should do?"

"Well, sir, if'n it was me a-making this decision, I'd leave the Sixth right here in Minnesota. The settlers are still so scared of the Indians that they mess their pants whenever they see one. They'd feel a heck of a lot safer if we kept Ridgely and Abercrombie open, and kept patrols out on the frontier. And as for relocating the Indians, that's going to be a mighty big job. They ain't going to leave peacefully, I don't care what they say, and the army will need to help out with that."

"Why do you think it's going to be such a big job?"

"Because I know people, that's why, and those Indians are people just like we are. Sir, how'd you like it if the government came along and said, 'Um, pardon me, Mister Miller, but you and your family have to pack up your duds and move your asses off this farm that you homesteaded and go where we tell you to.' How would you like to be told that, huh?"

"I never thought of it that way." Miller drew a deep breath. "Yeah, we may be seeing Indian service for a long time yet."

"Couldn't agree with you more, but if Lincoln ships us south, that relocation job ain't a-going to get accomplished. And with no one to guard the frontier, the Sioux and the other warriors just might get spunky again. Word has it the southerners are supplying them with weapons because they want to use them as a diversionary tactic against the Union. And a little bird told me that they're getting some of their supplies from the British too."

"I've heard those rumors also," Miller said. "But frankly, I doubt that either the southerners or the British would put much stock in the Indians because they are so unpredictable."

"I bet you six months' wages you're wrong."

"One thing for sure is that neither you nor I will determine our fate," Miller said. "Where we are this time next year will be determined by the commanders in Washington, not us."

"There I agree with you." Ryker stood and stretched. "Sir, I'd like to go into town for a bit tonight if you don't mind, tomorrow being Christmas and all. Thought I'd celebrate. Have you seen Father Ravoux?"

"He's up at the church celebrating Mass with Father Sommereisen and the Catholics on behalf of the Indians. He hopes to take up a collection too, him being a missionary amongst them all these years and all. Will you be back for guard duty tomorrow?"

"Yes, sir."

"Will you be sober?"

Ryker withdrew his flask, held it to his ear, and shook it. "Reckon I'll be sober enough for guard duty, that is, unless some pretty young thing over at the Mankato House gets me all liquored up and wants to celebrate Christmas a little bit early."

"I doubt you'll have to worry about that, you old toad."

"I doubt it too."

Miller chuckled. "Even though you have a stabilizing influence on the Indians and the younger recruits as well, I guess I can spare you for a few hours. Now get your carcass out of here before I change my mind."

"Thank you, sir." Ryker saluted. "I'll be back before long so I can get a little shut-eye. Plan to relieve the night guards at the jail when they go off duty at seven o'clock."

THE NEXT MORNING, CHRISTMAS DAY, was cold and blustery. A front had moved in from the Dakota plains, bringing with it five inches of snow and temperatures below zero. Ryker entered the jailhouse carrying several bundles and two suitcases. Ignoring the curious onlookers, he went to the far end of the compound and began to rummage in the supplies he brought. Within five minutes he had set up a Christmas manger scene and a small altar complete with candles and bread and wine.

He nodded toward the door, and Father Ravoux, dressed in clerical garb of purest white and accompanied by an altar attendant, entered carrying a golden chalice beneath a white cloth, starched to perfection, with the letters IHS embroidered in gold on the front. The families of the condemned followed behind the priest and fanned out to stand with their warriors. Ryker began to sing "Silent Night," and as he did so, he walked among the condemned and those granted stays of execution and passed out rosaries, small statues, and Saint Christopher medals to all of them, Saint Christopher being the patron saint of travelers. The wives and children and many of the warriors joined him in song.

When the hymn concluded, Father Ravoux launched into the Latin Rite Mass. "*In nomine Patris, et Filii, et Spiritus Sancti, Amen. Introibo ad altari Dei.*"

"*Ad Deum qui laetificat, juventutem meum,*" the altar attendant replied, making the sign of the cross along with the priest.

Communion was offered to those in attendance, and all but Cut Nose and Black Wolf partook of the sacrament. Ryker noted that Cut Nose stood alone with no family about him and stared at the ceremony through hostile eyes. When communion was finished, Father Ravoux removed the blessed hosts to the safety of his quarters as the crowd sang the recessional hymn.

185

After the service, Father Ravoux rejoined the prisoners and helped the scout pass out more religious gifts to the assembled families. Ryker told no one that he'd paid for the gifts out of his wages and the collection that the priest had taken up at the church. After all had enjoyed opening their presents, he leaned back and smiled at the Indian children, so innocent of the horrors that their fathers committed. As they played and squabbled and argued amongst themselves over the gifts, they could have passed for their young white counterparts. The entire compound then sat down to a sump-tuous Christmas feast. Mathias Ulman at the Union Hotel catered it, keep-ing his cooks up all night preparing the repast. In a sudden spirit of holiday generosity, he sold the food to Ryker at cost. It still set the scout back sev-eral weeks' wages, but he figured it was money well spent.

Making his way through the crowd, he stopped to visit, to hug children, and to speak words of encouragement to the condemned pris-oners. The celebration went into the evening, and Colonel Miller, moved by Ryker's generosity, allowed them to continue beyond curfew. He doubled the guard however, because the executions were less than twen-ty-four hours off, and martial law had been declared.

Approaching Black Wolf, who was now sitting with warriors Cut Nose and Tazoo, Ryker offered both of them a sack of smoking tobacco and papers. The three warriors accepted the gift and invited Ryker to sit with them in council. For a moment, Ryker's spirits soared because he thought the two Indians were prepared to atone for their shameful behav-ior against the settlers.

"So, the ace scout of the Sixth is back," Black Wolf said.

Ryker's spirits were dashed as he quickly discovered that Black Wolf was simply in a joking mood and intended to make coup on him.

"Say, Cut Nose, did I tell you that Ryker and I were hunting the white-tail deer on the prairie one time when all of a sudden, two hun-dred Dakota warriors appeared on the horizon. This made the great scout for the Sixth as nervous as a cow with a buck-toothed calf, so he turned to me and said, 'What do we do now, Black Wolf?' And I looked back at him and said, 'What do you mean we, paleface?'"

186

"What do you mean we, paleface?" Cut Nose laughed. "That's a good one, Black Wolf."

"Oh yeah, that's a real knee-slapper," Ryker said, also pretending to laugh. Then he stopped laughing abruptly and reversed the coup. "With jokes like that, Black Wolf, you ought to be on the stage, rather than," he emphasized the word, "*hanging* around here. The next one leaves in ten minutes."

Not missing a beat, Black Wolf added, "Sounds good to me. I'll give you free tickets to my next performance if you release me now."

Ryker adjusted his hat. "I wish you would have used your great mind for the good of your people rather than for going to war against the settlers. You directed your wrath at the wrong parties, Black Wolf."

"Maybe," Black Wolf said, "but we fought with whom we could find, and you must admit, we got everyone's attention."

"I have to admit that," Ryker said. "But what I can't accept is the innocents you sent meet their God and holding them personally responsible for that over which they had no say."

Tazoo, who sat quietly and listened to the exchange, now stood and faced Ryker. "What is done is done. When this hanging party is all over, tell our friends that we are being removed from this world over the same path they must shortly travel. We go first, but many of our friends will follow us in a very short time. I expect to go direct to the abode of the Great Spirit, and to be happy when I get there. We are told that the road is long and the distance is great, therefore, as I am slow in my movements, it will probably take me a long time to reach the end of the journey, and I should not be surprised if some of the young, active men we will leave behind us will pass me on the road before I reach the place of my destination."

Ryker nodded. "I don't doubt the truth of your words, Tazoo."

Cut Nose threw the rosary Ryker had handed him earlier back at him. "Take your beads, you half-breed whore of the white soldiers. You cannot buy my favor this cheaply. I have no use for them."

Controlling the urge to pound Cut Nose, Ryker picked up the holy object and placed it in his pocket. "You're bound and determined to die a heathen, aren't you, Cut Nose?"

The Indian spit on the floor. "One day, you will join me in hell." He then screamed "Ki-yi-yi!" in Ryker's face.

Ryker arose and looked down at the two smirking Indians. "I certainly hope not." He turned and walked over to where Stands Tall and Louis stood with Wa-kan-tan-ka. "Hello, Wa-kan-tan-ka. I understand you've been baptized."

"Yes, I have been," the Indian said. "Although I would prefer that tomorrow did not come for me, I understand it, and I accept it." He smiled at Ryker. "I am told you have shown great compassion to Stands Tall and Louis. For that, I thank you."

"You are very welcome."

"One last thing, Toby. I would appreciate it if you would keep my wife and son in your heart and see after their welfare, since I will not be here to care for them myself."

"Consider it a pledge," Ryker said, shaking hands with Wa-kan-tan-ka. "Stands Tall, Louis, I'm afraid you must go now."

"We are ready," Stands Tall said. She embraced her husband as did Louis his father, and all three began to sing the death chant. The other families in the compound took up the chant, and they and the warriors continued to sing with great feeling.

Ryker escorted the last of the family members to the door of the enclosure then turned back to listen to the mournful chant.

Although they looked sad, they also looked at peace with their fate, dressed now as they were in their finest ceremonial garb. All except Cut Nose, that is, for he still wore the bloody clothing he had on during the massacre and on the battlefield.

Watching the soldiers chain the condemned to the floor, Ryker shook his head sadly and walked out into the night.

15

BLACK FRIDAY, DECEMBER 26, 1862, arrived cold, gray, and blustery, a fitting day for an execution. Ryker was up at dawn, watching the relatives and friends of the condemned Indians return to bid them a final farewell. Gifts and trinkets, locks of hair and other items were exchanged as a final remembrance. The warriors told their loved ones that they wished to die happily, not sadly, and to join the Great Spirit as proud Dakotas. They wished to make a good appearance as they prepared to march to their doom, and carefully adjusted their eagle plumes and owl feathers. Glancing into their small mirrors, they touched up their faces with vermilion and ultramarine until they looked perfect.

Ryker moved outside and saw the crowd beginning to filter in, hundreds of them, and despite the cold, they gathered in groups behind the troops who stood now at parade rest. Martial law had been declared. The saloons were closed. The hotels were crowded. A group of Catholics led by their pastor, Father Sommereisen, prayed the rosary.

In another area, the Protestant groups were addressed by Reverend Williamson who, after delivering a rousing sermon on the wages of sin and the evils of drink, led them in singing songs of hope, including "When the Roll is Called Up Yonder," and "A Mighty Fortress Is Our God."

In yet another section, the minstrel from the Union Hotel placed a derby hat on the ground and began to strum his guitar to the tune of "The Streets of Laredo:"

> As I walked out in the streets of Mankato
> As I walked out in Mankato one day
> I spied a dead Indian who still was a-danglin'
> He still was a-danglin' but cold as the clay.
> Now beat the drum slowly and play the fife lowly
> These words he did say as I slowly walked by
> Come stand here beside me and hear my sad story
> Got hanged by the Sixth and I know I must die.

Several bystanders cheer him on and drop coins into his hat. He nods to them and continues with the second verse, which he wrote especially for this occasion.

> Go fetch me some water, a cold cup of water
> To cool my stretched throat now the Indian then said
> Before I returned his spirit had left him
> Had gone to damnation, the redskin was dead
> So beat the drum slowly and play the fife lowly
> The Indian beast has now gotten his due
> Drag down the gallows and bury him shallow
> No more to cause terror he's just a dead Sioux.

Colin O'Shaunassey, an enterprising Irishman who was more than a little tipsy with spirits already this morning, had concocted the idea of cutting up small pieces of deer hide chamois and selling them as parts of white scalps taken by the Indians in the massacre. He did a lively business, selling the fake tokens for two bits apiece.

Several newspapermen were again on hand as they had been earlier in the week. They gathered to record the final throes of the condemned and to again take souvenir pictures of families against the backdrop of the gigantic gallows.

"Now stand still and smile," a photographer said to a dour German farm family who hadn't come into Mankato since they voted for Lincoln in the presidential election. The photographer stood behind his large daguerreotype camera and made a slight adjustment to the lens. "Now smile and stand perfectly still." he said again. "Don't even blink. This'll take several minutes." The family's faces remained entirely expressionless as the photographer opened the shutter and immortalized their images on a silver plate. "Next!"

To the rear, coming from the direction of the great elm tree, Ryker saw Stands Tall and Louis and several other Indian families. They too were dressed in ceremonial garb, and eyes downcast, moved quietly towards the gallows to stand between it and the guardhouse.

Ryker watched as Officer of the Day Captain Burt approached McQuiston, who stood at the base of the gallows along with Mister Duley from Lake Shetek. Both men had lost children in the massacre.

"Come up here on the scaffold, gentlemen," Burt said. "I'll show you what your assignment is and how it's done."

McQuiston rubbed his hands together gleefully, breathing into them to ward off the cold and ascended the scaffold, followed by Mister Duley, who was silent. As McQuiston passed by, Ryker smelled the odor of alcohol on his breath.

"This rope is attached to the platform," the captain said. "Here, I'll stand on it a minute. See how it moves under my feet?"

"This is quite a gallows," McQuiston said.

"It's my own special design to hang forty men all at the same time. Actually, we started out with forty, but two of the brutes got a reprieve at the last minute. You are about to witness history in the making, gentlemen. Not only is this the largest mass execution in the history of our great state, but also, of our great nation."

"Yeah, yeah," McQuiston said, "enough with the speeches. What do I get to do?"

Captain Burt pointed again to the rope that held up the platform. "It'll be really easy. You take this ax," he held up a hatchet, "and sever that rope. It lies against the support beam, and the blade's very sharp. Strike the rope hard, so you separate the strands instantly."

"Then what?" says McQuiston.

"Then enjoy the show," Burt replied. "The Indians will be in the nooses attached to those beams up there. When the floor gives way, they'll drop several inches until their necks break and they die."

"Tidy!" McQuiston replied. He glanced at Duley. "I'll flip you for the honor." Before Duley could reply, McQuiston removed a silver dollar from his pocket and flipped it into the air. "Call it."

"Um, heads," Duley said, scowling at McQuiston. "You're really enjoying this, aren't you?"

"You damn right, I am." McQuiston tossed the coin again and stood back. The coin landed on the platform but not flat, instead bouncing from side to side and making a rattling sound as it wobbled faster and shallower until it lay flat. "Shit! It's heads."

"Why don't you both cut it?" Captain Burt said.

"Nah, that's okay," McQuiston replied. "I'd rather watch their faces while they twitch anyway."

"You won't be able to do that. They'll be hooded."

"Confound it all, you soldiers are taking all the fun out of this."

Ryker looked at McQuiston in disgust. *Geez, what an asshole!*

AT SEVEN-THIRTY, THE INDIANS were removed from the chains that locked them to the floor and were pinioned for their final walk, a process that took two hours. They began their death chant once again.

Father Ravoux entered the compound and devoutly commended the souls of the condemned to the mercy of God. Some responded solemnly to his prayer, others sobbed, and their tears fell to the floor.

Black Wolf listened to the minstrel outside singing his version of the "Streets of Laredo." "Hey, Cut Nose, hear that?"

"You mean that sidewinder outside?" Cut Nose responded absently. He was looking out the barred window and studying the gallows with great interest.

"Yeah, he's giving us a special serenade."

"He's probably a sissy," Cut Nose said, turning to Black Wolf. "Listen to that squeaky voice."

"I suppose so," Black Wolf replied. "I wonder if he looks pretty in a doeskin dress."

"Probably," Cut Nose said, glancing around. "Where the heck is my knife when I need it? I bet his scalp would look handsome hanging on my lodge pole."

"Cut Nose, you are so amusing," Black Wolf said, chuckling.

"Who? Me?" Cut Nose spat outside.

Captain Redfield moved among the prisoners, checking and double-checking their pinions to make sure they were secure just as Ryker entered. The scout had bathed, gotten a haircut, trimmed his beard, and wore army-issue dress-uniform trousers tucked into the fringed buckskin leggings topped by the Ojibwe ceremonial buckskin coat given him by Fawn at the time of Oliver's death. On this coat was displayed the insignia of a second lieutenant in the Union Army. At Ryker's request, but kept secret until now, General Sibley ordered Colonel Miller to allow the scout to dress in this fashion for the hanging.

Just as the military garb and insignia represented law and order, and the white Minnesota settlers, and the overwhelming support received from the army, the buckskin coat and Indian leggings represented the multitude of the Indian nations. Ryker believed his garb also signified coexistence between the military and the many Indian and white cultures across the state and the country, but he knew Sibley did not share this view.

The general intended to be the superior force of the federal government that drove the Indians from their native lands, and that made Ryker sad. He doubted anyone would convince either Sibley or the Union army to forsake this quest, for it was the way of progress, the way of the future, the way of the conquerer wresting control from the conquered, which was the basic struggle of humankind that had happened throughout the ages. The scout would fight to change this course of history if he thought there was any chance of success, but he knew the battle would be a futile effort. "It's pushing nine-thirty, Captain," he said, saluting his superior officer.

Redfield checked his timepiece. "Mine says nine-fifteen."

"Well, yours is wrong." Ryker hauled out his pocket watch. "I reset mine just this morning by the clock at the courthouse. It says nine-twenty-five."

"Glad you told me," the captain said. "It wouldn't do to be late for this occasion. The telegrapher is waiting to contact General Sibley with the news as soon as it's all over."

"We'll have them buried by early afternoon. I checked the burial trench. It's ready."

"Good, although I doubt they'll rest in peace for long. The morbid will want souvenirs."

"A bigger problem is the physicians. I hear they're looking for cadavers for the medical schools."

Redfield looked at Ryker, surprised. "Surely they'd have more respect than that."

"Don't count on it," Ryker said. "They'll take bodies from wherever they can get them, dissect them in front of their students, and then burn the remains."

"That's positively barbaric!"

"Folks are saying the same thing about us." Ryker raised his eyebrows at the speechless officer and headed toward the door, stopping beside Wa-kan-tan-ka.

"Wa-kan-tan-ka, I bid you farewell. Under better circumstances, I think you and I could have been good friends."

"I consider you a good friend anyway," the Indian said. He looked at Ryker pensively. "I fear I will soil myself in death."

"To do so is quite common." Ryker saw the pained expression in the pinioned warrior's eyes. "Do you have to go now?"

"Yes."

Ryker looked around and spied a chamber pot. He approached Captain Redfield and spoke with him briefly then returned and removed the pinions from the warrior's arms. "Come with me." He stood in front of the warrior to shield him from the eyes of the others as the man used the chamber pot.

"Thank you, Toby," Wa-kan-tan-ka said when he was finished. "You don't know how much I appreciate this kindness. I shall never forget this, or you."

"You look just fine," Ryker said thickly. He cleared his throat and hugged the warrior then eyed him up and down. "And you will pass into the next world with honor." He returned the warrior to his place in line and pinioned him again, finishing just as Captain Burt, the Officer of the Day, entered the enclosure and approached Captain Redfield. The two saluted.

"Captain Burt, I present you with the condemned prisoner detail. They're all prepared and ready for execution," Redfield announced formally.

Burt took a deep breath. "Yes, and as it nears the time, I'm wishing that someone else had drawn this detail."

"It needs doing and the time has come, and I know you'll do just fine," Ryker said. "I'll be right beside you."

"You don't know how much I appreciate that," Burt replied.

Captains Burt and Redfield, both nervous, saluted again, and Burt took charge. "Men," he said to the guards, "assist those prisoners. Lieutenant Ryker, here are the hoods."

The drums and fifes begin to play outside the enclosure. Ryker stepped outside and, looking around, secretly took a nip from his flask. He heard the Indians singing their death chant, loud and strong:

HIU-HIU-HI-AH-H! HIU-HIU-HI-I-AH-H-HIAAA-H-H!

Ryker felt his pulse quicken until it was fairly pounding in his ears. He felt himself flush and the hair stand up on his neck. He trembled a bit. Forcing himself to regain control, he looked to the skies and saw that they remained overcast. A light drizzle had begun.

High above the gallows, he counted thirty-eight bald eagles wheeling and soaring as though waiting to escort thirty-eight souls to a better place. He marveled at the power of the death chant to summon the Great Spirit of the Dakotas to this place. He knew the warriors would be inspired by their Great Spirit while they endured their final struggle. He glanced over at Stands Tall, now standing behind Louis with her arms about him, and he nodded to them. They nodded back. *Oh, Pappy, Pappy, Pappy* . . .

The door to the compound opened and Captain Burt, in full dress uniform, stepped out and walked slowly through a column of soldiers toward the adjacent gallows. The guards, their guns loaded, their bayonets fixed, followed beside the pinioned condemned, whose hands were tied behind their backs.

A cheer rose up from the crowd, hats were tossed into the air, and confetti floated down from the rooftops. The death chant grew louder, now interspersed with the piercing "Ki-yi-yi!" war cry.

Wa-kan-tan-ka saw Stands Tall and Louis. He tried to walk with dignity. He smiled at them and winked at Louis.

When the Indians and their guards halted at the base of the gallows, the crowd surrounding the deadly contraption on all four sides grew restless. Some began to sing hymns again. Others taunted and shouted:

"Kill them!"

"Dirty butchers!"

"Filthy heathens!"

"Hang them all!"

The guards facing the crowd raised their guns with bayonets fixed, on the ready in the event hysteria overruled reason.

While they stood at the steps to the scaffold, the splendid warriors in all their finery sang their death chant to their Great Spirit. The

196

chant grew in volume as Ryker, with the hoods, and Captain Burt ascended to the gallows.

The crowd began to surge toward the soldier guards, and they pointed their weapons at them. The crowd fell back.

The condemned were now in place, ten to a side, on the gallows. "Lieutenant Ryker, follow me," Captain Burt said, approaching Cut Nose.

Cut Nose took this opportunity to look at the crowd and holler: "When you find a dead man outside New Ulm with his head cut off, know that it is I, Cut Nose, who killed him."

The assembly booed the Indian. Ryker, now bearing the full weight of the understanding that he was about to snuff out the life of thirty-eight fellow human beings, took some comfort in the reaction of the crowd, and saw it as an indication that he was doing the right thing, the lawful thing.

Cut Nose saw a comely young woman in the crowd and leered at her. "Come here, honey. I got a use for you." He made an obscene gesture at the crowd and laughed as they booed and hissed him loudly.

The noose encircled his neck and the hood was drawn over his face. His shoulders still shook with laughter after he was hooded, for he could hear the angry shouts from the crowd. "You bastards," he muttered.

The other thirty-seven condemned Indians stood quietly as the nooses were placed and as Ryker and Captain Burt approached each one with a hood. "I'll bid them farewell, and after I ask them if they have any last words, you place the hood."

"Aye, sir," Ryker said.

"Te-he-hdo-ne-cha, May God have mercy on your soul," Captain Burt said. "Do you have any last words?"

"Thank you, Captain. Good-bye."

Ryker placed the hood.

"Wy-a-tah-to-wah, May God have mercy on your soul. Do you have any last words?"

Silence. Ryker placed the hood.

They continued around the scaffold. None of the condemned had anything to say until they came to Wa-he-hua.

"Wa-he-hua, may God have mercy on your soul. Do you have any last words?"

A cigar stuck out of the Indian's mouth. "Yes. Ryker, when you put that sack on my head, leave me smoking room, will you please?"

"Where'd you get the cigar?" Ryker said.

"A nice settler handed me one through the window of the jailhouse the other day. All I had to do was stand there and look at him while he drew a sketch. I forget his name, but it starts with an 'H.'"

Ryker thought of prominent names from Mankato. "Um, let's see, Hoffman, maybe? How about Hodapp, Hiniker, Huettl . . . ?"

"Huettl! Yes, that's the name! Huettl!"

"Oh, yes, the Huettl clan," Ryker said, smiling faintly. He placed the hood so the Indian could puff on the cigar for the few remaining minutes of his life.

"Sna-ma-ni, may God have mercy on your soul. Do you have any last words?"

The Indian looked at Captain Burt, terrified. "I'm frightened. Oh, please do not do this!" He began to sob as Ryker placed the hood.

The two men proceeded around the gallows.

"Shan-ka-ska, may God have mercy on your soul. Any last words?"

The Indian looked sadly into Captain Burt's eyes and opened his mouth to speak, then closed it again and shook his head. A tear ran down his cheek as Ryker placed the hood.

This was the saddest, hardest job Ryker had ever had to do, but he tried as they went from man to man, to offer some support with his eyes and kind expression.

"Chas-kay-don, may God have mercy on your soul. Do you have any last words?"

"Good bye, Captain."

Captain Burt shook the Indian's hand as Ryker placed the hood.

"Baptiste Campbell, may God have mercy on your soul. Do you have any last words?"

When he said nothing, Ryker placed the hood on his head.

"Tali-ta-kay-zay, may God have mercy on your soul. Do you have any last words?"

"Yes. Good bye to my family and friends."

Ryker pat him on the shoulder, then placed the hood, glad they had passed Cut Nose.

"Wa-kan-tan-ka, may God have mercy on your soul. Do you have any last words?"

"Yes. Good-bye to you all. I forgive you for what you are about to do, as I hope you forgive me for what I have done, and I shall rejoice when we met again in paradise."

Ryker removed his hat and dabbed away the sweat from his reddened brow on the sleeve of his buckskin coat, overcome at the sincerity of Wa-kan-tan-ka's statement.

Burt looked out over the crowd a moment then wiped his eyes on a handkerchief. "Thank you, Wa-kan-tan-ka. I needed to hear that."

"Splendid behavior, Wa-kan-tan-ka," whispered Ryker as he hugged the Indian. "Your family is proud of you. We are all proud of you. The Great Spirit, after whom you are named, is proud of you." He pointed above the gallows. "Your Great Spirit is up there now, smiling down on you and waiting for you to join him."

Wa-kan-tan-ka glanced overhead briefly. "You can see them, Toby, the eagles?"

"Yes."

"Our Great Spirit only shows himself to Dakotas. I have never known him to appear to a white man." Wa-kan-tan-ka smiled faintly at Ryker. "He sees you as one of us now."

Ryker also looked skyward for a long moment before looking back at Wa-kan-tan-ka and nodded solemnly. He placed the hood so that the warrior's royal features remained exposed, and so he could spend his last moments gazing at his family.

"Thank you, Toby. Thank you very much."

"You are welcome. I'm grateful I have known you. Say hello to my Pappy Oliver."

"I will."

They continued along the sad line of condemned men.

"Pa-zee-koo-tay-ma-ne, may God have mercy on your soul. Do you have any last words?"

"Good-bye, until we meet again in a better world."

Ryker placed the hood.

In like manner they prepared Ta-tay-hde-don, Wa-she-choon, A-e-cha-ga, Ha-tan-in-koo, Chay-ton-hoon-ka, Chan-ka-hda, Hda-hin-hday, Oh-ya-tay-a-koo, May-hoo-way-wa, Wa-kin-yan-na, the ten remaining men. Ryker placed the last hood.

FIVE MINUTES LATER, ALL WAS READY, and a hush fell over the crowd. Ryker looked at McQuiston, standing on the gallows next to Mister Duley. The man appeared to be crazed, with a look of pure rapture on his face, while he glared from warrior to warrior and licked his lips.

Captain Burt removed his saber and raised the shining blade over his head. The Indians, sensing the end was near, attempted to clasp hands even though they were pinioned. Some succeeded. A tom-tom beat began, then grew louder, and the death chant became an intense wail.

Major Brown of the Third Regiment, the designated drummer for this occasion, nodded to Captain Burt and began the executioner's cadence. He made three low beats, slow, steady, measured, dismal, and funereal. One . . . two . . . three . . . and Burt's sword dropped.

Mister Duley swung the ax and caught the rope squarely. It separated, and the floor of the scaffold fell away, leaving thirty-eight bodies to twist and writhe and spasm in the air.

The body of Cut Nose, however, fell to the platform base, and McQuiston jumped down to it, grabbing the severed rope above the noose and pulling upwards in a choking motion even though the man's life was already extinct. Cut Nose had chosen this noose purposely because he saw that the rope was of poor quality, and even at this, his hour of doom, the warrior planned his escape, although it proved to be a futile effort. With the help of the guards, his lifeless body was hoisted back into position and the rope retied so it swung some more.

The Indian beast has now gotten his due
Drag down the gallows and bury him shallow
No more to cause terror he's just a dead Sioux

The crowd went wild! They cheered, and hooted, and guffawed, and even the soldiers join in. The hanging Indians, those not immediately killed with broken necks, heard it, and it was the last sound to reach their ears in their dying moments. Retribution had come! A witness to the spectacle wrote of the execution:

On every side is a jubilee, and the Angel of Judgment seems to intone the solemn "Amen." Justice alone, in that hour of excitement, retains her composure and looks on the scene with a face undisturbed and calm. Tragic end, not less tragic than the massacre itself!

The reporters scribbled their reports, but had to wait their turns in line behind the military telegrapher, who wired the official announcement to General Sibley in St. Paul. The commander, upon receiving the wire, prepared one of his own to be sent the following day.

ST. PAUL, MINN.,
December 27, 1862
The President of the United States:
I have the honor to inform you that the thirty-eight Indians and half-breeds ordered by you for execution were hung yesterday at Mankato, at 10:00 A.M. Everything went off quietly and the other prisoners are well secured.
Respectfully,

H.H. Sibley
Brigadier General

Ryker eyed the hanging corpses and felt drained of all emotion, totally spent. He saw the hanging body of Wa-kan-tan-ka swaying gently in the cold December breeze and noted that the warrior's eyes remained fixed on Stands Tall and Louis as though to lock their images in his soul forever. He saw that Wa-kan-tan-ka had not soiled himself, and was as pleased as he felt the warrior's spirit must be.

He watched as Captain Burt and John McQuiston and Mister Duley descended from the scaffold. At the base, Stands Tall approached the men and held out her hand in a gesture of peace. Captain Burt did not notice her and continued on by. McQuiston looked at her and scoffed. Mister Duley stopped in front of her and looked into her eyes a long minute. Then he clasped her hand, and the two embraced.

Ryker smiled. The process of healing had begun.

Epilogue

LITTLE CROW, ALSO KNOWN AS Ta-wai-o-ta-doo-tah (His Red Nation) was the acknowledged leader of the war party that waged Minnesota's Great Sioux Massacre of 1862. Although he knew what it would ultimately cost the Dakota if they went to war, he also knew he had to be the leader of his people. After he fled from Camp Release in the fall of that year, he headed northwest into the Dakota Territory, but his destiny was still tied to Minnesota. On July 3, 1863, while picking berries with his son near one of the scattered lakes north of Hutchinson, the Sioux chief was shot dead by two farmers, Nathon and Chauncey Lampson. The government had placed a bounty on him as though he were a rabid coyote or some other common vermin. After his death, his body was taken to Hutchinson and dragged through the streets of town where it was severely mutilated and souvenirs taken from it. On the 4th of July, townspeople celebrated by again abusing the body. They placed fire crackers in his ears and nostrils, and further mutilated the corpse before throwing it into a pit. This behavior has caused future generations to wonder if the Indian or the white culture was more savage, for neither culture acted civilized throughout this dark period in Minnesota history.

Little Crow's scalp and arm bones were also taken as relics. They were eventually placed on public display then placed in the vault at the Historical Society in the state capitol building, St. Paul, Minnesota, until 1971, when his remains were returned to his ninety-four-year-old grandson, Jesse Wakeman, and finally interred respectfully in Flandreau, South Dakota.

Thus ended yet another sad chapter in the ongoing history of man's inhumanity to his fellow man.

www.ingramcontent.com/pod-product-compliance
Lightning Source LLC
Chambersburg PA
CBHW020557250626
47154CB00004B/1255